DESPERATELY SEEKING LANDLORD

USA Today Bestselling Author
MICALEA SMELTZER

UNTITLED

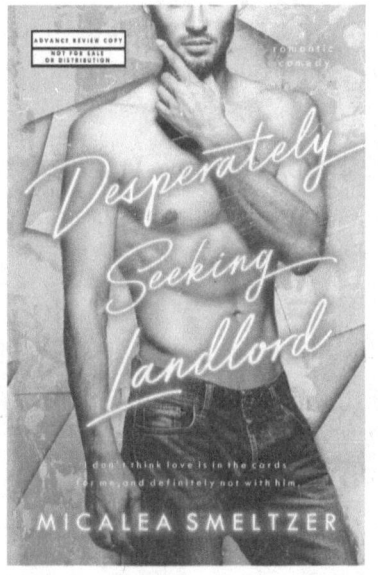

It was just supposed to be a fling.
It would end and we'd go our separate ways.

I should know by now nothing in my life is ever that simple.

When Jamie Miller knocks on my door ten months after we ended our ... whatever it was, I promptly punch him in his smug face, for no other reason than I feel like it and he deserves it.

It's probably not the best way to handle things, but I've never been good at doing things properly.

When he tells me he's my new landlord, my whole world is rocked.

But Jamie? He wants to prove to me he's more than an egotistical jerk and for some reason he's decided he wants *me*.

I don't think love is in the cards for me, and definitely not with Jamie, but he's determined to prove me wrong.

© Copyright 2019 Micalea Smeltzer
All rights reserved. This book or any portion thereof may not be reproduced or used in any manner whatsoever without the express written permission of the publisher.
This is a work of fiction. Names, characters, businesses, places, events and incidents are either the products of the author's imagination or used in a fictitious manner. Any resemblance to actual persons, living or dead, or actual events is purely coincidental.
Cover Design: Emily Wittig Designs
Editing: KBM Editing
Formatting: Micalea Smeltzer

CHAPTER ONE

Miranda

The picture comes to life before my eyes with each stroke of my paintbrush. In the past, I haven't taken commissions because I don't like to be paid to create someone else's vision, but recently I changed my mind so I could make more money to put back and save. With my senior year of college a month away from starting, it's crunch time. Real life is staring me in the face. Soon, I'll be clamoring for a position as an art teacher, while a pile of student loan debt gets dumped in my lap.

Fun times.

The snowy owl stares back at me, my tongue sticking out slightly in concentration. Feathers are a bitch to paint. It's a good thing I like a challenge.

A loud knock at the door makes me jump. Normally I have my headphones on, but they broke, and I haven't had a chance to grab new ones.

I lay down my palette and brush, wiping my hands on a towel before I make my way to the door.

The knocking starts up again and I roll my eyes. "I'm coming, I'm coming. Calm your tits."

Swinging open the door I stop in surprise. The last thing I expect to see on the other side is *this* man. I haven't seen him in months, eight months to be exact, and my first instinct is to slam the door in his face.

As it flies closed, he reaches out like a ninja and captures the edge in his hand, preventing me from closing it.

"Go away." My eyes narrow and my lip snarls. Everything about me screams *aggressive*.

"No can do, doll." Jamie grins back at me, ever the cocky asshole. You'd think for being thirty-four years old he'd have more maturity. But no, not James Miller. He's a dick through and through.

"Why are you *here?*" I blurt as it suddenly connects in

my head that Jamie is *here*, at my apartment building, in front of my door, nearly a year after we stopped hooking up.

Having sex with my best friend's landlord probably wasn't my brightest idea, but we both wanted a casual hook up. That's all it was, and it should've ended amicably, but there's nothing *amicable* about Jamie. He has a great cock and knows what to do with it, but that's about all he has going for him. It's not like he's sexy as sin or anything.

He totally is.

All the trash that leaves his mouth should have been enough to keep me away, but I've never been that smart.

It still doesn't explain why he's here after his asshole move the last time I saw him. He'd been ignoring me, which was fine, he's not my boyfriend—but what set me off was running into him at the bar, *our* bar we always went to, to find him snaking his hand up some woman's skirt. He made sure I saw too and when I marched up to him, to demand an apology or I don't know what, the dick face laughed and told me I was an easy lay and he was looking for more of a challenge.

He stares at me, those hazel eyes of his doing things to me they shouldn't. His lips quirk into the cockiest of half-smiles and then he says something I'm not prepared for.

"Not happy to see your new landlord?"

Unable to control my reaction, my arm coils back and my fist slams into his perfect nose. It's what I should've done in the bar months ago. Guess I'm making up for lost time.

He stumbles back in surprise, his hands coming up to cover his nose.

His shocked eyes flicker to mine. "You hit me!"

"Why do you sound so surprised?" I fire back indignantly. "You're an asshole and deserve much worse. I could've dick-punched you."

He wipes a tiny trickle of blood. It's not much, but I smile anyway because I still made him bleed.

He narrows his eyes and wiggles his nose. "You like my cock too much for that."

I roll my eyes at his outrageous comment. Yeah, Jamie's great in bed but it's not like he's the only fish in the sea.

But he might be the best you've ever had.

I tell my brain to shut up.

"Are you going to let me in?" He arches one brow and I narrow my eyes, crossing my arms over my chest.

His eyes zero in on my breasts, pushed up against my t-shirt and I snap my fingers. "Eyes up here, asshole. And no, why would I ask you inside?"

"Because I'm your landlord, you punched me, and I need to clean myself up." He waves a finger at his face where blood is smeared under his nose.

"You're *not* my landlord. You're Lou's landlord," I remind him unnecessarily.

His shit-eating grin spreads. "Oh, doll, I'm yours now too."

Color drains from my face. "B-But *Howard?*" I stammer, thinking of my sweet-faced elderly landlord I've had for the last two years. He owns several apartments in this complex for the specific purpose of renting them to college kids. He even brings cookies when he comes to collect the rent or check on things, like he's trying to soften the blow or something. Am I never going to have Howard's cookies ever again? Okay, I didn't know cookies could sound dirty but now I'm questioning everything. *Wait...* "He's not dead is he?"

Jamie shakes his head, taking a step closer to me. Everything in me tells me to step back, but if I do he'll have easy access to my apartment—and possibly my vagina since I have no self-control when it comes to him.

"He's not dead." He pulls his full bottom lip between his teeth and lets it go. "But he was looking to sell and I was looking to buy." He shrugs like it's oh-so-simple.

"So ... now you're my landlord." It's slowly beginning to sink in that Jamie, is in fact, my landlord. Which means...

"Oh my God, I punched my landlord!" I cover my mouth, trying to hide my horror.

He grins wickedly and looks me up and down. It's not

a slimy look, just pure seduction, and dammit if I don't tingle all over from it. "Guess you owe me a favor then."

I don't know whether to be scared or giddy about what a favor might entail.

"Now, can I come in?" He arches one brown brow at me.

I step aside. Jamie walks in and immediately heads for the sink. He rolls off a paper towel, dampens it and holds it to his nose before he turns around to face me.

Standing at the edge of the kitchen, trying to keep distance between us, I cross my arms over my chest once more. It's feeble protection. I don't think even middle age armor would be enough coverage. It's not my heart I need to protect either, it's my body, because Jamie brings out my inner hoe and she loves to say hello when he's around.

He tosses the paper towel in my trashcan and stalks closer. He's tall, but lean, with enough muscle that I know he takes care of himself but not too much that he looks like a juiced up meathead.

His eyes narrow and my breath catches as he leans closer. I hold my breath, convinced he's going to kiss me. I war with whether or not I want him to or if I should punch him again.

Neither comes to fruition.

"Is that *cum* in your hair?" His tone is almost angry—no, it *is* angry, which makes no sense at all.

That was not what I was expecting.

"What?" I blurt, jumping away from him. "Are you crazy? *No.*"

"Are you sure I didn't interrupt a sex fest?"

My jaw drops. "Are you kidding me? I said *no*—and even if you did, it's none of your business. I really don't know why you're even here. I'm sure the news of your ownership could've been shared via email, or maybe, I don't know, through the *mail.*"

"I wanted to tell you personally." He tries to hide a smirk.

"Oh." I place the back of my hand to my forehead and pretend to swoon. "Don't I just feel so special, that *the* James Miller, came to tell little ole me *personally.*"

He suppresses a laugh at my dramatic and fake southern accent.

"What's in your hair then?"

"Seriously, bud? We're back to this?" He gives me a look that says he isn't going to drop the subject until I answer. "It shouldn't make any difference to you, but it's *paint.*"

"Paint?"

I nod my head down the hall and he follows me. I sweep my arm into the spare room and he pokes his head inside to see the canvas resting on the easel.

Turning to face him with my hands on my hips, he reluctantly looks at me.

"Now, tell me Jamie, how would it be any of your business if I was having sex when you arrived? I haven't seen you or heard from you in eight months."

"It's not." He makes it sound so simple, like he doesn't actually care, but he can't erase the relief in his eyes. It doesn't make any sense to me, but men are confusing creatures. They can never just say what they think or feel. It's all a big secret.

Maybe that's why Jamie's dick is so big. It's full of secrets.

We stand there awkwardly in the hall, and I try to ignore the fact that my bedroom is at his back. We've spent a hell of a lot of time there in the past.

I wait for him to say something, but he doesn't.

"Well," I step aside, "now that you've informed me you're my..." I pause, choking on the word, "landlord, you can go."

He stares down at me, his blue button-down shirt taut across his chest. It's been way too long since I've gotten laid. I might be pissed at Jamie, but my lady bits didn't get the memo.

I try to ignore how seriously he stares at me. It's strange. Our relationship was completely physical. We barely spoke, but now he's looking at me like he has a lot to say and it's ... baffling.

Finally, he tips his head. "Later, doll."

He brushes past me, his arm grazing my breasts, and

my treacherous nipples tighten in response at the memory of what he's done to my body.

He looks back one last time, smirking when his eyes zero in on my chest. Before I can tell him to look elsewhere he swings the door open and is gone.

CHAPTER TWO

Miranda

Sliding into a seat across from my best friend Lou I let out a dramatic sigh. "You're never going to believe my news."

I stab a straw into my iced coffee. Her brow arches as she watches me. "Uh ... I take it this isn't good news?" She hedges, taking a sip of her own beverage.

I exhale heavily, pinching the bridge of my nose. I

lean heavily over the table, grinding out to the words, "Jamie. Bought. My. Apartment."

She snorts. "Be serious." I stare at her and her lips slowly part. "You're not kidding?"

"Wish I was," I grumble, staring at my coffee. I wanted the caffeine desperately, but now I know it isn't going to help the headache simmering behind my eyes—no, it's completely Jamie induced.

"Wait, *wait*. How is that possible?"

I shrug. "Apparently Howard decided to sell, and guess who was there to swoop in and save the day?"

"You're not still sleeping with him, right?" Lou tilts her head, giving me a *mom* look.

"No," I growl indignantly. "But even if I was, you have no right to judge. Not all of us are lucky enough to bag a smoking hot football player."

"Physical therapist," she corrects with a pointed finger.

"Right." I keep forgetting Abel graduated and is now an adult-*adult*—like one who has to be responsible and wear real clothes and call people sir and ma'am. "Jamie and I stopped sleeping together nearly a year ago now. He might be the best sex I've ever had, but I won't be hopping on that ride any time soon. He's too much of an asshole."

Again, Lou hits me with a stare that says *really*.

She's right to doubt. I have no self-control when it

comes to dick. It's like all rational thought goes out the window, I rip my clothes off, and I'm like *give it to me good.*

"I wish Abel and I could move somewhere else," she confesses. "Dealing with Jamie is such a headache, but the apartment is in a good location and a decent size."

"Jamie's ... *Jamie.*" There is no other explanation for him. I've often wondered if there's more to him than he lets on, sometimes he'd get this far away look, but then a dickish comment would usually leave his mouth and I'd change my mind.

"I guess it could be worse." She gives a simple shrug, like *that's that.* "Jamie might be a gigantic pain, but when it matters he does come through."

Like last month when her shower broke in her apartment and the place flooded. It was July fourth of all days, and somehow he managed to have one of his contacts come in to clean up the water and fix the plumbing. He even had the floors replaced within days. As a landlord it *is* his responsibility to keep those things up, but with his attitude you'd think he'd evil laugh and cackle out a *suffer peasants.* When Lou called to tell me about it, I was honestly surprised he'd taken care of it so quickly.

"Yeah, but at least you haven't seen him naked," I point out, and she chokes on her drink.

"Even though I'm aware of your ... *relationship,*" she side eyes me, "with him, it still makes me feel gross."

I sip my straw delicately and then whisper, "Huge." Just because I love watching her eyes widen and her cheeks blush.

Lou isn't a prude, not by any means, but she does *not* enjoy me boasting about Jamie's monster cock. I tried to show her a picture one time and I thought she'd crawl under the table. Thankfully, our gay friend Tanner was more than game to check it out. After all, I was just trying to spread the love via dick pic—that I took myself in person, because I'm a classy lady and don't except that kind of intrusion in my DMs.

Lou's phone vibrates against the table and when she peers at the screen a goofy smile splashes across her face.

My heart pangs, not with jealousy—I'm insanely happy my best friend has found true love—but with my own desire to have that. I haven't been lucky enough yet to find that one guy who clicks with me. Abel and Lou are a perfect match, seeing them makes me even more determined to find my right guy and not settle for anything less.

Even though I'm only twenty-two years old, I've been putting so much pressure on myself to find *a* guy, that I haven't been focusing on *the* guy. The one who's worth waiting for. The last thing I want to do is make the mistake of rushing into a relationship for the sake of not being alone. After all, I'm the best company anyone could ever have, so I can keep myself plenty entertained. In more ways than one, if you catch my drift.

Besides, nothing says at my age I need to be married and settled with five kids by the time I'm thirty.

This is my life and I can do whatever the damn well I please.

"Earth to Miranda." Lou snaps her fingers in front of my face, trying to get me to refocus.

"What?" I blink owlishly at her. There's no point in trying to pretend I heard her because I obviously didn't.

"*I said*, Abel wants to know if you want to go to the movies with us. He's getting the tickets now."

I crinkle my nose. "I'm always the third wheel. I feel pathetic."

"You're not a third wheel *or* pathetic. Now come on, you should go."

I frown. "Fine." While my agreement is reluctant, I also do want to go. Mostly because I don't want to sit around my place sulking about Jamie. Invariably that'll lead to dirty thoughts about him and me, spread eagle on my bed, going to pound town with my vibrator. "What time does the movie start?" I pick at my nails, pretending I'm really not all that interested in the answer.

She looks back down at her phone, fingers flying. "Seven, tonight."

I exhale a breath. She might say I'm not a third wheel but anything scheduled after five pm with your boyfriend is definitely a date, and I'm about to be tagalong Suzy because they feel sorry for me.

Honestly, I'm not unhappy on my own. It's nice. I think every person should have a time in their life when they're single and living by themselves. It gives you a chance to grow and learn who *you* are.

"Abel got you a ticket, so you better go," she warns, setting her phone down and replacing her empty hand with her plastic cup. Eco-Friendly Sasha at the table beside us glares, her own reusable cup sitting pretty beside her.

I give a thumbs up and forced smile. "I'll be there."

Reason number one why I'm single: I third wheel to the movies with my bestie and her boyfriend.

"Excuse me. Sorry. Excuse me. Oh, ma'am, I apologize." I pick up her purse from the floor where I knocked it from her lap with my giant caboose. I have a lot of junk in the trunk, what can I say. Blessedly, I finally make it to the empty seat beside Lou. I drop unceremoniously into the seat and she looks over at me.

"You bring chaos wherever you go."

I look back toward the pathway I had to take to reach our seats in the middle of the last row—aka the best seats in every movie theater—and sure enough, everyone is having to readjust from the stampede that is me and my badonkadonk.

"Oh, well." I shrug, wiggling around as I get settled.

"You could've climbed through." Lou points to the opening in front of all the seats, a walkway where servers can drop off food on top of the slender bar in front of us.

"I don't crawl on floors."

She snorts. "Likely story."

She has a point.

"I don't crawl on dirty movie theater floors covered in God knows what," I correct.

She smirks. "Okay, okay. But honestly, you've probably knelt on worse."

She's not wrong.

Abel passes me the menu he was perusing. "You want popcorn, Miranda?"

"Only if it's the herb parmesan one."

He chuckles. "Always, it's Lou's favorite too, and you've both turned me into a believer."

"It's way better than regular popcorn." I nod emphatically, flipping open the menu. I don't know why I ever bother to look. I always order the same thing. I grab the piece of paper and pencil provided and scribble my order on it beneath theirs.

Pizza with basil, feta, red peppers, and spinach. I know it's an upcharge for more than three toppings. Bite me.

I folded it up and stick it in the holder so they can grab it.

Digging in my purse, I toss twenty-five dollars across Lou to Abel. It falls in his lap and he leans forward glaring at me.

"What's this for?"

We do this same song and dance every time. Lou's boyfriend is chivalrous, that's undeniable, but I always refuse to let him pay for me too.

"Don't argue with me, Farquad, take the money."

"Farquad? Like from Shrek?"

"Exactly." I snap my fingers. "Not that you bear any resemblance, it just sort of rolled out in the moment. Go with it."

He shakes his head and folds the money up, trying to pass it back to me.

"I don't mind, Miranda, seriously."

"Nope." I push his hand away, Lou caught between us.

The back and forth continues for a solid thirty seconds before Lou snatches the money, stuffs it in her bra, and doesn't look or say a word to either of us.

Abel and I make eye contact and look at her slowly. She blinks straight ahead at the screen.

The previews start, and I sit back, determined to enjoy myself.

The movie isn't bad, the food is delicious, and at the

end I say goodbye to Abel and Lou before driving to the opposite side of town where my apartment is.

Opening the door I flick on the lights and sigh as the door closes behind me.

I'm happy on my own. I don't need a man to complete me. I'm a bad bitch.

So why do I feel so lonely?

CHAPTER THREE

Miranda

Stalking into the local Michaels I'm on a mission for paint supplies. I'm running too low and I have commissions to finish, with not enough time to order what I need from my favorite online vendor. There used to be a specialty art store on the west side of town, but apparently not enough people want decent art supplies, so alas I'm stuck dealing with the bane of my existence. Michaels is a mockery of my artistry.

Dramatic? Yes. A lie? No.

They call themselves an arts and crafts store, but the *arts* part is sorely lacking.

I wrinkle my nose at the ridiculous watermelon pool float hanging from the ceiling. Why are they selling pool floats?

I let out a disgruntled breath and narrow my focus until I reach the back.

Their paint choices are cheap brands, with jacked up prices, which makes me even angrier. I don't have a problem dropping a lot of money on paint and art supplies when I *know* it's the best quality. But this is probably better compared to Crayola grade.

However, I don't have a choice.

I gather the paints I need and hold them against my chest. I should've grabbed a cart, but I was too mad to think logically. Turning around, I nearly drop the bottles of colors, because Jamie is standing at the end of the aisle.

Why the hell is Jamie Jack-Ass Miller in Michaels of all places?

"Jamie," I blurt. "Hi."

Hi—the one word seems so idiotic coming out of my mouth, but I suppose it's a better greeting than punching him in the face.

"How do you know my dad?"

Down, down, down my eyes go the length of Jamie, connecting with the kid beside him.

Holy fuck, it's a mini-Jamie.

Jamie's hand on the boy's shoulder looks stiff and when my eyes dart from the child to him, he looks panicked.

"Uh..." Now I'm the panicked one. I can't exactly tell the kid I'm well acquainted with his father's dick.

"We're friends," Jamie tells him.

"I wouldn't say that."

Jamie glares at me and I press my lips together.

"I didn't know you had friends."

Ah, kids, so blessedly honest and blunt.

Jamie's jaw tightens, his hazel eyes full of an emotion that looks like fear.

Oh my God.

Suddenly, I'm connecting the dots.

He's married.

Oh, fuck.

Jamie is *married*.

I've fucked another woman's husband.

Holy shit.

I'm a homewrecker. That's what I am.

Unintentionally, of course, but that doesn't mean it's not true.

I think I'm going to be sick.

The paints drop from my arms and I run my ass away from them, straight out the store, to my car. I make one stop on the way home, because this news ... well, it definitely requires alcohol.

CHAPTER FOUR

Jamie

The last place I should be is standing outside Miranda's door, pacing incessantly. I've been debating for the last ten minutes whether I should knock or not. Normally, I wouldn't care. I would demand entry. But this is different.

I saw the look of horror on her face before she fled. I know exactly what she's thinking and she's wrong. I might be an asshole, it's better not to get attached to people when they always leave, but I'm not a big enough prick to do *that*.

Finally, I knock on the door and wait. It's late, and chances are she won't come to the door.

Surprisingly, it swings open. "You're not the delivery boy," she growls, starting to close the door.

"Wait!" My hand shoots out, keeping her from closing the door.

She glares at me, trying in vain to close it anyway.

"I need to talk to you."

"There's nothing to talk about. You're *married*. You have a kid and you're *married*." She keeps emphasizing that damn word and it's making me see red.

"Miranda," I growl her name pleadingly, "let me explain."

"No, get out." She kicks blindly at me, but fails to make contact.

"I'm not married."

She stops. "You're not?"

"People can have kids and not be married," I remind her. "Now, please, let me in so I can explain."

I'm more than a little surprised when she acquiesces and stops fighting me, stepping aside to let me enter her tiny apartment. It might be small, but it's cozy. I would know; I've spent a lot of time with her here.

She closes the door behind me and turns to face me, crossing her arms beneath her breasts. She's wearing a t-shirt with her university's mascot, but it's faded and worn with small holes around the collar. Her pair of sleep shorts hug her thighs and I greedily lick my lips, my thoughts straying to a dangerous place.

I never did get my fill of her, and that was the problem. I'm not sure anything can quench my thirst for this woman.

"Stop undressing me with your eyes and speak. So, you're not married then? Because if you are I'll murder you. I've watched enough shows to get away with it too."

I stifle a smile. God, she amuses me and she has no idea how much. I've gotten good over the years at hiding my emotions. It's best that way.

"Not married."

She exhales an annoyed breath, her arms falling to her sides. "Divorced? Widowed? A random hook up? Excuse me for being irritated Jamie, I know we never talked all that much about serious things, but we did talk some, and never, not once, did you mention having a son. Does Lou even know?"

I shake my head. "No one knows. I mean, people know—but I choose who I tell." She flinches and I realize I've hurt her, because this means she's someone I specifically chose not to tell. "My son ... he's the most important person to me." I know it's probably surprising, and sucky explanation, but it's the truth. "I was married," I finally force the words out of my throat. Sometimes I still feel the phantom touch of the platinum band I wore. "Things ... didn't work out."

It's the truth, but not the whole truth. She's getting more from me than any woman has since Shannon left me.

"So..." She hedges. "You share custody, then?"

"Tobias is *mine*." She winces when my tone comes out sharp and cutting, but if she knew the hell I'd went through to keep my son she'd understand. Softening my tone, I hold out the bag that's been clasped in my hand since the moment I got out of my car in the parking lot. "Here, I got these for you."

She takes the bag, brows wrinkled in puzzlement. She holds it open, peering inside at the items she dropped when she ran from us.

"Thank you."

"You're ... you're welcome."

I'm surprised, but thankful, she doesn't ask why. Frankly, I don't know what possessed me to buy her fallen items in the first place. It just felt like the right thing, and I'm not accustomed to doing the right thing, at least when it comes to anything that isn't related to Tobias.

"Where is your son? How do you have so much time to...?" She flicks a finger between us, and my thoughts drift to memories of her soft skin rubbing against me, the sound of our bodies joining.

"My mom. She lives with us."

My mom is one of the best people I know—scratch that, *the* best. When everything was going on with my ex, she was there, my rock and support system as I fought tooth and nail for the little boy who owned my heart.

"I thought your parents were dead?" She blurts.

Honestly, it's sad how little we truly know about each other, especially considering she's the longest ... relationship, if you can call it that, I've had since Shannon left us. Everything else has always been one-night stands, and contrary to popular belief, few and far between. With Tobias, it doesn't leave all that much time for sex, and I refuse to bring women back to my home. But it's easier to have people think I'm an asshole womanizer. I don't want people to know the real me. I shared my vulnerabilities with someone once, I won't make that mistake twice considering it blew up in my face.

"My father died when I was young, so I was raised by mom, but my dad's parents were heavily involved in my life."

"Hmm," she hums.

As things are settling between us, I'm starting to feel the familiar zing of fire between us. It's palpable. Thickening the air. My whole body becomes hyperaware of her proximity. The way her lips are so full and kissable. How fucking amazing her breasts look in her t-shirt. She's not wearing a bra and her nipples peek through the cotton.

I wait for a snarky remark from her. She's queen of them and I love trading barbs with her, but when I look in her dark eyes—so brown they're nearly black—I see the same thing I'm sure is reflected in mine.

Lust.

Desire.

Heat.

I want to move and close the distance between us, press my mouth to hers. It's a selfish thought, especially considering how I ended things—and by ended I mean ghosted and then rubbed another woman in her face.

A woman I didn't even take home and fuck, even though I wanted to. God, did I want to, because I wanted to erase the memory of Miranda from my skin, but I couldn't do it. I haven't been able to do it since. It's like my dick's grown a conscience all of a sudden.

Miranda inhales a shaky breath and lets it out slowly.

Before I can blink we're both moving, closing the distance between our bodies.

My fingers tangle in the hair at the back of her head, holding her to me. This isn't a picture perfect kiss, but it's still fucking amazing. It's rough, and raw, desperate on both our ends.

I nip at her full bottom lip, angling her head back.

Maybe this is why I can't seem to quit her. We're fucking explosive. I came over here to explain myself, that was all, I didn't want to get wrapped up in whatever this insane chemistry is with us, but it can't seem to be controlled.

We stumble down the hall to her bedroom and I lower her to the mattress.

I don't know what I'm doing or even thinking. All rational thought goes out the window.

I'm good at playing the part of the skeevy asshole. I know what to do to piss people off, keep them at arm's length. I like to keep my life as simple and uncomplicated as possible. The less people involved, the better.

But with Miranda I keep coming back.

I move the cotton of her shorts aside and grin against the skin of her neck when I feel that she's not wearing panties and she's already wet.

"Jamie," she moans my name low and slow. It's music to my ears. I slide two fingers into her, curling them, and her back bows off the bed.

I hold back the words I want to say. That she's fucking gorgeous. That I love hearing her moan my name.

I kiss her lips again and her fingers rub against the stubble on my cheeks. She raises her head, kissing me deeply as I continue to pump my fingers in and out of her. I swallow her mewling sounds as her orgasm builds. When she reaches her climax there's a loud knock on the door. My fingers still inside her and her body freezes. It makes it all the more noticeable the way her pussy squeezes mine like a vice.

I slip my fingers from her body. Licking them clean.

"Someone's at the door," I say unnecessarily, my tone sharp.

"T-That ... that'll be my Chinese food." Her skin glows with a slight sheen of sweat and her hair is a bit wild. She definitely looks like she just orgasmed and it makes me selfishly pleased that she'll have to answer the door like this.

"You better get that then."

She nods woodenly but doesn't move, not until there's another sharp knock. She scoots off the bed, righting her shorts, and runs from her bedroom.

I adjust myself and sigh, looking at the rumpled bed.

This shouldn't have happened and I definitely shouldn't feel forlorn at the fact that I didn't get to fuck her properly.

But it did and I am.

I stroll out of her bedroom just as she closes the front door with her hip. Her arms are wrapped around a paper bag full of food. The smell of spices permeates the air.

"I would ask you to stay, but..." She pauses. We both know she wouldn't ask me to stay. She never has in the past. It was always fucking and done with us. Tonight isn't any different.

"I have to go."

I really do. I always do. I have responsibilities. Ones that Miranda is now privy too.

I open her door and pause. I feel her eyes on me, watching inquisitively.

Shaking my head I step past the threshold and close the door behind me.

I lean back against it, exhaling a breath.

A second later I hear the lock click into place.

CHAPTER FIVE

Miranda

Plopping on Lou's couch, I cross my legs under me. I hold the paper plate with two slices of pizza close to my chest, terrified it might fall on the floor. But let's be real, at some point I will get sauce and cheese on my boobs.

From the small kitchen to my right, Abel and Lou are the picture of domestic bliss as he bends to kiss her. He's just come home from work and brought the pizza with him. When I asked Lou why it couldn't be delivered, she mentioned something about a delivery boy seeing her naked. It made no sense to me.

They each grab a plate themselves and Lou sits beside me while Abel takes the chair. I wish I could get over this feeling of always crashing their good time. Lou is my best friend, and Abel is clearly the man she's going to spend the rest of her life with, so he's not going anywhere. It just feels so lopsided though. Them in love, and then there's me.

Reason number two why I'm single: I spend the evening eating pizza with my best friend and her boyfriend instead of going out.

"I have something to tell you guys," I announce around a stringy mouthful of pizza.

"You're becoming a stripper?" Lou questions at the same time Abel says, "Sounds serious."

"I ran into Jamie." They both roll their eyes. "And he has a kid—a son."

Lou's jaw drops and Abel looks confused.

"Jamie doesn't have a kid," Abel blurts. "That's impossible. Who would procreate with that prick?"

"Well, apparently someone did."

"You're lying," Lou accuses. "I've known Jamie since I moved in here. I've never seen a kid and he's never mentioned one."

"Did you know he's divorced?"

Abel sputters. "Who the hell in their right mind would marry him?"

Abel particularly hates Jamie. I don't blame him. In the past Jamie has made lewd comments and been downright rude to Lou. Abel has no tolerance when it comes to that. You'd think that would've been enough to keep me from getting involved with him, but I'm not always the brightest crayon in the box when I get a hankering for a good dicking.

"Well, he's divorced. Clearly she smartened up and left him. I still can't believe you've slept with him," she gripes, biting into her crust.

I wince. "I think there's more to it than that. He has custody of his son." Last night he gave me more information than he ever has, but there was still so much left unsaid, but I could infer some things by reading between the lines. "I think a lot of the way he acts is to keep people at a distance. I don't know how long it's been since his divorce, but I got the impression his wife did a number on him."

Last night showed me there was more to Jamie than any of us have ever given him credit for. I mean, he gave me an unbelievable orgasm and didn't wait around expecting one in return. But more important than that, he bought the paint I dropped before fleeing. I really needed it and there was no way I was returning to get it after that fiasco. But he bought it and brought it to me anyway. He didn't have to do that but he did.

"How did you even find all this out?" Lou asks, perking up as she becomes invested in this story.

I exhale a sigh, the pizza I was eating now sitting heavy in my stomach.

"I ran into him when I went to Michaels. His son was with him and I *might've* freaked out thinking he was married and cheated on his wife with me. Surprise, surprise, he actually showed up at my apartment later, after I ran away from him, to explain."

"I have such a hard time picturing Jamie *married*." She says the word like it's dirty, and I guess when it comes to him it is. Any guy who is as rude, crass, and arrogant as he is definitely isn't the marrying type.

"I hope he's not raising the kid to be just like him." Abel lets out a disgusted breath, setting his empty plate aside. He grabs a bottle of blue Gatorade and gulps some down. Lou eyes him, making sure he sets the bottle down on a coaster.

"I'm sure he's a better father than person." I cringe, because Jamie's not *all* bad. Only, mostly.

Abel raises a dark brow and I frown back.

Me defending Jamie is laughable, especially in such a poor way. I don't even like the guy. Yeah, our sex is great —*was*—but it never went beyond that and when he ended things the way he did, it just reinforced what an asshole he is.

But you sure didn't have a problem letting him finger your pussy last night did you?

I bat those thoughts away, like literally motion with my hand trying to get rid of them and Abel gives me a funny look.

"What are you doing?"

"There was a fly," I lie easily.

Lou shakes her head at me and they exchange a look. We all know there was no fly. I'm just crazy.

I finish my pizza, toss the plate away, and grab my purse.

"I better get going, guys. I have ... to knit a sweater."

Lou rolls her eyes. "Likely story."

I shrug. "It was the best I could come up with on the fly ... no pun intended."

She laughs and Abel hides a smile.

"But really," I continue, "I want to go home, take a shower, get in my pajamas, and watch this documentary I recorded on JFK Jr. With me gone y'all can have some hot freaky sex or whatever it is you do when I'm not around ruining the fun."

Lou tosses her head back laughing, her blonde tresses swinging around her shoulders. Abel merely covers his face with his hands.

"I'll see you guys ... well, let's just be realistic, tomorrow. I'll see you tomorrow."

"Love you," Lou calls after me with a wave.

I blow a kiss and close the door behind me.

On my way across town to my apartment I blast Lizzo's new album, doing some awkward car dance moves every time I reach a stoplight. Her music makes me feel like a bad ass and I just have to move.

Turning onto Airport Road I make an immediate right into my rundown apartment complex. The sun is beginning to go down and I grab my bag, heading inside.

"Hi, Miranda." I bristle at my name on the lips of Mr. Creepy Creeper Guy as I call him. His real name is Stan —short for Stanley, which he continuously reminds me of, not that I care. While Jamie might come across as a rude douchebag ninety-nine percent of the time, he doesn't give me the impression he might murder me and cover his body in my skin. Stan does.

"Stan Shunpike," I mutter back, not making eye contact as I step pass him, heading for the stairs. Thank God he doesn't live on the same floor as me—not that he can't climb stairs if he feels like murdering me, but it does give me a sense of ease.

"Still don't know who that is." I can tell from his voice he's sporting his smarmy smile.

I pause and look back at him. He's probably in his

late twenties, but he looks more like forty. He's losing his hair, his skin has a grayish hue, his acne scars look like gigantic craters, and his teeth are a rotted gravestone color. It's druggie city over here and Stan is their leader.

"Still don't care that you don't know."

He chuckles, but it's not a pleasant sound. It's more like glass raining down on my body. "One of these days, Miranda. One of these days." He wags a finger at me and I make a break for the stairs, hurrying up to my apartment.

I don't know what he has planned for *one of these days* but I don't want to be finding out.

Opening the door, I slip inside and make sure everything is locked before I set my purse on the floor. I start taking my clothes off as I move through the apartment, leaving them in a trail behind me.

Hopping in the shower, I scrub and buff my body, taking extra care to shave. It's totally dumb of me since what happened with Jamie last night will *not* be happening again. Ever.

I get out, wrapping my body in a towel and another around my hair. Padding across the hall to my bedroom to change into my pajamas I realize how quiet it is. It didn't used to bother me, being alone, and I hate that it does now. It's not that I'm not independent, but there is comfort in having another person around.

Doing my best to dismiss those thoughts I turn the TV on and slip beneath the sheets. The documentary comes on and I let out a hefty sigh.

Reason number three why I'm single: I watch documentaries about dead people.

CHAPTER SIX

Jamie

"Tobias! You have five seconds to get downstairs!" I glare down at my watch, running two minutes late already to drop Tobias off at his summer day camp. Two minutes might not seem like a lot, but when you're a parent two minutes turns into twenty in the blink of an eye. "Tobias!" I raise my voice in irritation.

At seven years old he's recently hit this stage where

he suddenly cares about what clothes he wears and has to style his hair *just so*. I don't get it. I expected that to come later, much later, in high school or something. But not with my son. He wants to be impeccably groomed every morning. I guess it shouldn't be *too* shocking since I'm used to wearing dress pants and shirts, hair neat, shoes shined—but kids are supposed to play in the mud and get dirty. At least, that's what I did.

My mom shakes her head as she steps out of the kitchen, wiping her hands on a checkered dishrag.

"Give the child a break."

I exhale a sigh. "I can't be late."

She walks forward a few feet and grasps my forearm. "I know."

My mom's hair is a light gray color, pulled back in a bun. Her age is showing around her eyes and mouth, but I still think she's beautiful, and the best mom I could ask for.

"It's going to be fine, Jamie. You worry too much." She stands on her tiptoes to kiss my cheek and I force a smile for her benefit.

"Tobias! We have to go!"

"I've *told* you, Dad, it's *Toby*." He appears at the top of the stairs in a pair of church clothes. Black pressed pants, a blue button down shirt he's carefully tucked into his pants, except for a bit sticking out the back that he missed, and a suit vest. It's easily ninety-five degrees outside.

This child.

"I named you Tobias, that's what I'll call you. You're going to get hot," I warn him, eyeing his clothes. I don't bother arguing with him to take them off, I learned months ago when this phase began, or whatever it is, to roll with it.

"Come here, child," my mother chides, tucking his shirt into the back of his pants.

"I'll be fine, Dad." He sighs heavily, like *I'm* the pain in his ass. I have to try not to smile. Not only does Tobias look exactly like me, but he acts like it too. Thank God on both accounts. I don't know what I'd do if he behaved like his mother. "What are you doing, Grandma Jo?"

"Tucking your shirt in, you loon. You missed a spot."

Once he's fixed, I place a gentle hand on his shoulder and direct him to the garage to get in the car. Tobias is easily distracted and if I don't watch, we'll be another five minutes late.

Tobias hops in the backseat of my black BMW X6 and buckles himself into his booster seat. A snooty elderly lady at the Quick Mart the other evening haughtily stuck her nose in the air and asked why a kid his age and size was in a booster seat.

"Safety, ma'am," I replied with a glower. Thankfully, that got her to shut up.

I might be a lot of things, but Tobias is my everything, and his safety is my upmost priority. I almost lost him once—twice, actually—and I won't let some careless mistake on my part be the reason he's taken from me.

Climbing into my car I wave goodbye to my mother who stands in the doorway of the house, watching us go.

The drive to the school is a short one and I walk him inside, making sure he's accounted for before I leave. The two teachers running the program have assured me my vigilance isn't necessary, but they don't know what I'm dealing with.

Leaving the school, I swing by the closest Starbucks for a black coffee. She shouldn't cross my mind, not at all when I have more important things to worry about, but I scan the parking lot for a lime green Kia Soul. There's not one there. My chest tightens. I want to lie and say it's relief that makes me feel this way, but it's not. I was selfishly hoping for one small peek at Miranda to make my day seem a little bit better than the shit fest I know is headed my way.

Grabbing my coffee from the drive-thru window, I drive an hour into Sterling to my lawyer's office. Don Bellamy is the best custody lawyer in the tri-state area. I made sure of it seven years ago when I had to fight for custody of my son from someone who didn't even want him, but wanted to keep him once she found out how much she could get in child support.

Parking in the lot I head inside, trying but failing to take meditative breaths.

I can be a raging asshole most days, but my ex-wife truly brings out the best in me.

"Jamie."

I look down a well-lit hall and Don strides toward me. A file is clasped in his hand and he holds out his other as he reaches me.

"Is she here?" I hate that my voice sounds shaky. Shannon has the ability to unravel me when I need to stay sane and level-headed.

"She is." He nods. "Just remember, this meeting is a formality. You don't owe her anything. She has no rights to Tobias, she signed them all over. But agreeing to meet with her makes you look good should she decide to start trouble."

I nod. It's things I all know already, but my stomach still feels unsettled.

I smooth my hands over my button down and gripe, "Let's get this over with."

Following him down the hallway he opens the door to a conference room with a round wood table and six chairs.

Shannon is seated at one, her blonde hair is cut short, almost in what I guess is a bob. She's makeup free, which is a rare sight since she was always caked in makeup before and is probably done intentionally so she can seem demure. She looks older, a little warier, but I guess that's to be expected since I haven't seen her in nearly seven years.

"Jamie." She looks at me in surprise, which is laughable considering she's the one who demanded this meeting.

"Shannon." I pull out the chair on the other side of the table from hers, careful to keep my tone neutral. "Where's your lawyer?"

"I didn't think one was necessary. This is just a conversation, correct?" She arches a brow, drumming her white tipped nails on the counter. *French*, the word comes to my brain and I recall her once telling me they're *French tipped*.

"I don't know." I cross my fingers together and lay them flat on the table. "You tell me."

Don sits down beside me with a Styrofoam cup of coffee, the steam filtering in the air.

She tucks a piece of hair behind her ear, but it's so short it immediately falls forward.

"It's been eight years since I got pregnant, Jamie. I'm a different person now. I've done a lot of growing and changing. Is it impossible to think I want to see my son?"

I look her over carefully. She doesn't look like a sad and grieving mother over the fact that she hasn't seen her son since he was an infant.

"Yes, yes it is."

Her face crinkles in irritation but she quickly schools it into a mask of sweetness. Out of the corner of my eye I see Don make a note on a pad I didn't even know he'd procured. The file sits to his left, grazing his fingertips of that hand.

Shannon's eyes narrow in on his movement and she sits up a little straighter, pursing her lips.

"You signed your rights away," I remind her stiffly.

She raises her chin. "It doesn't change the fact that he shares my DNA."

I want to slam my hand down on the table, snarl at her, let loose everything I've ever wanted to say to her. But I can't. I have to keep my head on straight. Tobias is my top priority and I can't let Shannon fuck with my head.

"And mine." My voice is forcibly soft. "But I'm one-hundred percent his parent. You can't say the same." She opens her mouth to argue and I cut her off. "A parent is the person who is there twenty-four-seven. The one who wipes asses. Checks temperatures. Cleans up vomit. Attends every school function. You've done *nothing* for him. Nothing." I jab my finger into the table and Don clears his throat. I release a pent up breath. "You wanted an abortion," I remind her softly, tamping my emotions down because even to this day this fact grates at me. When I look at my amazing, brilliant son, I can't imagine what possessed her to even consider the possibility.

She rolls her eyes. "I was twenty-seven. We'd just gotten married."

Rage. My fists curl beneath the table. I don't want to hit her. Just metaphorically knock some sense into her.

"Twenty-seven isn't too young to have a kid, *sweetheart*," I mock and she flinches. "And as you pointed out, we were married. Established. We had the money to handle a child, a home, but you didn't want him."

"You knew I didn't want kids."

Booyah.

I lean back, smiling like the fucking cat who ate the canary because I've snared her right where I want her. "Then why do you want him now?"

Her mouth opens and closes like a fish out of water.

I stand up and look down at Don. "I think that'll be all. As always, great seeing you Shannon—next time, go easy on the botox."

Her face turns red and before she can retort my long legs are carrying me from the room and out of the building.

CHAPTER SEVEN

Miranda

My legs are crossed under me, my tongue stuck slightly out between my lips. Using my thumb, I smudge the charcoal a bit on the sketchpad balanced on my knee. My playlist is on softly in the background as well as the TV. Working in silence is the bane of my existence.

The whole right side of my hand and arm is covered

in charcoal, and there's probably some smeared across my face from the repetitiveness of which I shove my hair out of my eyes. My dark hair is long, thick, and curly. Most days I straighten it, I find it easier to control that way, but I didn't feel like messing with it after my shower. I'm sure I resemble Medusa.

I'm so focused on drawing I don't hear the knocking at first. Looking at the time, it's nearing ten at night.

I swear to God if it's Sour-Breath Stan I'm going to smother him with a pillow.

I lay my sketchpad and charcoal pencils on top of my dresser. Looking at the palms of my hands I let out an exaggerated sigh. It's no wonder my place always looks slightly dirty. I'm constantly getting pencil everywhere.

Crossing the apartment, which only takes a few feet, I grab the baseball I keep in case of emergencies.

But it's no creeper when I open the door.

"Jam—"

I have no time to finish the sentence before he's bursting into my apartment, kicking the door closed behind him with a loud bang. The baseball bat drops from my hand. He takes my face between his two large hands and holds me captive, his lips a brand on mine when they connect.

My heart comes to life, beating like I've just attempted an aggressive workout—which actually seems to be exactly what Jamie has in mind, based on the hard curve of his erection pressing into my stomach.

I don't have a chance to ask him why he's here or what he thinks he's doing, because he keeps kissing me. I know I could push at him and he'd stop, but even if I tell myself I don't want anything to do with Jamie, that I don't even like him, it's all a lie. There's something about this man I can't seem to quit. I hadn't seen him hardly at all since our original tryst ended, just the occasional accidental run in if he happened to be at Lou's apartment complex when I was there. Now he's shown up here three times in less than a week. I'm beginning to think he can't get me off his mind either.

His hands move from my cheeks to the back of my thighs and he lifts me up. My legs coil around his waist, pushing his erection into my center. I moan against his lips, his kiss dizzying. I feel him walking and a moment later my back is pressed against my bed. He doesn't break the kiss, his long body leaning over mine.

My hands move up his chest and make quick work of the buttons. I shove the fabric off his shoulders and he steps away only long enough to discard the fabric like a meaningless scrap. Sadly, that shirt probably costs more than my rent.

Our kisses are frantic, the room filled with the pants of our breath.

Somewhere, deep inside my brain, my logical self is

screaming at me to stop this. That I promised I would never ever go down this path again. Not with Jamie, not with any guy. I deserve more, something real.

But my horny side tells her to shut up and that I'd rather have Jamie deep inside me instead of her logicalness.

"Why are you here?" I somehow manage to ask as his hand curves around the back of my thigh, spreading my legs.

I belatedly realize how underdressed I am. Since I was home alone for the evening and would soon be going to bed, I'm only wearing a pair of panties that say *epic babe* on the back and a ratty pajama shirt.

Jamie seems to have a knack for showing up when I'm dressed to impress.

His left hand climbs under my shirt and he squeezes my right breast, his thumb rolling the nipple. I'm soon tearing my shirt off and he captures my taut nipple in his mouth, then pays attention to my other breast. I've always hated my boobs. They're too big, saggy, and boast stretch marks, but Jamie pays that no mind. He never has. When we were doing this thing before he always told me he couldn't get enough of my body. It's the sexiest thing any man has ever told me.

"Why are you here?" I ask again, realizing belatedly that he hasn't answered me.

His lips press to my neck, right at the point where my pulse jumps. "Because I needed you."

I grip his hair in my fist, tugging him away from my skin. Not forcibly, just enough to make sure those laser-beam hazel eyes are looking at me. "Why would you need me?"

His eyes are sad, lost, even a little confused. His lips are red from our kisses and I can't stop myself from rubbing his bottom lip with my thumb. His hand on my hip tightens, and he pulls me closer so my lower half is lined up even more with his. I can't stop my moan at the feel of him pressing into me. I'll never ever open my mouth and tell him this, but I haven't had sex in eight months, not since our last time. I swore to myself I was waiting for something real, but here I am again, about to do this same bump and grind with Jamie. What is it about him I can't quit?

"I don't know," he admits, and I see the truth in his eyes. He's not lying or trying to goad me. "I just ... today was a bad day, and after I put Tobias to bed, I told my mom I had to get out. Somehow I ended up here. It's like..." He pauses and his Adam's apple bobs as he swallows. "There's something about you that's addictive. I can't seem to quit you."

My eyes widen, my breath catching, as he throws my thoughts back to me. I don't have time to catch them, study, and analyze them like I want to because he returns to doing delicious things to my body and I can't think straight.

I know this is crazy. I shouldn't be doing this with him. True, it's just sex, but Jamie is Jamie and I should've never slept with him in the first place.

My thoughts are a scrambled mess inside my brain and he must sense it.

"Get out of your head. It's just me."

The fact that it's Jamie should be the last thing to comfort me, but it does.

Pushing all my rational thoughts away, I let go, allowing my body absorb the pleasure.

Maybe it's because Jamie is the only man I've slept with that's significantly older than me, but no guy has ever been able to wring pleasure from my body like he can. It's as if I'm a musical instrument and he's the maestro.

He takes his time worshipping my body. You'd think he'd be all about his pleasure, but he's not. I have to give him credit, he's a very generous lover, and I think it gets him off when he can turn me on and make me come.

It feels like hours pass before we're both completely naked and he sinks into my body.

"Oh, fuck." My body bows off the bed at the feel of his cock inside me. "God, I forgot how big you are."

His chuckle vibrates my skin. "You know how to stroke my ego."

"And something else." I swivel my hips and watch the way his length disappears in and out of me.

His hands are braced on my sides, muscles taut, veins pronounced. God, his body is incredible. Mine, by contrast, is not—at least according to magazines. My thighs are thick, my hips flared, my legs too short, my belly pudgy, and stretch marks are a road map upon my skin. But I don't see what society calls imperfections. This is *my* body. It's a living, breathing, beautiful thing.

Jamie buries his head into my neck, his voice rasping against my skin. "What is it about you? Why can't I stay away? I always need more of you."

He lifts my hips, changing the angle and I gasp. "You stayed away plenty long," I pant out.

He shakes his head and his scruff rubs against me, making a scratchy sound. "It was … torture." His breaths are laborious, his jaw clenched as he holds himself back.

"We make no sense."

Not our words, but us. He's twelve years older than me, he has a child, he's a jerk. By contrast, I'm quirky and kind of weird. I'm loud and overprotective like an aggressive mama bear, and a complete free spirit. Opposites doesn't even begin to cover what we are.

He kisses my jaw gently. "Do you feel that? Do you

feel how we fit together? Do you feel how *right* this is? It's not logical, but it doesn't have to be, it just is."

I let out a whimper, feeling him rub against my G-spot. My fingernails dig into his arms, leaving behind little half-moons. "I love your cock," I moan, my legs shaking as my orgasm builds, ready to crest.

He looks down at me, forehead to forehead. "At least someone loves something about me."

I have no time to process his words before we're both coming. My orgasm seems to go on forever with little after shocks raking my body.

Sex with Jamie is always pretty fucking great, but this was out of this world.

He rolls off my body and I instantly miss the weight and heat of him against me. My body is slick with sweat from our sex. He gets up and I watch his firm backside as he steps into the hall for the bathroom.

When he comes back I'm still laying where he left me. I couldn't move if I wanted to. My body is spent.

He starts grabbing his clothes and I feel a sting in my chest.

"You're leaving?"

He nods, yanking his pants up his long legs.

"Is it because you want to or because you have other responsibilities?"

His eyes dart over me and he pauses, his now wrinkled dress shirt clasped in his hands. "I've never stayed with any of my hookups." I flinch like I've been slapped. His eyes soften with vulnerability. "But if I was going to stay with anyone it would be you."

He looks my naked body over carefully, like he's trying to memorize every dip and curve like it's the last time he's going to see me like this. Maybe it is, this shouldn't have happened anyway. I don't know why it makes me sad to think that it could truly be the last time. I've already went through Jamie withdrawals once, I don't relish the idea of doing it again. But really, this needs to stop. We're all wrong for each other and I'm looking for something real. I want what my best friend has. I *deserve* that kind of love, a man who worships me and looks at me like I'm everything.

Kind of like Jamie is looking at you right now?

My conscience needs to take a hike, because Jamie isn't, and can never be, the guy for me.

He buttons his shirt and puts his shoes on, pulling his keys from his pocket. His dark brows are pulled together and he looks away, jaw ticking.

"We can't do this again."

I sit up on my elbows and his eyes reluctantly stray to my breasts. I swear I hear him groan. "We can't," I agree.

His eyes darken and his voice grows husky. "But we will."

There's no chance for me to utter a response before

his heavy footfalls are leaving the room. A second later the door closes.

Reluctantly I get up, tossing my shirt over my body to lock the door.

I stand no chance when it comes to Jamie Miller. He's my undoing.

CHAPTER EIGHT

Miranda

"Jamie fell and his penis penetrated my vagina."

Lou spits out her coffee all over the table, causing more than a few people to turn and stare. Tanner lets out an uproarious laugh and high fives me.

"Somehow," Lou begins slowly, her fingers wrapped tightly around her coffee cup, the nails painted pink except for each of her ring fingers, which are yellow, "I doubt that's how it happened."

I cross my arms over my chest. "That's my story and I'm sticking to it."

"Oh, no." Tanner grabs onto my arm, looking at me imploringly. "You cannot leave me hanging there. I need details. My love life sucks, let me live vicariously through you."

I pick up my own iced coffee, sipping for a bit too long. "Fine," I drop my shoulders when they both continue to stare, "I'll tell you." Trying to explain to them what happened three nights ago feels impossible. I know neither of them would ever judge me, but I also know Lou doesn't approve of Jamie, and why would she? "He showed up at my apartment and when I opened the door he bound inside, grabbed me, and kissed me like I've never been kissed before. It was like he was drowning and the only way he could get any air was to kiss me."

"It sounds like he forced himself in," Lou hedges, looking unsure.

I shake my head. "It's not like that, trust me. I could've pushed him away and he would've let me, but … I didn't want to."

She exhales a sigh that sounds a lot like a groan. "Why can't you stay away from him?"

"I don't know," I whine, crossing my arms on the table and burying my head between them.

Tanner rubs between my shoulders. "Don't be ashamed."

"I'm not." I sit up. "I just wish I could understand it myself, it's frustrating. Why can't I like a normal, sweet guy?"

Tanner coughs. "Because normal sweet guys are overrated."

"Hey," Lou exclaims defensively.

Tanner rolls his eyes and waves his hand in dismissal. "Abel might be sweet, but he's not normal. Not with a body like that."

Lou snorts, but her eyes are serious as she looks at me. "I don't want you to feel like you can't talk to me about him. Do you have feelings for him?"

"No!" I blurt, more quickly than necessary. My automatic defensive response takes even me by surprise. Both Tanner and Lou give me wide-eyed expressions. I curl in on myself, trying to hide. "It's complicated," I decide on. "I don't *think* I have feelings for him, but I don't dislike him or this wouldn't keep happening. Jamie and I ... we're just..." I struggle for the right words and literally grab at the air as if they'll magically appear and I can shove them in my mouth to spit back out. "We're just us."

It's a shitty explanation but it's all I've got.

"I think you should go for it and not feel bad." Tanner shrugs, taking a bite of muffin.

"I've already been down this path with him before. It didn't end well."

"What exactly happened?" Lou probes, voice soft like a concerned mother.

I roll my eyes. I'm over the whole thing, truly I am, but that doesn't mean talking about it doesn't sting. "We were having casual sex—exclusive sex," I add when she opens her mouth. She promptly closes it and waits for me to continue. "And instead of telling me he was ready to move on with someone else, he rubbed some leggy blonde in my face." I rest my elbow on the table, head in my hand as I exhale a gusty sigh. "It was rude and … it hurt my feelings. As long as we were hooking up I felt he owed it to me to say, 'Hey, Miranda, it's been nice fucking you. Your pussy is supreme, the best ever, but it's time for me to move on. I'll never find a better lay than you, but I have to try.'"

Lou snorts and tries to cover it with a cough. "You're crazy."

"Tell me something I don't know."

"Do you think you'll hook up with him again?"

I turn to Tanner. "Well, since I didn't intend for the other night to happen, I'd say probably." Sipping my coffee, I draw my finger through the condensation on the table. "At least classes are starting back up soon. I'll be too busy for this to keep happening."

Lou laughs. "Yeah, like you were too busy last year."

I stick my tongue out at her, but it's a valid point. Despite my classes and workload, I still made time for Jamie.

"I just don't want you to get hurt," she continues. "You're my best friend, practically my sister."

I snort, waving a dismissive hand like I can bat away her concern. "Getting hurt would imply I have feelings, which I don't. It's just sex."

"Whatever you say." She leans back in her chair and slurps at her coffee until it makes the annoying sound of sucking in air.

Her comment stirs something inside me.

I don't have feelings for Jamie, right? I couldn't possibly.

CHAPTER NINE

Jamie

I stand for a moment, watching my son on the playground with the other children from the summer day camp at his school. He doesn't know I'm here to pick him up yet and watching him laugh, smile, and be a normal kid makes fighting for him all the more worth it.

Shannon was my high school sweetheart. I fell for her hard when I was a sophomore, but she wouldn't give me the time of day until our senior year. We were married our junior year of college. I thought we were blissfully in love, and everything was perfect. I started working for my family and made good money. She worked as a buyer for a fancy boutique.

I found the pregnancy test by accident when I was removing the trash from the bathroom.

I didn't say anything to her at first, afraid she was planning to surprise me with the happy news and didn't want to ruin it by telling her I already knew.

But a week passed, then two, and she still didn't tell me.

Unable to take it anymore I said something to her and was horrified when she told me she hadn't told me because she was considering getting an abortion.

"It's not the right time, Jamie," she told me.

"What do you mean? This is great, a baby, we talked about having kids—"

"No, *you* talked about wanting to have kids. I never said I did."

Her words were a shock to me, having been with her for nearly ten years at that point.

"You don't want kids?" My response was surprised.

She shook her head, tears shimmering in her eyes. "I'm not meant to be a mom, Jamie."

I'd stared at her for a full minute before I said, "But I'm meant to be a dad."

That was the beginning of the end for us. She ended up deciding, obviously, to keep the baby—mostly because I begged and pleaded for our child's life. She became even more withdrawn when an ultrasound revealed Tobias had an atrial septal defect. In layman's terms, a hole in his heart. By the time she was eight months pregnant she served me with divorce papers.

When Tobias was born, she didn't even hold him.

After he was clean and swaddled, he was given to me. "Congratulations, Dad," one of the nurses told me, giving Shannon a dirty look.

I took Tobias home and was immediately a single father, taking care of an infant facing open-heart surgery. I'm the one who stayed up with him when he cried. I fed him. Changed him. Burped him. Loved him.

Shannon was going to sign over her rights, he was going to be mine without any hassle. Our divorce would be final and we'd go our separate ways.

But then she learned how much money she'd get from me with child support. Whether she figured it out on her own or if someone mentioned it to her, I'll never know. That's when things got nasty and we spent months in court. Most judges always side with the mother, even when they're a piece of shit, but somehow this judge saw Shannon for what she really is and awarded me sole custody.

After everything she did, and the fact she made it

abundantly clear she didn't want him, I still feel a sting of guilt for denying her the opportunity to see him. I don't *want* to keep Tobias away from his mother, but I *do* want to protect him. Right now I can't trust her motives. Tobias knows about her, I've shown him pictures, spoken about how we fell in love. I've never said anything bad about her to him, because no matter what, he has half her DNA. For me, I feel like bad mouthing her to him would be like saying half of him is horrible too, and that's not true. He's perfect. He's asked where she went, why we're not married anymore, and if it was his fault. I've told him adamantly it's not his fault, and that she just wasn't ready to be a mom. I know he doesn't quite understand, but he grasps it enough.

He finally spots me and his whole face lights up. "Dad!"

My answering smile is as big as his.

If I'm remembered for anything in this world, I want it to be for being a good father.

Tobias plows into my legs, hugging me. "I missed you, Dad."

"Missed you too, bud." I hug him back, ruffling his hair. I know it won't be long until he doesn't show me affection like this anymore, which makes me try to soak it up every chance I get.

"Ready to go?"

"Yeah. Let me get my backpack." He runs away before

I can respond and grabs it from the pile by the side of the school.

He runs back to me and we walk side by side to my car.

"In you go." I open the back passenger door for him to hop inside.

He tosses his backpack onto the opposite seat and plops onto his booster seat.

"How much longer do I have to use this thing?" He wiggles the arms of it before reaching for his seatbelt.

I shrug, peering at him over the top of the door. "Until it's safe for you to not use it."

"Dad." He rolls his eyes.

"Tobias," I echo, rolling my eyes back and he laughs.

Once he's buckled I close his door and get in. The engine has barely purred to life when he asks, "Can I get a Happy Meal?"

I look at him in the rearview mirror. "No, your grandma made a nice dinner. We're going to go home and eat that."

He sighs heavily like I've crushed all his hopes and dreams with one simple refusal. "But Levi said his parents were taking him to Chuck E. Cheese tonight. A Happy Meal is nothing compared to that."

"Well, I'm sorry I'm not Levi's parents." I flick my blinker on, waiting for traffic to clear before I pull out of the school lot.

"Can I get one tomorrow?"

"No."

"When can I get one?"

"When you stop asking."

"You're so annoying."

I chuckle. "I'm your dad. I'm supposed to be annoying."

"Well, you're doing a great job at it."

I have to stifle my full-blown laughter.

I used to give my parents the same attitude as a kid. I guess this is my payback.

Pulling in the driveway of the two-story home, I click the button for the garage door and it whirs up so I can park.

Tobias unbuckles, grabs his backpack, and runs inside all before I can shut off the car.

"Grandma Jo!" I hear him call as I step out. "I'm hungry and something smells good!"

I laugh. It seems like the Happy Meal is completely forgotten.

Locking the car, I close the garage door and head in.

Tobias is right, something does smell good.

I stroll into the kitchen and find my mom setting down plates on the table. There's a formal dining room in this house, but we never use it.

"Thanks, Mom." I bend and kiss her cheek before I take a seat.

Not a day goes by where I'm not thankful for all my mom's help. I might be a single father, but I definitely haven't raised Tobias alone. My mom didn't want to continue living by herself, not that she isn't capable, she just said it was lonely, and I really needed the help. Having her around has been a blessing and I think it's good for Tobias.

"Yeah, thanks Grandma Jo."

"You're welcome, Toby."

"Don't encourage him with the nickname, Mom." I stand up and grab a beer from the fridge.

I hear the scrape of a chair as she sits down. I pop the cap before I rejoin them. She made some kind of chicken and rice meal that smells like heaven. I wish I could cook like her. Even though she's tried to teach me, I don't have the knack she does.

"The boy should be allowed to go by a nickname if he wants," she chides me.

Exhaling a breath, I turn my eyes to my son who's already stuffing his face. "I named you Tobias for a reason. Do you know why?"

He shakes his head, a piece of rice stuck to his lip. I reach over and brush it off.

He makes a face and pushes my hand away. "Stop, Dad."

Ignoring him, I continue, "I named you Tobias because it's a strong name. It means God is good. I'm not a religious man, son, but God was good to me when he gave me you."

Tobias's face quirks as he thinks. "I still want to be called Toby."

I throw my hands in the air. I can't win with this kid.

My mom laughs and I shoot her daggers.

"Of course you do," I groan.

He's only seven. I don't know how I'm going to survive when he's a teenager.

CHAPTER TEN

Jamie

The flat out sprint I'm running on the treadmill should have me exhausted, but I'm nowhere close. I keep thinking if I run fast enough I can get Miranda off my brain. It's not working. I haven't seen her in two weeks, and it's been hell fighting with myself not to show up at her place. I keep telling myself it's sex I need, but it's a fucking lie, which frustrates me more. If it was about sex I could go anywhere and find someone just as willing, but I haven't bothered trying, because I know no one will be her.

After everything that happened with Shannon, I haven't been interested in pursuing a relationship. I loved Shannon deeply, with all my heart, and she hurt me more than anyone ever has. Tobias was two years old before I slept with another woman, and that was only by mistake. I'd gone out with friends for my birthday, my mom watching him, and got so wasted I didn't realize what I'd done until I woke up the next morning. Up until then, Shannon had been the only woman I'd had sex with.

I'm not sure it's even a relationship I want from Miranda, but I know I haven't had my fill of her. It frustrates me to no end.

Before her, my hookups were occasional. I know it's probably surprising to some people, the way I act, but it's true. But after we slept together the first time I needed more.

I'm a fucking addict when it comes to her.

I know I can't keep running at the pace I am, so I shut off the treadmill and head for the showers. It's after seven and the gym is relatively quiet. I'm not ready to go home, though, but have no idea what to do.

My mom took Tobias to the movies, it's something they do just the two of them at least once a month depending on what has released. His school starts up in only a couple of days. He'll be in second grade. It blows my mind he's growing up so fast. It still feels like I was just holding him as a newborn.

Changing into jeans and an old t-shirt, I leave the gym, driving around for an extended period of time, while I try to avoid the direction of Miranda's apartment.

I'm a fool.

I stop by Chick-fil-A and then there's no more avoiding it.

Gathering the bags of food, I head up to her apartment, knock, and wait.

The door swings open and she stands there in an old ratty t-shirt covered in paint splatters. A loose pair of jeans are barely holding onto her body.

"What kind of pants are you wearing?"

She looks down and back up at me, shaking her head. "Boyfriend jeans."

"Boyfriend jeans," I blurt, my voice higher than normal. "What the fuck do you mean your boyfriend's jeans?"

She rolls her eyes, leaning against the open doorway. "Not *my* boyfriend's jeans. It's the name of the style. Chill. Why are you even here? You've got to stop showing up like this."

Tell me something I don't know.

"I don't know why I'm here." It's perhaps the most honest answer I've ever given her. "But it just felt like where I needed to be."

She continues to lean there, her straight white teeth digging into her bottom lip as she contemplates.

"That for me?" Her eyes flicker to the Chick-fil-A bag. "Because I'm starving."

I nod. "Both of us. You gonna let me in?"

She lets out a dramatic sigh and playfully rolls her eyes. "I guess." She steps aside to let me in. "It's late. What are you doing out?"

She closes and locks the door while I set the bags and drink carrier down on the kitchen counter.

"My mom took Tobias to a movie, so I'm on my own."

She shakes her head. "It's still weird you're a dad."

"Well, I am."

The quiet settles between us and it's a little bit awkward.

She pushes me aside with a bump of her hip. "I need food."

I watch as she grabs plates from her cabinet and begins fixing us each a plateful of chicken nuggets and waffles fries.

"Ugh, yes. You got sauce. My favorite." She pulls out two packs of honey mustard. "You want any?" She holds the sauce bag out to me and I take the Chick-fil-A sauce.

"I got you a lemonade." I wave my hand at the drink carrier where a large lemonade and sweet tea sit.

Her dark brows furrow. "How do you know I like lemonade?"

Because one time when I kissed you, I could taste it on your lips, and now I can't think of the sweet and sour flavor without thinking of you.

"Just a hunch."

She shakes her head, still looking confused. Grabbing her drink, she heads for the couch. I take my sweet tea and follow her. She turns the TV on.

"This is weird." She gives me a funny look as I settle on her small couch—it's actually more of a love seat, and there's no way for two people to sit on it without touching.

"What's weird?" I pop a fry into my mouth, waiting for her response.

"This. You. Us. I mean, we're sitting on my couch eating food. Normally we're naked."

"We can get naked."

"Jamie." She lightly whacks my shoulder with the remote and I laugh.

Fuck, it feels good to laugh.

"Don't you think it's weird?"

"No," I reply honestly, and I swear her cheeks flush.

Sighing, she wiggles around. "Should I put a movie on or something?"

"Sure, whatever you want."

I can tell she's tense as she scrolls through Netflix and finally settles on National Treasure. "I love this movie," she admits, looking down at her plate.

"Me too." She looks at me in surprise. "What?" I blink innocently. "I know you and Louise think I'm the Devil incarnate, but I'm not really."

In fact, my heart is so sensitive I've had to build a fucking fortress around it. Somehow, though, when I'm around you the walls are starting to crumble.

"I don't know what you are." Her reply is soft, almost mumbled.

"Most people don't." I shrug and take a bite of chicken.

I'm not trying to be purposely mysterious. I don't let most people close enough to get to know the real me. Not anymore. I suppose it's my fatal flaw. Everyone has to have one.

We eat in silence, both watching the movie like we've never seen it before.

"I want to change," Miranda announces, pausing the movie. "Do you need to go?" It's a fair question. I am always leaving it seems.

I look at my watch and shake my head. My mom will have taken Tobias to get ice cream and will be putting him to bed. These are the only nights he's allowed up past his bedtime and he cherishes them.

Miranda tugs on her shirt. "Well, I'm going to … uh … put pajamas on."

"Okay." I pick up my tea and drink while she continues to stare at me.

"This is so weird," she mutters to herself before walking off.

"I can take my shirt off if it'll make you more comfortable!"

"Shut up, *James*."

I hear her banging drawers in her room and muttering under her breath.

When she returns, in a plain t-shirt and Eeyore pajama bottoms, I wait for her to sit down before I say anything.

"My name isn't James."

She looks at me wide-eyed. "Uh ... yeah it is."

"No," I drawl slowly, "it's Jamie."

She snorts and shakes her head. "Mhmm, I know. That's your nickname."

"No," I repeat. "Jamie is my *actual* name. It's on my birth certificate and everything." I smirk when her jaw drops.

"What? I ... everything I know is a lie. Lou, calls you James."

"She assumes James is my first name, like most people do. It's Jamie."

"Is that why you call her Louise? Because it's her actual name."

Fuck, she sees too much.

"Yeah," I admit, stretching my arm over the back of the couch. I don't do it intentionally to get closer to her, but when my fingers graze the edge of her shoulder and she shivers I'm glad I did. "Tobias wants me to call him Toby and I refuse."

She laughs. "Why the hang up on names?"

I think for a moment, looking at the paused still on the TV of Nicolas Cage holding the Declaration of Independence in an elevator.

"A lot of people called me James growing up, because they thought that was my actual name. After a while it grated on me. I'm Jamie. Not James."

She bites her lip looking chagrined. Curling her legs under her, she faces me. "Now I feel like a bitch for calling you James. I just assumed that was your name and you didn't like it." Her lower lip pouts slightly. "I can't believe I'm saying this, but I feel bad. I'm sorry."

"I didn't tell you." I don't bother to correct most people these days. It's a waste of breath.

She stares at me a moment longer before clearing her throat and grabbing the remote. The movie starts back up and the conversation drops off.

Miranda eventually settles her body against mine, falling asleep before they enter the church.

I should get up, leave, but I don't.

Miranda wiggles her body against mine, making a soft noise in her sleep.

Why am I here?

In this tiny ass apartment, with a woman twelve years

younger than me, is the last place I should be but the only place I seem to belong.

I glide my fingers over the curve of her cheek and she curls into me more. There are dark circles under her eyes and even though I know her classes have only started, she's clearly exhausted.

I tell myself not to do it, but I do it anyway, and bend over to place a gentle kiss on her forehead.

I don't know who I am anymore, at least when I'm around her, and it terrifies me. I haven't given anyone the power to break my heart since Shannon, but I'm very close to letting Miranda do the same. It's why I walked away the first time, put that distance between us. Despite it, I couldn't stay away. She's my bad habit, one I can't quit, one I don't want to.

CHAPTER ELEVEN

Miranda

Awareness slowly creeps into the recesses of my brain. My whole body screams in protest at my contorted position. My head rests on something hard, my nose pressed against something that smells vaguely of wood and a hint of orange. I feel an arm wrapped around my body.

Where the fuck am I?

I force my eyes open and find my face pressed against

the softest t-shirt. I inhale the scent again, certain it's the greatest thing I've ever smelled. Slowly I sit up, unwinding my body from the pretzel shape I was in. The arm drops like a heavy leaden weight. Looking around I see I'm in my apartment, my clothes are intact, and…

"Oh my God." My hands fly to my face as I take in Jamie asleep on my couch. He's sitting upright, his head angled in a position that can't be comfortable. One arm hangs limply, no longer around me, with the other resting on the edge of the couch.

Grappling for my phone on the coffee table my jaw drops further when I see the time. Six in the morning.

Holy shit.

Jamie spent the night.

Unintentionally, but still.

And to think, we didn't even have sex.

I know he's bound to be pissed. This couldn't have been in his plan.

Sucking it up, I shake his shoulder. He barely wobbles. I push him harder and he jolts awake, bleary hazel eyes looking around in confusion.

"Miranda?" Confusion heavy in his voice as well as sleep. He stretches his arms above his head, twisting his neck. "Fuck, what time is it? I've got to get home."

"It's six."

He rolls his eyes and stifles a yawn. "No, I got here at like nine."

"Six in the morning, Jamie."

"Fuck." He jumps up from the couch, patting his pockets and no doubt making sure his keys are there. "Shit. Fuck. Dammit all to hell."

"Calm down." I follow him to the door and grab his arm, but he shakes my hold loose.

"I can't calm down. My son is usually up by now and I'm not at home." He thrusts his fingers through his unruly hair. "I have to go."

"I'm sorry," I say. I don't know why I feel the need to apologize. I'm not the one who invited him here. He showed up. He fell asleep. He's a big boy and can deal with it.

His shoulders soften at my words. "Not your fault. I..." He clenches his jaw. "Thank you for last night."

My lips part in surprise, but he doesn't give me a chance to respond before he's opening the door and fleeing my building.

Shaking my head, I lock the door behind him.

I used to say I liked older guys because they were less complicated, but Jamie?

He's the flashing neon light of complicated.

Classes are over for the day, and I want nothing more than to go home, dive into my bed, and sleep for days.

But, alas, adulthood calls.

Grocery shopping is a must. Especially considering the only things in my refrigerator are a container of yogurt, a pack of English muffins, and a bottle of mustard I'm certain was expired when I bought it.

Behind the wheel of my car I stifle a yawn, and drive to Food Mart.

I'm convinced grocery shopping is the most mundane thing to ever exist. You have to browse the aisles, pile your cart full, check out, and then go home, carry it all in, and put it away. This isn't a one step process. It's more like a million.

I push the cart through the store, getting things necessary for meals I'll probably never make, and a smorgasbord of snacks. Snacks are a college student's fuel. That and coffee.

I pause in the bread aisle, scanning for the one I always get.

My phone buzzes in my pocket and I pull it out.

Lou: Abel and I are going to Griffin's tonight. A couple of bands are playing. You want to go?

Me: No. I have a date.

Lou: OMG! WHAT?! A DATE?! WHY DIDN'T YOU TELL ME?!

Me: With my bed. I have a date with my bed.

I find the right bread and add it to the cart, moving on to the next aisle.

Lou: That was mean. You got me all excited for no reason. How rude.

Me: Okay, Michelle.

Lou: Jeez, you must be tired. It was Stephanie who always said how rude.

Me: Whatever. I'm getting groceries and then I'm going home to sleep.

Lou: All right. Fine. If you change your mind, just come.

Me: Have fun.

I put my phone away so I can finish shopping and get home. I don't like being this tired, but I know I can't half-ass anything. I want to get the best grades I can, and hopefully have an awesome student teaching position next semester. I need everything to go smoothly, so I can get a job no problem. The last thing I want to do is graduate with a mountain of debt and no job, but realistically that seems to be what happens to a lot of people these days and then you end up with a minimum wage job that has nothing to do with your degree.

"Come on, Dad, they're Spiderman cupcakes. You have to get them for me."

"No. No, I don't. The last thing I need is you hyped up on sugar."

My cart comes to a screeching halt, banging into a table of freshly made bagels. One pack topples onto the floor and hazel eyes turn in my direction.

I wish I could back the fuck out of here and not be seen, but it's too late.

Jamie stares at me and I stare back. Neither one of us makes a move closer and everything else dulls around us. I can't even hear anything. It's as if most of my senses decided to shut down.

I went months never seeing Jamie, and now he's everywhere.

At my apartment.

At Michaels.

Now at freaking Food Mart.

What. Is. Happening.

"Fancy running into you here." I finally find my voice and of course it's something stupid to leave my mouth. Where's Ursula to steal my voice when I need her?

Jamie says nothing, but his mini-me pops around the corner.

"Oh, hi. You're the lady from the store."

Panic clogs my throat looking at the boy. It's still crazy to me that Jamie is a father. It doesn't suit the preconceived notions I have about him.

"Uh, yeah, that's me."

So smooth Miranda.

"Dad, it's your friend. You should say hi." Mini-Jamie pokes Big-Jamie's side. *"Dad."*

Jamie shakes his head. "Right … um … didn't expect to see you here."

"Well, it is the grocery store closest to my apartment."

Why can't I rein in my sarcasm just once in my life?

"Do you paint?"

My eyes drop to Mini-Jamie. The kid is wearing dress pants, a button-down shirt, and red suspenders. "Uh…"

"You dropped paint at Michaels."

"Oh, yeah." I shake my head rapidly. "I'm an artist."

It always feels weird to label myself an artist. I feel undeserving of the title. With every project I always see things I feel need improvement and it seems wrong to call myself an artist when I can't achieve perfection. That's the thing about art. It isn't perfect and it's always a little messy. Kind of like life.

"That's cool. I like to paint too. I like lots of things."

I look from Big-Jamie to Mini-Jamie. "What other things do you like to do?"

"I'm a boy scout," he says proudly. "Just like my dad was."

Jamie groans. "Thanks for throwing me under the bus, son."

"You're welcome." Mini-Jamie grins at his dad.

Jamie shakes his head back and forth, pinching the bridge of his nose.

"Boy scout, huh?" I arch a brow, fighting a grin.

Picturing a young Jamie in a cub scout uniform is actually pretty adorable.

"Yeah, he made it all the way to Eagle scout," Mini-Jamie exclaims in praise.

My eyes widen and I fight a grin. "Wow, Jamie. I'm impressed."

Jamie mumbles, "I was a dorky kid."

I laugh. "Somehow, I doubt that."

Mini-Jamie interrupts, clearing his throat. "Since you're an artist, do you think you could teach me sometime? I want to get better, but my dad can't even draw a stick figure and Grandma Jo says she'd rather teach me how to cook instead."

"Um..." I bite my lip.

"Tobias, I think Miranda has other things to do besides teach you how to paint. She's very busy."

"Oh." His face falls and he toes his shoe against the floor.

My heart pangs and I feel bad. "Actually, I'd love to if it's okay with your dad."

Mini-Jamie lights up and Big-Jamie looks panic-stricken.

"Can you come now?" Mini-Jamie asks. "You can ride in our car. There's plenty of room."

"Son—" Jamie begins, but I cut him off.

"I actually can't right now. I'm really tired, so I need to go home and take a nap, but your dad has my number so he can let me know when it works in his schedule."

Mini-Jamie scrunches his face. "A nap? Only babies take naps."

I laugh. "You'll reevaluate that statement when you're older."

He shrugs. "I doubt it, but whatever you say."

I lift my gaze to Big-Jamie. "I really don't mind, if it's okay with you."

He nods, jaw clenched, but no response is uttered from his lips.

Somehow, I feel like I've stepped on his toes even though I didn't intend to.

"Well, um, I guess I'll be going then." I back my shopping cart up to skedaddle awkwardly away.

Behind me I hear Tobias ask, "So, cupcakes?"

Jamie sighs heavily, a weary, exhausted kind of sigh. "You can have the cupcakes."

I smile to myself.

The ice man isn't so icy after all.

CHAPTER TWELVE

Miranda

Yoga normally relaxes me.

It's something I look forward to, especially when Lou and I can attend class together. Tanner tags along sometimes too. He's ridiculously good at it, and I'd be lying if I said I wasn't jealous of his downward dog. I look more like a llama having a seizure. You'd think after all this time I would've mastered such a simple position, but regrettably, I have not.

"You guys are making me look ridiculously horrible at this," I hiss to my friends, over the voice of the instructor in front of the room.

Lou turns her eyes to me. "You need to get out of your head. That's your problem."

"She's right," Tanner pipes in. "You look awfully distracted."

"I am *not* distracted."

Defensive? Yes.

Distracted? ...Perhaps.

I was surprised to get a text from Jamie this morning. I thought after the grocery debacle a couple of days ago that I wouldn't hear from him again until he magically showed up looking for a one-way ticket straight into my vagina. Which, let's be real, he already has the all access pass.

Jamie: If you really don't mind teaching Tobias, could you come over this weekend? Either day is fine. If you're free. Which you're probably not.

I don't know what exactly he was trying to hint at. My social life is severely lacking. Tanner, Lou, and Abel are really the only three people I know around here, except for Jamie. Don't get me wrong, I've dated while I've been at college, gone to some parties, but look where that's gotten me.

Basically, I'm a certified cat lady minus the cat. When I'm not at school, I'm at home either doing homework, painting, or watching reruns of Beverly Hills 90210. My mom watched the show religiously on repeat when I was growing up. To this day I still have a major crush on David Silver. I'm convinced Brian Austin Green is a god among men. Megan Fox is one lucky lady.

See, clearly you've had a thing for older guys right from the start.

"Are you constipated? Because you look like it." Tanner looks me over carefully.

"That's her thinking face," Lou tells him before I can reply.

"That's your thinking face? Are you sure?" Tanner's brows scrunch. "You really need to work on that, because you look like you need to take a shit."

I snort and fall from my position, face planting onto the mat.

"You okay back there?" The instructor asks, and before I can even right myself I know every eye in the room is on me.

"I'm fine." I raise my hand waving it, and she gets back to instructing.

"Do you need a laxative?" Tanner hisses under his breath. "There's a Walgreens across the street."

"Oh my fucking God, Tanner, I'm not constipated! My bowel movements are just dandy!"

If I thought everyone was looking at me before they definitely are now.

Lou busts out laughing, falling spread eagle on her mat as she rolls around clutching her stomach. Tanner presses a hand over his mouth to stifle his own laughter.

Maybe I should be embarrassed, but I'm not.

I look around at everyone staring at me. "What? You guys don't talk about your poop with your friends? Think about it, are you really even friends if you can't talk about this kind of shit? Literally."

I stand up, brushing my black leggings off, and walk out of the room.

Yoga is pointless when I can't get Jamie off my brain and know I need to reply to his text message instead of continuing to put it off.

I put my sneakers on and hang out in the front area waiting for Tanner and Lou to finish up.

Bringing up Jamie's text I stare at it for a while longer before I finally respond.

Me: I don't have plans. Whichever day is better for you works for me.

His reply is almost instant.

Jamie: Saturday at 3?

Me: Perfect.

My heart tap dances in my chest. It's silly. Technically I have plans with Jamie's son, not him, and yet I'm excited at the prospect of being around him. I'm baffled by the fact I even want to be near him. Emotions and feelings are weird, pesky things. They get all tangled and knotted like a yarn ball and there's no making sense of them.

Tanner and Lou join me a few minutes later.

"Wanna grab lunch?" Lou asks, pointing across the street to a café.

"I have time."

"Yeah, I'm starving." Tanner wipes sweat from his brow with the edge of his shirt.

The three of us head across and sit outside at one of the tiled tables with an orange umbrella.

"You really did seem distracted today," Lou remarks, pretending to look at her menu, but I can feel her eyes on me.

"Just thinking about school."

"School or Jamie's dick?"

I choke on my tongue, coughing like a beached whale.

"School, definitely school," I tell Tanner, holding up a hand in a *please have mercy on me* gesture.

"I feel like there's a lot you're not telling me." Lou sets down her menu and when I reluctantly look her way I wish I hadn't. I can clearly see the hurt she feels. It's not that I don't want to confide in her, but it feels impossible when I can't even comprehend my own thoughts.

I get a small reprieve to think about what I want to say when the waitress drops off waters and takes our order.

"I'm not intentionally trying to hide things from you, or leave you out, but I don't know how to talk to you when I barely know how I feel or what I think. It's made worse because you don't even like Jamie."

"So, this is about Jamie?" She raises a brow. "And I might not like him, but I don't really know him. Obviously you know him better than I do. But I can't begin to understand things if you don't talk to me about them."

I stare at a loose tile on the tabletop. "That's the thing, though, I don't understand it myself."

Her lips downturn and she's quiet. Tanner is busy checking out a guy at the next table.

I'm surprised when I feel her hand grab onto mine.

"Remember, no matter what, I'm your best friend and I'll always have your back. I only want you happy. That's the most important thing."

"Thank you." I squeeze her hand back.

I don't know how I got so lucky having a best friend like her, but I know what Lou would say it is.

Fate.

CHAPTER THIRTEEN

Miranda

"Arrived! Your destination is on the right," my navigation system says in a too pleasant tone. My car rolls to a stop in front of a sprawling brick front suburban home.

It doesn't scream Jamie to me, but I guess he's not just Jamie anymore.

He's *Daddy* Jamie.

Okay, that's fucking weird.

I park my car against the curb, but leave it on so the AC can blast my heated skin.

"Why am I sweating so much?" I groan, fanning my pits and contorting my body to get them closer to the vents.

I cannot roll up to Jamie's front door drenched in sweat. That's not an attractive look.

I pull down the sun visor and wipe smeared mascara from beneath my eyes. I grab some chapstick from the cup holder and swipe it on.

I'm acting like a complete crazy person.

"Get over yourself, Miranda."

I'm so good at giving pep talks to myself.

I give myself one more moment to catch my breath before I grab supplies from my car, walk up the fancy walkway past flowers I'm sure his mother lovingly takes care of because I can't imagine him doing it, and finally stop in front of the cheery robin's egg blue door.

One, two, three. On the count of three I push the doorbell.

I don't have to wait long before the door soars open.

"You're here!" Tobias exclaims, giving a little hop. "Dad, she's here!"

"Tobias," I hear Jamie grunt from somewhere nearby, "what have I told you about opening the door?"

Tobias looks up at me and rolls his eyes as Jamie appears around the corner.

My breath catches. It should be illegal the way he makes a pair of jeans, simple white tee, and bare feet look absolutely sinful.

"That only murderers and Jesus freaks ring the doorbell."

I snort and Jamie's expression is amused behind his son.

"Man, I'm totally failing at this already. I left my crowbar at home and my ax is stuck in a tree. But I can do this." I stand up straight and clear my throat. I knock the air and Jamie tilts his head curiously. "Hello, such a beautiful day. Can I tell you about our Lord and Savior Jesus Christ?"

And then Jamie does something I never, not in a million years, thought I'd bear witness to.

He laughs.

Not a simple manly chuckle.

No, he tosses his head back, his whole body shaking with laughter.

I give myself a mental pat on the back for a job well done.

"My grandma is making cookies," Tobias says, grabbing my arm and urging me inside. "Do you like cookies?"

"Who doesn't?" I scoff in disbelief.

"What is in those?" He nods at the bags in my hands, tugging me along to the kitchen I presume.

Jamie follows behind, now a silent guardian. I mentally picture him in a suit of armor and I hate to say, he could even rock that. It must be a curse to be that good looking.

"Grandma Jo, this is Miranda," Toby introduces me as we reach the kitchen, a light and airy space.

Grandma Jo sets a tray of cookies on the counter and pulls off her oven mitts.

"It's nice to meet you. You can call me Mama Jo." I can already tell she's a warm, caring person, and probably as ooey gooey sweet as the chocolate chip cookies starting to cool.

"Nice to meet you too." For a moment I want to joke about how Jamie came from someone so sweet, but I think better of it. It's becoming obvious to me that his ex did a number on him, completely altering him. "Not going to lie, I would love to have some of those cookies."

She laughs, her cheeks flushed. "I'll bring you and Toby some in a bit."

"Mom," Jamie groans, and I turn to find his tall frame leaning against the refrigerator with his arms crossed over his chest. "Don't spoil his appetite."

"Jamie, Jamie, Jamie," she sighs his name with a shake of her head. "A cookie has never hurt anyone. Don't think I haven't figured out that it's *you* who steals the cookies, not Toby."

Jamie's lips twitch. "False accusations get you nowhere."

His mom shares a conspiratorial look with me. "He thinks he's so clever. A mother always knows." She taps the side of her forehead.

"Is there somewhere I can put these?" I hold up the heavy bags that are beginning to take a toll on my hands and arms.

Mama Jo grabs one of the oven mitts and tosses it at Jamie.

"What was that for?" It bounces off his body, landing useless on the floor. That'd be like attacking a bear with a needle.

"Take the bags from the young lady. I taught you better than that."

"Oh, right. Give them here."

He grabs them from me.

"Jamie," she scolds again. To me, she adds, "He has manners, I swear. I didn't raise a complete heathen."

Jamie rolls his eyes. "Miranda likes me without my manners," he mutters, and my jaw drops.

I give his mom a horrified expression and she looks between the two of us with intrigue.

Fuck me.

Jamie looks at me with a smirk and I swear he can read my mind.

Not that way, I ping back and hope he hears it loud and clear. He frowns, so I think he does.

Or it could be because you're staring really hard at him?

Shoving my hands in the pockets of my work jeans as I've dubbed them since they're speckled with every color of paint imaginable I rock back on my heels awkwardly. "So ... uh ... where do you want me?"

Jamie stifles a laugh.

"I mean," I glare at him, "where do you want me to work with Toby?"

He sobers, exhaling a breath. "I set up a table in the basement."

He starts walking, which leaves me to assume I'm meant to follow. Toby scampers ahead of me and I follow the two Miller boys into the basement.

It's a finished basement and I look around in awe at the TV and living room set up, bar, and pool table.

I keep following Jamie around to another side where he's set up a foldable long table on top of plastic sheeting to cover the carpet, with more of the sheeting draping the table.

He notices me taking in all the plastic. "I don't like messes."

"Are you sure you're not planning to Dexter me?"

"Did you just make Dexter a verb?"

I pause, swaying back and forth. "Maybe," I drawl.

He shakes his head and places the bags on the table.

"Thanks for carrying those."

"Mhmm," he hums.

Toby starts going through them, vibrating with excitement. "What are we going to paint Miranda? Can I paint a dinosaur? I love those. My whole room is dinosaurs. Can I show you later?"

"Tobias, one question at a time," Jamie scolds lightly, ruffling his son's hair.

"We're going to do a couple of different things," I answer his first question. "You can definitely paint a dinosaur and if we have time, and your dad doesn't mind, you can show me your room."

"Cool." He grins and again I'm blown away by how much he looks like Jamie. If only I'd see Jamie smile that big, so carefree and happy.

Jamie stands there and I make a shooing motion. "You can go now. Toby and I have things covered. We don't need an overseer."

His lips turn down. "But—"

"Dad," Toby pleads, clasping his hands in front of his chest, "we don't need a babysitter."

Jamie exhales, hands on his hips. "Fine. No messes."

I take a dramatic look around the space. "I think with all this plastic, I'll be fine."

Another sigh. "I'll be in my office. You know where to find me. Be good," he says to Toby.

Toby rolls his eyes. "I'm always good."

Jamie shakes his head, fighting a smile. "The sad thing is I know you believe that."

I watch him leave and then begin pulling out canvases—I got a bunch of small ones—paint, brushes, and other supplies.

"Why do you like to paint?" Toby picks up a canvas, holding it between his hands and turning it like he's steering a ship.

I place a cup on the table that I'll need to fill with water. "Because there's something pretty cool about taking that white, blank canvas, and creating something from my mind. It can become anything I have the ability to think up."

"Like a rocketship?"

"Yep." I spread the brushes out. "Or a dinosaur. You can paint people, pets, places, objects. But you can also take the paint and just have fun with it, see what happens when you mix different colors, make a complete mess. When it comes to art, you don't have to grow up."

After everything is set up on the table I fill the two cups I brought with water from the basement bar.

Toby pulls out one of the chairs Jamie had set out with the table. Like me he's wearing clothes that won't matter if they're dirtied. This is only the third time I've seen the kid, but it's the first time he hasn't been dressed up.

I grab one of the paper plates I brought and squirt different colors of paint on it, then place it in front of Toby before doing the same for myself.

"If you want to lighten a color you're going to mix white and the color together. Always do a little at a time. If you want to darken a color, add black to it, again only a little to start."

"Won't it look muddy if I add black?" His brow crinkles in confusion.

"Only if you add too much. That's why you do it like this." I demonstrate and his mouth becomes a tiny O shape.

"Wow! I never thought of that!"

I laugh and sit down in my own chair. "That's why I'm here, right?"

"Right," he agrees, nodding. "What first?"

"How about that dinosaur?" I grin at him.

He beams up at me and my heart squeezes. I don't know how any mother could walk away from this brilliant boy.

Several hours later I've cleaned everything up, eaten more cookies than I should have thanks to Mama Jo, and my body is speckled with paint. But I have to admit, it was fun working with Toby. He's a funny kid and it was good practice for when I'm an art teacher.

"Toby, I need to run to the store, why don't you come with me?" Mama Jo says to him as he runs past.

I set the bags down by the door, digging through my purse for my keys.

"Why?"

"Because I want you to."

Jamie comes from somewhere in the back of the house. "Are you leaving?"

I start to speak but Mama Jo cuts me off. "Toby and I are going to run to the store. We'll be back in a little while."

Jamie's brows draw together and he watches his mom urge his son down a hall. A minute passes as the two of them leave, and then Jamie's staring at me like some fascinating specimen under a microscope.

"I cleaned things up and left the canvases drying, mine included since I can't exactly have wet paint in my car. I can pick them up later in the week."

Jamie watches out the window over my shoulder as the car pulls away.

"She thinks she's so sneaky."

"W-What?" I stutter.

He fights a smile, rubbing the stubble on his chin.

"She's giving us time alone."

"*Oh.* But why? She doesn't know about me. Or us. Or any of the totally indecent things we've done."

He fights another smile.

"You're an attractive woman, Miranda. I haven't been in a relationship in eight years. My mother wants to see me find someone, fall in love, and preferably give her more grandchildren."

My mouth parts and my cheeks color at the image he's conjured in my mind. One of a blissfully happy married Jamie and me with a butt load of kids running around.

Clearing my throat, and wishing I could Etch-A-Sketch that picture right out of my brain, I point over my shoulder. "I should be going."

He shoves his hands in his pockets, raising his shoulders up. "You should be."

I let out a breathy, "But?"

"Stay."

One word.

I never knew one word could have so much meaning. That it could impact me in a way I don't expect.

Looking up at him, I try to hide the shaking in my hands, because I'm afraid.

Absolutely petrified of my feelings for him. I've tried to keep them locked away, but the fact is, they're there. I *like* him, and if he keeps showing me bits of the real him,

I'm afraid that *like* might grow into something even stronger.

"Why?" *Why should I stay?*

"Because I want you to."

He extends his hand to me and I stare at it like it's a poisonous snake, ready to strike. He quirks his fingers and I place my hand in his.

Once my hand is in his grasp he pulls me to his body. I'm surprised he's not pushing me away, hauling me out of his house like yesterday's trash. He's so hot and cold I never know where I stand with him.

My heart is beating out of control, my mind spinning.

I want to say something silly or stupid, anything to break the intense stare he has going with me, but I can't. All words have fled my brain, tunneling out like annoying little ... well, whatever animal tunnels. I can't think straight when I'm in Jamie's arms like this.

"I feel like I shouldn't be here," I say instead.

"Why?" His eyes are on my lips.

"Because you're you and I'm me and we don't make any sense."

"Do we have to make sense?"

I close my eyes. "It'd be easier if we did."

He lowers his lips to my ear and my eyes drift closed. "It's taken me my whole life to learn nothing ever makes sense," he whispers lowly. "I want to show you something."

My eyes fly open and I take a step away from him. "If you whip out your dick I'll punch you again."

A small laugh bubbles out of his throat and dammit if I don't feel some kind of satisfaction about that.

Sobering, he says, "You've already seen it and you haven't punched me yet, so I think I'm safe. Admit it, you love my cock."

My mouth drops and he wears a satisfied grin.

He reaches out, curling his index finger underneath my chin and pushing it up so my mouth closes.

"That's not what I want to show you."

He tugs my hand and pulls me down the hallway and around the corner into a tucked away office space.

If you told me to close my eyes and imagine Jamie's home office, honestly, I'd probably picture a sex dungeon. Not ... this.

The walls are filled with bookcases crowded with books and knick-knacks. His desk is huge with an iMac on one end, one of those desk calendars, a cup for pens, and a holder for papers and envelopes. It's all surprisingly neat and tidy. There's a sturdy desk chair, a built-in bench beneath a window, and two leather club chairs that make me want to dive bomb into them and stay for hours with a soft blanket, cup of coffee, and a good book.

"Why are you showing me this?" I find myself asking, walking away from him to study some of the book spines.

I feel him move behind me, his presence warm and heady.

"Because I want to show you more of me."

I turn around and he's so close I have to crane my neck back to look at him. Poking my index finger into his chest I say softly, "Why don't you show me more of what's in *here*?"

He swallows thickly and grabs my hand before I can pull it away, flattening it over his heart. "I'm trying." He looks pained, whether by his words or the idea of truly letting me in, I don't know.

It's all so confusing, him and I.

He lowers his forehead, pressing it to mine. His eyes close. Then mine.

"Stop making me feel, Miranda."

"Stop making me want you."

He pulls away from me and I instantly miss his warmth.

I quickly turn around and return to perusing the shelves, pulling some books off to read the backs.

I pull off Pride and Prejudice, my lips quirking with a smile.

"What?" Jamie asks from the corner, having spotted the movement with his laser focus.

I hold the book up for him. "Another reason I'm single—books have given me an unrealistic expectation of men." I return it to the shelf, ignoring his frown. "You and Darcy are kind of alike, you know?" I muse and out of the corner of my eye I see him cross his arms.

"How so?" he prompts, his voice suddenly deeper.

I give him a coy smirk. "Always judging everything."

He shakes his head but lets me look through his office, even keeping quiet when I snoop through the drawers where the most interesting thing I find is a Matchbox car, most likely hidden by Toby. Everything is normal, if not ridiculously orderly. He's a definite neat freak, which surprises me.

"I should be going," I finally say. I've been here longer than I planned, and even though I'm only going home to an empty apartment, I feel jittery with the need to get away.

He nods and turns off the light, following me to the front door.

"There's something else I want to show you."

"Now?" I raise a brow.

He shakes his head. "What are you doing tomorrow?"

"Nothing."

I already turned down Lou's offer to go to the American History museum in D.C. with her and Abel.

"I'll pick you up at eight."

"At night?" I blurt.

"In the morning."

"Um ... yeah ... nah ... it's Sunday and that's too early."

"Eight, Miranda." His tone turns bossy.

I stick my tongue out. "Don't tell me what to do."

"Eight. In. The. Morning. Be ready."

"Ugh." I grab my stuff and he opens the door. "Have I ever told you that you're super annoying?"

"I think you've mentioned it once or twice." He smiles, a small one but a smile nonetheless. That smile, it's mine. I grab it, cradling it close before tucking it away into the recesses of my memory.

"I guess I'll see you at nine," I grumble.

"Eight."

"Nine."

He chuckles. "We'll see who wins."

"Me, I always do," I call behind me, already halfway down the walkway.

After my car is loaded and I'm in the driver's seat, I look, and he's still standing in the open front door.

He lifts his hand in a wave.

I give him the finger.

And he laughs, a big belly laugh. I wish I could hear it, but it doesn't really matter because no matter what happens come morning I know I'm the real winner.

CHAPTER FOURTEEN

Jamie

I knock on her door at 8:01 in the morning.

The door blasts open—she can't open a door in a normal manner—and she huffs, "You didn't think I'd be awake, did you? Ha! Fooled you. I'm up. Dressed. Even brushed my teeth, but you better have coffee."

I hold up the drink carrier and her eyes light up.

"My savior." She takes one of the iced coffees and gulps a quarter of it down.

"All right, let's go." She steps out and closes the door behind her, making sure it's locked. "This better be worth it." She catches me staring at her clothes and punches me in the shoulder. "You better not be judging me for what I'm wearing. You didn't tell me what this was for, and considering the early time, I wasn't getting fancy."

"I just thought your ass looked nice in those cotton shorts."

Instead of snapping back at me, she has a pleased smile instead.

The pair of gray shorts hug her curves and the cropped white shirt she has on leaves little to the imagination. Despite her bra, her nipples are pebbled against the fabric. She wears a pair of tennis shoes and her hair is thrown back in a messy ponytail. There's not a stitch of makeup on her face. She looks fucking sexy, and if I didn't have something planned I would haul her ass inside so I could take time exploring her body.

"We better go," I say, ushering her down the stairs.

We reach the bottom level and a door opens.

"Going somewhere this early, girly?"

Miranda whirls around and I find some creepy looking guy with yellowed teeth looking her up and down.

"It's not *that* early Stinky Stan. Mind your own business."

He gives her a nasty smile but when he notices me

glaring at him he quickly scurries back into his apartment.

"That guy give you problems?" My voice is deep, fighting the edge of anger I feel. I place a possessive hand on the small of her back and guide her to my car.

She shrugs, reaching for the passenger door but I grab it before she can.

"He's nothing I can't handle."

"You shouldn't have to handle him."

She rolls her eyes as she slides in. "You're acting like a jealous boyfriend. I don't need you to protect me."

I'm sure Miranda is more than capable of taking care of herself, but that doesn't mean she should have to.

Putting a lid on my temper so I don't walk back and beat down Stan's door, I walk around the front of the car and get in the driver's seat.

"This car is nice," she whistles, rubbing her hands on the leather seat. "This feels like butter."

"It should with what it costs."

I hate the frown that suddenly appears on her face. "Yeah, I'll never be able to afford something as nice as this."

"One day."

She shakes her head, giving me a small smile. "On an art teacher's salary I'll be lucky if I can afford to eat anything other than ramen noodles. Let's face it, I'll probably have to resort to one of those awful, so called, life hacks where I cook them in a coffee maker."

"You'll do better than you think."

She snorts, rolling her eyes. "Jamie, I want to be an art teacher because it'll make me happy, not because it'll make me rich. I'd rather be poor with a rich heart, than have all the money in the world and a cold heart."

Well, fuck.

Clearing my throat, I back out of the parking space. Turning right out of her apartment complex I don't drive more than a mile before I pull into the small local airport terminal.

"Why are we here?" Her brows are scrunched together like the two furry caterpillars Tobias dumped in my hand this morning for shits and giggles. He has no idea I ate a worm once on a dare. The disgusting fact still haunts me to this day. But it's probably no worse than the mescal I drank in my college days. "This is an airport, Jamie." Her tone implies I'm too dumb to know where we are, and I have to suppress a laugh.

"I know it's an airport."

"Then why are we here?" she challenges, crossing her arms over her chest and lifting her chin haughtily.

It pains me not to laugh at her attitude. She's so fucking defiant. That might be a turn off for some guys, but I love it. She speaks her mind and takes no shit. Her confidence and boldness is part of the reason I'm attracted to her.

"Reasons."

"That's not an answer."

"It's the only one you're getting." Her glare turns deadly. "For now," I add.

Parking the car, I shut off the engine. I undo my seatbelt, turn in my seat to face her and arch one brow. "Get out of the car, sweetheart."

She snorts. "Don't call me sweetheart."

I grin and I notice the way her breath catches.

She likes when I smile.

"Come on," I encourage. Leaning into her, I brush hair from her shoulder. "You're so close to answers, let's not stall now."

Her eyes zero in on my lips and I back away, quickly exiting the car. It's not that I don't want to kiss her, but I know if I do I won't want to stop at kissing. I'm addicted to her and she doesn't even know it.

She follows me into the small terminal, looking at me curiously when I offer no explanation as we're checked by the security.

"How are you today, Mr. Miller?" Joe, one of the security guards asks, even as he checks my ID. He's a "by the book" kind of man.

"I've told you, call me Jamie." I walk through the metal detector and wait for Miranda to do the same.

Even though the airport is as small as they come and only for privately owned planes, we still have to go through a small search. It's definitely not as extensive as flying out of Dulles, the nearest international airport, but it still seems overboard to me.

Joe hands me my ID back and I return it to my wallet. Now that we're clear, I reach for Miranda's hand. She looks at my outstretched hand with surprise before slowly taking it. I lead her out of the building, feeling the pulse and vibration of all the questions in her body as she struggles to keep them all inside.

I'm sure at this point she's connected the dots, but I still don't want to say anything yet. I'm bringing her here to offer her a small piece of me. Yeah, it's not a lot, but it's something—more than I've ever given anyone and I hope she knows that. I don't share much of myself willingly with anyone. I've learned the hard way that people have the tendency to use you, but this brings me joy, and I guess selfishly I want Miranda to see that side of me.

We reach the hangar, and I pull out my key, unlocking the side door.

I flick all the switches and the overhead lights illuminate, blinding us for a moment.

"Holy. Shit." She exhales, her eyes wide as she looks around.

The hangar is one of the largest ones at this airport, housing three planes.

"Does your friend own one of these?" she asks, still spinning.

"I do."

She stops, brown eyes wide like a cornered doe. "You own one of these?" She looks at them with even more awe and surprise. "Which one?"

"Take your pick."

Her jaw drops. "All of them?"

I nod. "That one," I point to the largest, "is the company jet. So technically *I* don't own it, but since I'm now the owner of the company, I do get the final say in its use." I turn to the middle one. "That's the newest addition. I wanted something I could fit more people in, but obviously not as big as the jet."

"How many can fit in it?"

"Ten." Shoving my hands in my pockets, I swivel to face my favorite plane. The one that means the most to me. "This one is my most prized possession." I start walking toward the yellow plane. "It can only fit two people."

She follows and makes a frown at it. "It's so ... tiny."

I chuckle. "That's kind of the point of an ultralight aviation."

"Why is this one special?" She cocks her head, studying me and then the plane. "Is it worth a lot."

I chuckle. "No, to a lot of people it's probably a piece

of junk. It's just a basic plane, but ... my grandpa got it for me when I got my pilot's license."

"That's why it's your favorite?" She looks surprised.

I nod. "You can't put a price on memories."

I may not seem like the most sentimental person, but I am. When my dad passed away, my grandfather stepped up to the plate, filling that fatherly role I was lacking. He taught me things I'm only beginning to understand. That's how he worked, though, planting seeds that would later turn into a sprawling forest.

"We're taking this one up," I tell her.

"Whoa, whoa, whoa, Christian Grey, back the fuck up. My ass is not getting in that plane." She holds her hands in front of her chest, waving them back and forth. When she starts to back up, I grasp her arm to halt her movements.

"I'm an excellent pilot."

She gives me a bewildered look. "I don't care if you're Sully Sullenberger, I'm not getting in that plane."

Her eyes dart back and forth in fear.

I startle in realization. "Have you never been on a plane?"

She snorts and looks at the ground. "Of course I have."

"Miranda."

She utters a reluctant and small, "No."

Where I still hold her arm, I rub my thumb in

soothing circles. "I would never let anything bad happen to you."

She looks up at me reluctantly, her eyes open but wary. "You can't make that promise."

I guess she's right. I'm something bad and I've already happened to her.

But I still want to get her on the plane, show her a piece of my world I don't share with anyone else.

The skies are where I go when I want to be alone, need the space and time to think. Up there is freedom, down here is chaotic madness.

I run my fingers through my hair, pushing the slightly curled ends away from my eyes. "Please," I beg, actually beg her. Letting her arm go, I hold my hand out, giving her the choice to take mine. She looks from my outstretched palm, to my eyes, to the plane. She makes the same trek with her gaze two more times. "Trust me."

She wets her lips with her tongue and closes her eyes. When they open I can see the resolve there.

"Don't make me regret this, Jamie."

"I won't."

But you might regret me.

CHAPTER FIFTEEN

Miranda

I wonder what series of choices I made in my life that have led me to this moment.

Jamie straps me into the *two*-passenger plane, making sure everything is snug and secure, before sticking some kind of noise blocking headphones over my ears.

There's a reason I've never flown in a plane before, just the idea absolutely terrifies me.

Big, hurtling, sheets of metal flying through the air at unnatural speeds seems like a recipe for disaster to me.

But if I *was* going to get on one of those tin can death traps, I always pictured it being a big, *normal*, plane. Not a kid's toy plane, because, let's be real here, this is basically the glorified version of that.

I might pee myself, and if I do, I hope the smell haunts Jamie for the rest of his life. It's the least of what he deserves for talking me into this mess.

"I'm going to make you do something you absolutely do not want to do as payback for this."

He places a headset on and shakes his head at me.

He thinks I'm kidding. I'm not.

"I'm thinking I'll paint you naked." He smirks. "Never mind, you'll like that too much. Hmm," I think, tapping my index finger against my lips. "Perhaps I'll make you my bitch boy for a day. No," I shake my head, "somehow that'll lead to sex. Everything seems to with us," I grumble. "Ooh, I know." I snap my fingers. "I'll make you get a pedicure with me—you're paying." He makes a face of disgust and I clap my hands, because ding, ding, ding we have a winner.

Jamie ignores me as he pushes buttons and speaks to someone through the headset. The hangar is open and he drives the plane out onto the runway.

I take breaths in and out, in and out. Having a panic attack is the last thing I need to happen right now.

"You ready?" Jamie asks.

I grip the seat between my hands, my knuckles turning white and the plane isn't even moving right now.

"No," I blurt. "I've changed my mind. I can't do this. Let me out. I am a flightless bird. I like the ground. The ground is nice. I like to get low, the lower the better."

Jamie busts out laughing at my rambling and I have to suppress my smile, because *damn* his laugh is sexy.

He says something else to the person through his headset, and then, before I can process, we're speeding down the runway.

"Jamie!" I scream, grabbing at anything I can hold onto. "I'm going to murder you! I told you I'm a flightless bird! I'm a mother-fucking ostrich in a sea of pigeons!"

Jamie, bastard that he is, doesn't care.

"Pretty sure that saying is something about flamingos, not an ostrich."

I glare over at him. "Flock you."

A scream tears out of me as he pulls back and the plane leaves the ground.

"Oh my God, I'm going to be sick."

"Vomit bags are under the seat."

I grab one just in case. As amusing as it would be to throw up all over Jamie's plane, I know most of it would end up on me, which wouldn't be cool.

As the plane steadies out, so does my belly.

"Whoa," I exhale, staring out the windows at the

views below. All the farmland laid out in a grid pattern, the tiny cars, and buildings. "The world looks so small up here."

"I think that's part of the reason I like it so much," he admits, flicking some buttons on the dash.

It's still scary as hell being up so high in this giant flying apparatus, but not as bad as I thought it would be. After all, I haven't fainted, piddled myself, or died yet.

I can feel Jamie watching me, and without looking at him I say, "Eyes ahead, pilot boy."

From the corner of my eye I see him shake his head but do as I asked.

I don't know how long we're in the air, or how far we go, but I do know when he lands the plane I'm actually a little sad for it to be over. Not that I want to tell him that.

When we're out of the plane, the first thing I do is pounce on him like some demented cougar—the animal, not the old lady kind—and he jolts back in surprise, but manages to catch my flailing body.

I kiss him, tangling my fingers into his silky locks.

Breaking the kiss, he gives me a little smirk. "Wasn't so bad, huh?"

I roll my eyes and step out of his embrace, giving his chest a light smack. "Shut up."

I start to turn away, but his arms wrap around my waist and he pulls me back into his hold. My hands land on his biceps and I swear he flexes them on purpose. I haven't told him, but he looks hot as fuck in his pair of jeans and white tee. It's the simplest outfit known to man, but one that makes me want to strip off my panties and toss them over my shoulder.

If Jamie ever learns the power this outfit has over me I'm in big trouble.

The *get me pregnant* kind of trouble, but without the getting me pregnant part.

"I think you like me," he murmurs, nuzzling his nose against mine.

My eyes drift closed.

"Never."

"Mmm," he hums, pressing his lips against my ear. "I know I like you." My heart skips a beat at his words. "I shouldn't, but I do. It scares me, but I can't stay away."

My fingers dig into his arms, but he makes no move to pull away.

"I swore I'd never go down this path again, but I can't stay away from you." My breath catches at his confession. "There are so many reasons why I should walk away from you. For starters, I'm no good for you. You're too young and deserve more than someone like me, a jaded, workaholic, single father. You're a breath of a fresh air and I'm the fire that steals all your oxygen."

I lean my body into his, not sure what to say in response. His hand comes up to cup the back of my neck and we stand there wrapped in each other, neither of us wanting to move.

Finally, I find my voice. "Maybe we shouldn't overthink things. Just enjoy the now. Think you can do that?"

His chuckle is warm. "I'm not very good at that, but I can try."

I hug him closer, resting the side of my face against his chest. "We're the most illogical of the illogical."

He combs his fingers through my hair. "I think I've spent way too much time with you, considering that made sense."

I roll my eyes even though he can't see. "I wish I didn't like you. This was easier when I hated you. It was just..."

"Sex," he finishes for me.

"Yeah." I swallow, trying not to let fear settle in my veins. I don't know where this thing with the two of us is headed, but I know in my gut there's a very real chance I could get my heart broken.

I look up at him, pressing my chin against his chest as I do. I love that he's taller than me, but not too tall. "What does this mean? Are we dating?"

He gently clasps my face between his hands like I'm something precious to cherish. "We'll see where things go. I think we're both the type of people who don't like labels, choosing to ride the wave instead."

Holding the back of his shirt in my fists so he can't

slip away from me, I ask, "Why did you never formally end things with me last time? Why rub another woman in my face?" I hate that this fact still hurts me this much. I normally have such a thick skin, but that hurt.

He exhales a heavy, weighted sigh, still holding my face between those large capable hands of his. I try not to think about how I want them on other parts of my body, especially considering I want the answer to this question more than I want practically anything—even art supplies, and that's saying something.

"Because I'm an ass." He rubs his thumb over my bottom lip.

"That's not answer."

His hazel eyes deepen. "Because," he swallows thickly, "I was beginning to feel things for you that scared the shit out of me. Things I hadn't felt since I fell in love with my ex-wife and we know how that turned out. I was afraid of giving you the power to break my heart. I hurt us both instead."

His answer both pleases and hurts me. "Life's full of heartbreak. Small fractures and big ones, and some that don't hurt at the time, but are a deep festering wound later. You can't avoid it."

"I can't avoid *you*."

God, I want to kiss him. So I do.

I feel like I'm always the one initiating it, but as soon

as our lips touch it's explosive. There's no knowing where I end and he begins.

He devours me slowly, like I'm a delicious dessert he wants to cherish every bite of.

My fingers skim under his t-shirt, tracing the contours of his chest. He's not a sex-pack abs kind of guy—like a six-pack, only sexier—but he's still fit and in shape. I trace the contours of his muscles and mewl in protest when he stops kissing me. Thankfully, it's only long enough for him to get rid of that pesky white shirt. I'm sure it's going to get dirty on the ground, but he doesn't seem to care.

"Jamie," I moan his name as he kisses the column of my throat.

I gasp when his tongue glides against my collarbone. I think my lady bits tingle too.

"I want you naked," he growls.

"Here?" I blurt out, coming to my senses. "Someone might see."

He shakes his head against me, already reaching for my shirt. "No, this is my hangar. They won't come out here unless I call them to."

"Oh."

"I've never taken a woman on my plane before. You're the first."

"Me?"

"I've never had sex in here either."

"You're being very convincing."

"Miranda," he pulls back, looking into my eyes. His hazel orbs are serious. "I've fucked you a million different ways, but please, I'm begging you—let me make love to you."

Jesus Christ, I can't argue with that.

I nod, a whispered "yes" leaving me breathily.

He takes my hand and I follow him onto the company jet he pointed out earlier.

"Jamie?"

He gives me a boyish smirk, causing my insides to twist. "What?" He blinks innocently. "It has a bed."

I shake my head, but I'm too turned on to care. Besides, the plane *is* his.

He tugs me down a hall, not even giving me a chance to check things out, and into a darkened bedroom. He flips a switch and a light turns on beside the bed, illuminating the room in an orange glow. I get a brief glimpse of the rich wood details, plush carpeting, and a king size bed, before Jamie kisses me once more, blocking everything out.

We fall onto the bed together, wrinkling the soft covers.

I expect him to tear my clothes off like usual, but he wasn't kidding when he said he wanted to make love to me. He kisses me gently, exploring my body carefully before he slowly removes my clothes one item at a time.

By the time I'm naked beneath him, he's only left in his boxer-briefs. I wiggle, needing to feel the press of his body into mine. His erection pushes against me and I reach between us, pushing the fabric down a bit to let the tip peek out.

I rub my thumb around the tip and air hisses between his teeth.

"Fuck, Miranda. I need you to touch me so bad."

I push his underwear down further and he does the rest of the work, shucking them on the floor with the rest of our clothes.

I wrap my hand around his cock, rubbing up and down and rotating my wrist.

He holds his body above mine, his arms taut, and I barely have to knock into him to roll him over and onto the mattress.

I sit up on my knees and lean over his body.

"Oh, fuuuuuck," he moans lowly, as I take him in my mouth. "God, your mouth." He gathers my hair out of the way and watches me suck his cock.

His eyes flutter closed and he crosses an arm over his face, muttering, "You'll be the death of me."

It isn't long before he's pushing me off of him. "Need to be in you," he murmurs, his hazel eyes nearly black.

I stretch my arms above my head and his eyes follow my movements and the way my breasts sway.

"You're way too fucking gorgeous for me." He looks at

me possessively. I've never had any guy look at me with such reverence.

He grabs the base of his cock and pushes into me slowly. Both of us watch him disappear inside me, letting out twin moans.

When he's all the way in, he just rests there, not moving. My fingers dig into his back, wanting him to fuck me like he always does, but knowing we both need this moment.

His eyes close briefly and when they open there's something in them I can't interpret.

"Slow," he says, and I think it's more for his benefit than mine.

He pulls back just a little before pushing back into me. I moan, my fingers moving down his body to grab his ass, urging him into me fully.

He kisses me deeply, rocking his hips in and out of me.

I whimper from the pleasure of it.

"You have no fucking idea how good you feel wrapped around my cock," he murmurs into the skin of my neck.

He peppers kisses all over my body while he makes love to me. I feel absolutely worshipped. Tears burn the back of my eyes because sex has never felt like this before. This beautiful and all-encompassing. I didn't know it was possible to feel something like this, let alone with Jamie of all people.

I place my hand on his stubbled cheek, our eyes locked.

"Oh, God, Jamie," I cry out with my orgasm. "Jamie, yes."

He growls and a moment later his own orgasm hits him.

Neither of us moves for a moment and then he pulls out. We lay together, his arms wrapped around my body. His lips press against my shoulder and I feel the annoying sting of tears again.

Because I think I might be falling in love with Jamie Fucking Miller.

Not cool, feelings. Not cool at all.

CHAPTER SIXTEEN

Miranda

"I've decided post-sex Popeye's is my new favorite thing in the world," I announce, stuffing my face with a bite of mashed potatoes.

Jamie chuckles, dipping a chicken finger in sauce.

Big, bad, Jamie eats chicken tenders.

I like him even more.

After we left the airport, both of us were starving, and since it was after noon, we knew food was a must. I have no idea how we ended up on the complete opposite side of town, eating Popeye's out of his fancy car, but I don't mind one bit.

"Are you going to yell at me if I get butter in here?" I ask, holding up a packet of butter.

He brushes his hands off on a napkin. "No," he says around a mouthful. "If you only knew half of the stuff Tobias has spilled in here you'd be horrified. I had to have the car detailed a couple months ago because he got slime in the back seat. *Slime*."

"Where did he get slime?"

"My mom," he laughs, and I can see the love he has for her and his son in his eyes. "Apparently he watched a YouTube video and wanted to make it, so they did, and it ended up in my car."

"Well, butter it is then." I put some on a biscuit and take a bite.

"What did you think?" he asks after it's quiet for a moment.

I quirk a brow. "Of the sex?"

He shakes his head. "No, of flying?"

"Oh." I bite my lip, not wanting to admit that I actually enjoyed it. "It was okay, I guess." I try, but fail, to sound believable.

He reaches over and grabs a strand of my hair, tugging on it lightly so I'll lean into him. *"Liar."*

"I don't lie."

My nose crinkles.

"Aha," he cries, snapping a finger and pointing at my treacherous nose. "You *are* lying."

I grab the end of my nose. "How do you know my tell?" My tone is defensive. I've always had this really bad habit of wiggling my nose when I lie. Most people are unaware of it, but of course Jamie would pick up on it.

He releases my hair and tugs my hand away from my nose. "Because, I notice things about you."

My heart stretches and yearns, begging for me to let it reach across and gather Jamie into its embrace.

I'm scared, though. I don't understand why I'm so fearful of having my heart broken. It's not like I had some great love at one time in my young life that went sour. I've never had the kind of love I read about in books. It's always been bad Tinder dates and even worse hookups. One guy I didn't even go on a date with still haunts me to this day because he slid into my DM's telling me how he's the pussy whisperer because he has eight cats.

I contemplated calling animal services, because that shit ain't right.

But here's Jamie, a man twelve years older than me.

With a son.

A fancy house and car.

A mother-fucking *plane* that doesn't even have snakes.

And he makes me feel things I didn't believe were possible.

"Now," he begins again, "did you like it, sweetheart?"

That word. It should grate on my nerves, not fill my belly with butterflies.

I nod, there's no point in lying.

"Words, Miranda. With words."

I lean into him until the console is the only thing separating us.

"It." His eyes follow my lips. "Was." His tongue flicks out. "Just." A muscle in his jaw ticks. "Okay."

His fingers thread in my hair until we're nose to nose. "I love when you fight me. It makes victory all the sweeter." He skims his lips against my neck and his teeth lightly bite my flesh. I'm thankful his car has such tinted windows or we'd be giving anyone driving by or sitting in the fast food restaurant quite the show. We're not even doing anything scandalous, but it looks that way. "Tell me the truth," he hums.

"Never."

I feel his smile against my skin.

And then he does something I least expect.

The bastard tickles me.

"Jamie!" I shriek, trying to get away from him. Food falls from my lap as I try to get away, laughing all the while. "Stop, please, stop."

"Are you going to keep lying to me?"

"Me? Lie? Never. Jamie, please." I push at his hands, laughing hysterically. I'm trapped with nowhere to go.

"I want the truth this time," he warns playfully and finally his onslaught ends.

"Never," I say in a serious tone, lifting a finger, "tickle me ever again."

He holds his hands up in surrender. "I can't promise that." I glare. "But I do promise to only use this against you in the most serious of situations."

I snort. "Because my opinion on aviation is a serious matter."

"It definitely is." He grins. "Now, come on. I want your real opinion." His smile disappears slowly. "Am I wrong? Did you actually hate it?"

I shake my head, biting my lip. "It was amazing. Truly. Thank you for sharing that with me. It means more than you can possibly know that you showed me something you love, and I might've been scared to death at first, but I'm so happy to have that experience with you." I squeeze his hand. "I can't believe I'm saying this, but I actually wouldn't mind doing that again."

This time it's his turn to joke. "The flying or the sex."

"Both," I admit.

"You really think you'd do it again?"

I pretend to think for a moment. "I mean, I did do you again, and again, and again, and plenty of other times, so I think I might be open to the idea of flying more."

"Always a smart ass."

I shrug, bending to pick up the mess. He's going to have to pay for another detailing, but it's not my fault he tickled me. That's all on him.

He looks at his watch and lets out a sigh. "I better get you home."

I look at him sadly, and that's something I never thought would happen, but I am unhappy about this day ending. It's been nice seeing this side of him and spending hours together having actual conversation ... and a little sex, I mean, come on we can't help ourselves.

"Yeah, I need to meal prep for the week."

"You meal prep?" He starts putting empty boxes into the bags.

"I'm a college student, I don't have time in the week to make meals. If I do it on the weekends, then I don't eat like shit during the week."

"Thank God I have my mom to cook or it'd be takeout every night."

He slips out of the car and throws away the trash.

"I really did have fun today," he tells me. "I'm glad you trusted me enough to get on the plane."

"That was not trust, buddy." I wag my finger at him.

"Then what was it?" A smirk twists his lips.

"I ... don't know," I admit.

His smirk widens and he buckles his seatbelt before reversing out of the parking lot.

All too soon he's parking in front of my building.

"What are you doing?" I blurt when he unbuckles his seatbelt.

He looks at me like I'm the crazy one—which, to be frank, is true.

"Walking you to your door. I've heard that's what a proper gentleman."

"A proper gentleman probably doesn't fuck a girl twelve years younger than him on his company jet. Wait, does this mean I can say I've joined the mile high club?"

He shakes his head at my antics. "First off, what we did today wasn't *fucking*. Get it right, sweetheart. I made love to you," he growls lowly, and I think he's genuinely offended I called it fucking. "And to join the mile high club the plane has to be in the air."

"If I give you a blowjob in the two-seater does that count?"

He chokes, turning it into a cough. "Um, no, and while that sounds fun it'd be extremely dangerous, so don't even think about trying it."

I mock pout. "Way to ruin all my fun."

He leans against the headrest. "You'll be the death of me, woman."

I grin. "That's the plan."

Grabbing my bag, I shrug it on and exit the car. As

promised, he follows me to my door, kisses my cheek, and waits until I'm safely inside.

I rest my back against the closed door, sliding my butt all the way to the floor with the giddiest smile on my face.

I think I might be happier than I've ever been, and it's all because of Jamie Fucking Miller. Who would've thought?

CHAPTER SEVENTEEN

Miranda

It's the middle of the week and I should be sleeping since I have classes early tomorrow. But I can't, because there's a ghost in my apartment.

Either a ghost or a raccoon.

But I'm pretty sure it's a ghost haunting my bathroom. I've been in and out of there multiple times, trying to deduce what it is and I'm coming up empty. Therefore, a ghost seems like the most logical explanation.

I roll over and look at the clock, finding it to be a little after one in the morning.

I have to be up at six and I haven't slept one solid minute yet despite trying.

With a dramatic sigh, I swipe my phone off the bedside table and bring up Lou's contact, complete with a pink Starburst photo, and ring her.

The phone rings and rings, finally her disgusted, "This better be important," comes over the line.

"There's a ghost in my apartment," I whisper in case ghosts can hear. I mean, they can, right? That's why all these ghost hunters are always talking to them on TV?

"You have to be fucking kidding me. I'm going back to sleep."

"Wait!" I cry. "There really is something in here. A raccoon or mouse or something. I can hear it moving around in the ceiling of the bathroom. Can you ask Abel to come over?"

"Miranda," she sighs, and I know she's shaking her head at me.

"Or it could be a bat," I ramble, "what if it flies out and bites me? I don't want to be a vampire."

"But it's okay if Abel gets bitten?"

"He'd be an attractive vampire," I reason.

"He has to be up at four in order to be at work at five. I really don't want to wake him."

"Right," I deflate. "It's fine."

"Why don't you call Jamie?"

"Jamie? Why Jamie?" My voice squeaks, because I haven't told Lou about our kinda-sorta date or how we're not quite a couple but are something more.

"Uh … because he's your landlord. If you can't sleep, see if he'll come over."

I bite my lip. She has a point, but I don't want to disturb him. Waking up Lou is a different story since she's my best friend and it's written in the blood contract that all besties must be prepared for late night or early morning phone calls.

"Fine, I'll call him," I grumble, sitting up and pushing my unruly hair out of my face. "I'm not happy about it, but I'll do it."

She gives me a small laugh. "Just make me a promise?"

"What?" I hesitate, a bit scared to agree.

"You tell him about the ghost theory."

"I hate you."

"Love, you love me."

"Mhmm, bye. Go back to sleep."

I hang up and call Jamie. "Hello?" he asks after barely two rings, sounding way too awake for the early hour.

"Um … hi … it's me … Miranda."

His soft chuckle is intoxicating. "Yeah, I know. Caller ID comes in handy these days."

"Oh, right."

"To what do I owe the pleasure of this late night call?"

"This isn't a booty call if that's what you think it is."

He chuckles. "Didn't think it was."

"Anyway, there's a ghost in my bathroom. I need you to extinguish it Ghostbusters style."

He clucks his tongue. "Sorry, my proton pack is charging."

"Don't laugh at me," I whine. "There really is something in my bathroom ceiling. It's making a lot of noise and I don't know what it is. Ghost, raccoon, bat, doesn't matter because I can't sleep. I need to be up for class in a couple of hours."

"I'll be over as soon as I can."

"Really?" I brighten. Some sleep will be better than no sleep at the rate I'm going. Besides, now I'm really curious about what *is* in the ceiling because my brain is conjuring all kinds of disturbing ideas. Like a trapped Furby reawakened by the demented Furby gods. I begged for one of those stupid things for Christmas one year, and then promptly threw the thing in my closet to never be seen again, though occasionally heard from when it would speak from the depths.

Oh my God, it totally is a Furby. The previous renter must've hidden one up there to torment me.

That makes no logical sense considering they

wouldn't have known me, but my brain likes to go on tangents.

Throwing my covers off, I pull a sweatshirt on to try to mask the fact I'm braless. Jamie might've seen me naked numerous times, but I still don't feel comfortable letting my girls flop around all willy-nilly.

Padding into my kitchen I pour myself some water and sip at it, trying to ignore the screeching and scratching coming from the bathroom.

Whatever is in there wants out *now*.

Maybe my ceiling is giving birth to a demon.

What if it's the portal to the Underworld?

Hmm, that might not be too bad. I've always thought there was something undeniably sexy about Hades. Clearly I have a bad boy complex.

After enough minutes for me to completely freak myself out there's a soft knock on the door.

As my landlord, he has a key, but I appreciate that he waits for me to answer.

God knows he rarely extends the same courtesy to Lou and Abel.

I swing the door open and my jaw drops.

If I thought Jamie in jeans and a t-shirt was sexy, that version has nothing on gray sweat shorts Jamie with an old faded college shirt and tool basket in hand.

I think my ovaries just sat up and sang a song in his honor.

I step out of his way and he joins me inside.

"Where's the ghost?" His stupid crooked grin sends my insides spinning.

"It decided to leave and left a demonic troll in its stead." Pushing his shoulder lightly I usher him down the hall to the bathroom. "It's somewhere up there." I point at the ceiling. It makes a noise and I shriek, grabbing onto the back of his shirt. "Save me," I beg him.

He sighs and sets down his bag of tools. "You're going to have to let me go if you expect me to save you."

"Oh, right." I let go of his shirt, leaving wrinkles in the shape of my fists.

There's a howl from above us and some scratching.

"Demon!" I scream and point. "There's a demon up there!"

Jamie slaps a hand over my mouth. "Shh, you're going to wake up your neighbors."

I stop screaming and he lets go of me. "Why don't you wait in your living room?"

I shake my head. "I can't let it eat you."

He looks me up and down. "Yes, you're very ferocious. I'm sure whatever is up there will be positively terrified."

I pout, sticking my hands on my hips. "I can be very scary."

He snorts. "Yeah, that's why you took care of it and I'm not needed here."

I glare. "If I could smite you, I would."

"Smite? Are you from the medieval times?"

"No, I've never actually been there," I quip, hands still perched on my hips.

"Not what I meant."

"I know," I say with a smile as he bends over to grab some sort of saw looking tool. I'm too busy looking at his ass to care what it actually is.

"Do you have a step ladder or anything?"

I snort. "Do I *look* like I own a step ladder?"

He glances at me over his shoulder. "Uh ... no." He steps up on the closed toilet lid. I don't bother chiding him on the possibility of breaking it, if he does he'll have to replace it anyway.

He begins cutting a large chunk out of the ceiling and I lean against the doorway.

"I didn't know you were handy."

He pauses and looks at me. "There's a lot you still have to learn about me, sweetheart." Returning to sawing the ceiling he adds, "My grandpa wanted me to not only learn the family business, but be able to handle what he called manly chores."

I can detect the hint of sadness in his tone. "You miss him."

His shoulders sag. "More than you know." He saws a large square and uses his hand to hold it in place, but that doesn't stop it from wiggling slightly. "I have to get whatever this is out, before it moves again, so ... watch out."

Before I have the chance to contemplate running into the living room and dive bombing onto the couch, he pulls the tile down, and dust explodes everywhere.

Coughing, from the onslaught of insulation falling out I jolt when something smacks into my chest.

I scream, ready to lodge the thing off of me when I hear the tiniest, most pitiful meow.

"It's a kitty!" I exclaim in surprise. It comes out sounding more like *kittaaay*. I see big blue eyes and dusty oatmeal fur before I hug the kitten to my neck.

Jamie steps off the toilet lid, sets down the tile he cut out, and rubs drywall dust and insulation from his hair. "A cat?"

"A kitten." I hold out the fluffy furball proudly so he can see. "My ceiling gave birth."

He frowns at the kitten. "It's dirty."

"She's perfect," I croon, cuddling the squirming kitten to my chest. I don't even know if it's a girl, but it feels like she is.

"You're not keeping the cat, Miranda," he growls in warning. "Animals are not allowed."

I jut my bottom lip out. "I should get special privileges. I *am* fucking the landlord." I wink at him while petting the kitten on the top of her fluffy head. To the cat I say, "How'd you even get up in my ceiling?"

Jamie sighs, scrubbing his hands down his jaw. "Its mom probably got on the roof somehow and this one got separated."

I hold the fluffy puff out at arm's length. "You can be the Beta to my Alpha. The Fettuccine to my Alfredo. Ooh, that should be your name, Fettuccine."

Jamie groans. "You're not keeping it."

"No, of course not," I assure him. "I'll take her to the animal shelter tomorrow."

"Mhmm."

He doesn't believe me. He's right to be wary. No way am I willingly giving up this cat. It feels like some sort of sign. If a kitten falls from your ceiling, clearly it's chosen you, right? The wand chooses the wizard, after all, so can't the cat choose the cat lady?

"I promise," I tell him, crossing the fingers of my left hand behind my back. "Fettuccine will be out of here before you know it."

Sure, I won't be able to keep this a secret forever, but hopefully I can come up with a way to persuade him later.

His eyes narrow and I hope to God my nose isn't twitching, because I'm in deep shit if it is.

"You shouldn't name it. Names lead to attachment."

"You shouldn't call me sweetheart. Nicknames show a kind of fondness," I mock playfully.

He leans his head back, looking up at the ceiling as if he's begging it for answers.

"Between you, Toby, and my mom, I'm headed to an early grave." I grin widely at him as he lowers his head and looks at me. "What?" he asks with confusion.

"You called him Toby."

"Dammit," he curses, bending to move the tile out of the way. "Don't tell him I slipped up."

Petting the cat, I lean my hip against the counter. "Ooh, blackmail. I won't tell if you let me keep the cat."

He glares and points at me. "Not happening. Maybe I should take the cat with me."

"No!" I shriek, holding her tighter against me.

His eyes narrow. "Miranda—"

"I don't trust you! You might hurt the cat." I cuddle her impossibly closer. I'm not letting him leave with her. She is mine and I am hers.

He sighs, shoulders falling. "I wouldn't hurt the kitten, Miranda. I'm not a monster."

"Do you not like cats?"

"They're messy," he grumbles, wrinkling his nose. "And they smell."

"So do kids but you have one of those."

He contemplates for a moment but smartly keeps his mouth shut, because he knows I have a point. He picks up his tools and looks around at the mess. "It's late, get some sleep and I'll send someone to patch the ceiling and clean up tomorrow."

I fake swoon, hand to the back of my head and all. Fettuccine meows in my opposite hand, probably not liking the way I've bent back. "My own personal knight in shining armor."

He shakes his head at a loss for words and heads out of the bathroom, brushing past me. His elbow grazes my boob and from his little smirk when he looks over his shoulder I know it was on purpose.

I follow him to the door. He opens it, turning around to stand in the threshold.

Lowering his head, he grazes his lips over mine. "Try to sleep."

"Thank you for coming over," I say as he pulls away, biting my lip slightly. "It..." I pause, sighing, because I hate being vulnerable. "It meant a lot. I was really freaked out."

"Any time, sweetheart." He points at Fettuccine. "You're not keeping the cat."

Oh, but I am.

"Absolutely not," I respond, nodding in agreement. I can tell he still doesn't believe me, but I can't say I blame him. "Text me when you're home."

He nods. "I will."

He kisses me one last time and then he's walking

away. I lock the door and clean up Fettuccine as best I can. She really is adorable.

"You look like one of the Aristocats," I tell her, holding her in front of my face as I carry her to my room. "A little Marie."

She meows in response like a good little kitty.

"Ooh, you're a *Pastacat*," I tell her and she yawns. "I'm so clever."

I climb into bed and the tiny furball makes herself comfortable in my pillow. I don't mind a bit.

Ten minutes later I get a text from Jamie saying he's home.

I've barely sent him a goodnight response with a kiss emoji before I'm fast asleep.

CHAPTER EIGHTEEN

Jamie

Don's name flashes on my phone screen and I curse from my office in Tysons, Virginia. I rarely work from the big office housing Miller Enterprises, but today is chockfull of meetings with executives, so it's where I need to be. I'm grateful most of the time I can work from home and be close if Tobias needs me.

"Hello?" I reluctantly answer the phone, knowing

there can't be a good reason why he's calling. I straighten a pen on my desk, trying to distract myself from what I'm sure is going to be a painful conversation.

"Jamie, do you have a minute?"

I look at my agenda. "My next meeting is in twenty minutes."

"Plenty of time." He clears his throat. "Shannon is requesting another meeting."

I pinch the bridge of my nose and lean forward, resting my elbows on my desk. "Why? We clearly didn't get anywhere the first time."

"She's threatening to return to court to fight for equal share custody."

The air leaves my lungs and I pick up the pen I previously straightened, stabbing it into a stack of papers. "Bull-fucking-shit. She doesn't want Tobias. She didn't want him then and she doesn't want him now. Any idea what she actually wants?" My tone is deadly, but Don takes it in stride. After all, he's paid to deal with this shit.

"I think we both know what she actually wants."

"Money," I hiss, throwing the pen across the room.

I was already not in the best mood having to be in the city dealing with all the dickish board members who think they know more than me just because they're twenty years older. Now, I'm fucking livid.

I'm not a monster.

I wouldn't keep Tobias from Shannon if I truly

believed she regretted her decision and wanted to be a mother to him. But I learned her true colors after she got pregnant. All she wants is a bank account padded with money so she can further Botox her already plastic face to match her plastic existence.

"I'm not giving her a penny," I warn in a grave tone. I point my finger roughly in the air like Don's there to witness it. "She's already taken more fucking money from me than necessary. She signed her rights away and that's that."

"I know, I know. This shouldn't be an issue."

There's a but implied. I know it.

"But," he continues, "she's a woman."

"What the fuck does that have to do with it?" I blurt, but I know. I already fucking know.

He sighs heavily, as irritated by this as I am. "Judges always sympathize with the mother."

Even when they shouldn't, he leaves unsaid.

It doesn't matter that she wanted an abortion, or that she only wanted him once she realized the amount she'd get in custody, or even that she hasn't bothered to see him, not even now. It doesn't matter that I'm the one who wanted him. Who stayed up late when he cried, fed him, changed his diapers. It doesn't matter that even now I'm the one who clothes him, who makes sure he brushes his teeth and does his homework. I'm the one who's been there for every birthday and bruised knee.

Because at the end of the day, I'm the man.

The dad.

And we're not together, so obviously I'm the deadbeat parent in this situation.

It pisses me the fuck off and I throw a stack of papers at the wall.

"Mr. Miller?" My assistant, a woman in her fifties named Claire, pokes her head in. "Is everything okay?"

I point to my phone and she nods, heading back around the corner to her desk.

"What should I do?"

He's quiet and I hear something ticking in the background. Maybe a clock, or perhaps his pen tapping against his desk.

"My suggestion? Meet with her. Play nice, but..."

"But?" I growl. I really fucking hate that word.

"I think in the end you're going to have to give her more money or she won't disappear."

I stand up, staring out the window of the building at the traffic surging below. This area outside of Washington D.C. is always bustling. I don't like it. It might be surprising to some, but I prefer my quiet suburban life.

"If I really thought she wanted to see Tobias this wouldn't be an issue."

"If she wanted to see your son she wouldn't be going through lawyers."

I know he's right. Shannon is money hungry, and

Tobias is nothing but a pawn for her to get what she wants. She doesn't love him, know him, or even care about him the tiniest bit.

I don't understand it.

I was a fucking dad the minute I figured out she was pregnant, but she's never realized she's a mom.

She's cold-hearted and I'll do everything in my power to keep Tobias away from her for that reason alone. I won't let her break his heart like she broke mine. It made me an angry bastard and I don't want my son to grow up with a chip on his shoulder. He deserves more than that.

"What are you thinking, Jamie?" Don probes.

I exhale a weighty breath and lean an arm above my head against the glass. Sirens blare.

"Set a meeting."

CHAPTER NINETEEN

Miranda

"Who's the cutest kitty in all the land? You are, Fettuccine, that's right it's you."

I tap him on his pink nose.

That's right, Fettuccine is a boy. I took him to the vet this morning and was informed that my sweet girl kitty has male genitalia. What a disappointment. It was going to be her and me against the world.

I think I still can be a good boy cat mom.

"You're absolutely insane," Lou says, walking beside me as I push the shopping cart through Petco.

"I think this whole thing is adorable," Tanner interjects, rubbing Fettuccine on top of his head. The kitten leans into Tanner's touch and purrs.

"You're not supposed to have pets," Lou reminds me for the thousandth time.

She's just a salty pretzel because she wanted to adopt a puppy and was denied by Jamie.

My pussy is his kryptonite, though, so I know I can persuade him.

He'll come to love the little fluff-ball. Who wouldn't? A fluffy cream-colored cat named Fettuccine is what dreams are made of—totally Lizzie McGuire in Rome vibes.

"I can be very convincing." I give her a smirk and sway my hips.

She pretends to gag. "Ick, gross. I don't want to picture you and my landlord doing the dirty."

"He's my landlord now too," I remind her, turning down an aisle of cat food and searching for the one the vet recommended. "But unlike you, I enjoy when he comes to collect rent."

Tanner chuckles and Lou looks horrified. "You know I'm the kind of person who blurts whatever is on my mind and I'm no prude, but *ugh*, why do you have to be bumping uglies with *Jamie*?"

Tanner leans around me to look at her as I stop, standing on my tiptoes to grab the bag of food from the top shelf. "If you'd seen his dick you'd understand."

"Should've looked at the photo while the offer was on the table," I sing-song, dropping the bag into the cart.

Fettuccine meows from the front child's seat and I scratch behind his ears. So needy, but I love it. I always wanted a cat growing up, but my parents were afraid I wasn't responsible enough. As Lou would say, fate sent one my way.

"Bleh." She holds her hands out in front of her. "I do not want to think about Jamie's dick *ever*, let alone actually *see* it. No thank you."

"It's a work of art," I continue, just to annoy her.

Tanner helps. "The Mona Lisa of dicks."

"Songs have been written about less worthy penises."

Lou shoves her fingers in her ears. "La, la,la I'm not listening to you."

"You're no fun." I pout. I'm used to being able to say anything I want to Lou, but Jamie repulses her.

I turn down another aisle and scan the cat toys. Bending down, I pick up a tiny blue mouse. "I really do like Jamie," I mumble.

Even though I can't see her I know she freezes in place behind me. Tanner is probably sporting a silly grin.

"Like ... how much do you like him?"

I bite my lip and stand up, tossing the toy mouse into the cart. "More than I should."

"Miranda," she sighs, her eyes sad. "I don't want you to get hurt."

I've been hurt a lot, just like she's been in the past until Abel came along. I understand why she's protective. I'm the same way with her. I'll fuck up anyone who messes with her, literally. Pretty sure one of Abel's former asshole teammates is still afraid of me. I saw him a couple months ago in Walgreens and he dropped a box of condoms before running out of there like the hounds of Hades were on his heels.

I can make grown men cower. It's kind of my super power.

But I don't want Jamie to cower. I want him to embrace me, let me melt in his strong arms, and that scares the poo out of me.

"Getting hurt is inevitable." I shrug, moving to her other side to look at a cat scratch post. There are some giant climbing ones that I know are far too large for my apartment.

"It might be inevitable, but that doesn't mean you stop in front of a moving car just to see if you get hit."

I flinch.

I know Lou didn't approve of me sleeping with Jamie when it was *just* sex, so I don't know why I would expect her to jump for joy over a relationship with him. She knows him one way, the way he projects himself to the world to keep people from seeing what a sweet squishy marshmallow he is on the inside, but I've seen more. The deeper, hidden parts of himself he only shares with a select few. If she knew him that way, she'd understand. He's pretty impossible not to like.

He's strong and capable. A hard worker. Compassionate. A loving father.

He's the whole package, more than I could've ever imagined for myself.

My best friend's approval feels necessary, but since I also don't know where this whole thing is going I don't want to push it.

Placing a tan cat post in the cart I move further down the aisle. Tanner has Fettuccine scooped into his arms, swaying with the cat. He's singing some made up song in a whispered voice to my cat.

Fettuccine is going to be the most spoiled kitty ever. He hit the jackpot when he fell through my ceiling.

As promised, Jamie sent someone to repair the damages. It's good as new, with absolutely no sign of the birthing of Fettuccine.

"I'm hungry," Tanner announces suddenly, cutting off mid-song. "Can we go to Olive Garden after this? I want..." He pauses, looks at the cat with wide, horrified eyes, and finishes in a whisper, *"fettuccine* Alfredo." His eyes dart back and forth from the kitten in his arms to me. "Is Fettuccine going to be offended if I eat that? He's not going to think I'm like ... eating his sibling or something, right?"

Lou busts out laughing. "It's a cat, Tanner. I think you're fine." She pats his shoulder.

"We can't do that unless we order it and eat it somewhere else," I interject, spinning one of those feathered dangly toys through the air. I throw it up and catch it like one of those flag people in band.

"Why?" Tanner asks.

I narrow my eyes on him. "Pretty sure they wouldn't take kindly to my kind of Fettuccine." I point to the fluffy kitten.

"Oh." He looks down at the cat. "That's not fair. Fettuccine would be a good boy."

Turning my back on them, I leave the cart for Lou to push and gather more items for Fettuccine including a necessary litter box. I don't want little turd burglars appearing in my apartment.

"Ooh, look. I have to get him a collar and nametag." I run over like an excited kid to the whole row of collars and leashes—leashes specifically labeled for cats. I can't imagine walking my cat, but maybe I should consider it.

My friends follow me and I nearly lose my shit when I notice Fettuccine sits on Tanner's shoulder like some sort of bird.

I scour the collars and finally pull out one I like. It's blue with little sundaes on it.

"Come here, Fettuccine," I coo, and Tanner reaches up and grabs the kitten from his shoulder, holding him out for me. I try the collar on and it's a perfect fit. "You look snazzy, buddy." I unclip it from his tiny neck and drop it in the cart with the rest of the goodies. I don't even want to think about how much this is going to cost me. It's a good thing I just took a partial payment for a large nude portrait—a gift from a woman to her fiancé.

Adding in some food bowls, a couple more toys since I don't know what he might like to play with, and even a small shirt that says #1 Savage, I finally move to the checkout. I pay for everything, including a nametag they conveniently have a machine for.

Lou and Tanner follow me over to the machine carrying the bags and Fettuccine. I think Fettuccine likes Tanner as much as Tanner likes him.

I put in the special coin they gave me and go about selecting the style and color I want, before I type in the information.

"But I want a guinea pig, Dad. They're so fluffy and cute."

I freeze at the sound of the child's voice breezing in through the automatic doors.

"Tobias, I told you—we're getting a beta fish. That's it.

We are not leaving here with anything that poops everywhere and requires maintenance."

I pray to every god I know offhand that Jamie doesn't notice me here.

Or Lou.

Or Tanner.

Or freaking Fettuccine.

Goddammit, why did I have to bring the cat? I could've totally passed this off as helping a friend.

Except Jamie knows your friends.

Shit, I'm screwed.

"Oh, hey Jamie," Tanner blurts and waves with his empty hand, the other one holding the cat.

Jamie freezes, his eyes swinging to the three of us huddled around the nametag machine.

I've never wanted to run and hide so badly before.

"Miranda!" Toby cries, running at me and throwing his arms around me.

"Hi, Toby." I hug him back.

He pulls away and grins up at me with a smile that's the twin to his father's. "Can you come over and paint with me again?"

My eyes flick up to Jamie.

Yeah, we're kind of sorta, but not really dating, but that doesn't mean he wants me spending more time with his son.

I shrug. "Sure, hopefully soon. I still need to pick up the ones I did with you before."

Mini-Jamie vibrates with pride. "They're so pretty Miranda. You're a really good artist. My dad is letting me keep them in my room. I promise I won't let anything happen to them." He crosses his fingers over his heart. "Well, the rest of them. My dad said one got messed up."

"That's okay. I trust you." I ruffle his hair.

Toby hurries back to his dad's side and Jamie narrows his eyes on the kitten and then me. "That cat better be going home with him." He points at Tanner.

"Oh, totally." I wave a dismissive hand.

Tanner tries to stifle a sort.

Lou rolls her eyes.

Some friends I have. They're not helping to cover for my ass at all.

"But it has your name on it."

Fuck.

My.

Life.

Toby points at the screen where loud and clear it says IF FOUND CALL MIRANDA HERSHEL.

My worried eyes reluctantly meet Jamie's.

"Miranda," he growls lowly. "You can't keep the cat."

"I told you so," Lou fake coughs. I glare at her and she backs away, setting the bags on the ground.

"I tried to take him," I explain, holding my hands up

pleadingly. "But they had no room." It's a lie, I didn't try, but I'm sure the animal shelter *is* full. "Besides, it's a kill shelter. I can't leave him there."

"Him? I thought it was a girl."

"Uh..."

"She took it to the vet."

"Tanner," I whine. "You guys are not helping." My treacherous friends are far too amused by my discomfort to care whether or not they're doing me a favor.

"Surprise, it's a boy," Tanner adds, wiggling the fingers of his free hand.

"I need new friends," I grumble under my breath.

"You can't keep the cat."

"Jamie," I plead, jutting out my bottom lip and clasping my hands beneath my chin. "He *chose* me. I can't just abandon him."

He sighs, looking dejected. "My hands are tied. I only own a few apartments, not the whole complex, and the rules are simple—no pets."

Tears burn my eyes and I look from Jamie to the cat. "I'm not getting rid of him. I'll ... I'll ... move somewhere else."

He pinches his nose and exhales sharply. "I've had a rough day and I don't want to argue with you right now." It's then that I noticed his disheveled appearance. His dress pants are wrinkled, his suit jacket gone, dress sleeves rolled up, collar unbuttoned, and tie askew. His hair looks like he's run his fingers through it a million times.

"Fine," I agree. "But I'm keeping him."

I push the button so the machine will start engraving the nametag.

Jamie shakes his head and his tired, bleary eyes look at the three of us. "I'll talk to you later," he mumbles, "this isn't over."

It's safe to say Jamie and I both have the same level of stubbornness. But I *will* win this.

"Come on, Tobias." He puts a hand on his son's shoulder and guides him away. "Let's get that fish."

"A *guinea pig*, Dad."

Jamie sighs heavily and I suppress a laugh, because clearly Toby is as strong-willed as I am.

Jamie might've gotten his way for years, but that isn't happening anymore.

Olive Garden takeout bags litter Lou's kitchen countertop. There's a smorgasbord of pastas, salad, breadsticks, and soup spread out so we can all have a bit of this and that.

Abel looked relieved when he got home and saw all the food. He grabbed a plate and immediately started piling food onto it. Him and Lou share a chair, her draped in his lap, while Tanner and I sit on opposite ends of the couch letting Fettuccine run back and forth between us. *Friends* plays as background noise on the TV. God knows Lou and I have watched every episode multiple times.

I pierce my fork through a bite of lasagna, popping it into my mouth.

Italian food soothes my wicked soul. Anyone who says they don't like pasta is a monster I don't want to meet.

"So," Abel twirls spaghetti around his fork, "you have a cat now."

"Temporarily," Lou interjects.

I glare at her. "Permanently. I'm keeping him." I smile as I watch the furry gremlin attack my toe.

"Mhmm," she hums doubtfully.

I toss a pillow at her and she laughs, knocking it away easily.

I know Jamie has to have some sort of sway over my ability to keep the kitten. Besides, whatever the others in charge don't know won't hurt anything. After all, it's a *cat*, not a dog. It's not like he can bark at all hours of the day and night. Cats mostly sleep, right?

Granted, my knowledge is limited, but I'm willing to learn and be the best cat mom there ever was.

Fettuccine dive bombs into my leg and I laugh when he falls back and rolls over.

Maybe it's stupid to feel so strongly about a kitten that fell through my ceiling, but I do. I smile to myself as the tiny kitten runs over to Tanner, crawling up his leg and digging his claws into his cotton shirt.

Abel grins, watching Fettuccine. "I think Jamie has met his match when it comes to you. I'm thoroughly looking forward to seeing who wins this argument. My bets on you." He tips his head in appreciation.

I place a dramatic hand on my chest. "At least someone is on my side." I glare at Lou.

"Hey, I am too," Tanner pipes in. "This little guy is the perfect new member for our friend group."

Lou frowns and leans forward on the edge of Abel's lap to get closer to me. "I'm not *against* you, I'm just trying to be realistic. Chances are, you're not going to be able to keep the cat."

"He fell from the *ceiling*," I emphasize, gesturing wildly. My plate of food nearly goes flying off the arm of the couch, but I grab it in time before it can splatter all over the pink-hued rug. "If you, oh believer in fate, don't think that *means* something then I'm convinced you've been body snatched."

"He is awfully cute." She bites her lip, watching Fettuccine scamper back and forth. "But I do think it'll be impossible to convince Jamie to let you keep him."

Tanner snorts and picks up the kitten, rubbing its nose against his. "If anyone can convince Jamie, it's you."

CHAPTER TWENTY

Jamie

"See, Dad, I told you a guinea pig would be *way* better than a fish."

I stare at the furry creature housed in the colorful cage on my son's dresser. It's black and white, with floppy ears, and a wrinkly pink nose. It's the ugliest thing I've ever seen, but he thinks it's perfect.

I could curse his school for their grand idea of having the second graders get a pet. Their suggestion was a fish, which I didn't like either, but was far better than the overfed gerbil looking thing I now share a home with.

"Oh, yeah, *way* better than a fish," I say sarcastically. My tone goes right over my son's head.

Tobias twists his head, watching the animal. "I'm going to name him Oreo."

"Very original," I comment, shoving my hands in my pockets, twisting my head the opposite way of Tobias's to inspect the guinea pig.

"Boys?" My mom pokes around the entrance to his room, wiping her hands on a dishtowel. "Dinner's ready."

"Can Oreo eat dinner with us?"

I eye the dirty looking creature. "No, he stays here."

"Can I play with him in my room after?"

"No."

My mom sighs from the doorway.

"Dad," Tobias whines, stomping his foot, hands clasped into fists. "I *have* to spend time with him. That's the *point*."

It's moments like this I'm so thankful I have a son, not a daughter. While Tobias can have his moods, a girl would be way worse, and God forbid I even think about the teenage years. I shudder at the thought of tampons, boyfriends, and questions I couldn't even begin to answer.

"You can't keep that animal locked up all the time," my mom interjects.

I am severely outnumbered.

"Fine, you can let him out after dinner."

Sometimes, there's no point in arguing.

It's a struggle for me, but I'm learning I have to let some things go when they aren't worth the argument.

"Come on, Monster." I ruffle Tobias's hair and place my hands on his shoulders, steering him out of the bedroom.

The two of us follow my mom downstairs to the kitchen. The smell of roasted vegetables permeates the air.

"What'd you make, Mom?" I bend and kiss her cheek. "It smells delicious."

"It's a pot roast. It's been cooking in the Crock-Pot all day."

"Have I mentioned lately you're the best?" I drape my arm over her shoulders.

She shakes her head. "Stop plying me with sweet words." She pushes me off her and I laugh.

I might not tell her all the time, but she knows how thankful I am that she's been here for Tobias and me. I couldn't have done all of this without her help. Being a single parent is hard. Knowing I have her in my corner helps.

We sit down with our plates, along with a beer for me, a glass of wine for my mom, and a water for Tobias.

"We should invite Miranda over for dinner sometime." Tobias drops the sentence in between us casually.

"Oh, what a great idea," my mother chimes in cheerily. She has this look in her eyes. One of hope and excitement. It makes a pit form in my stomach.

I know she hopes desperately I'll meet someone and fall in love, that all the stars will align, and whatever other magical stuff she probably thinks up, but I'm not sure I can go back down that path again. I like Miranda, I do, and I want to spend more time with her doing things other than taking our clothes off, but it doesn't mean we have a future, just a right now.

"She probably wouldn't want to do that."

It's stupid to be scared to have her in my home again, but I think I enjoyed it too much the first time and I'm scared of what might happen if she comes back. I know Tobias wants to take more lessons with her, and I don't want to hold him back, but it's all fucking confusing. Even with Shannon I wasn't this confused and torn up over things. Is this what it's like to be a woman? Questioning every little thing and detail. It's exhausting.

"But she likes you, Dad." Tobias points at me with his fork and I realize he's seen me do that one too many times and now he's mimicking the gesture.

Kids. They're our tiny little clones, perfectly projecting our nuances.

"She's nice," he continues, shrugging his shoulders. "You should ask her on a date."

Technically I've taken Miranda on a date, not a *real* date, but taking her flying was sort of that.

"I'd be okay with it," he adds, looking at me with eyes the color of my own. "If that's what's holding you back from getting a girlfriend, just know, I won't mind. Especially if she bakes cookies. I really like cookies. Do you think Miranda makes them? You should ask her."

This kid.

"Maybe, if we keep her, the stork will bring me a brother or sister. That's what Tommy in my class said happened to his parents. He has a baby sister now. I wouldn't mind having a baby around, but don't expect me to change its diapers or hold it when it cries."

I choke on my beer, and I know this is how I fucking die.

Drowned by a fucking Michelob Ultra thanks to my seven-year-old and his declaration of desire for a sibling.

My mom hides her laughter behind a napkin.

"You should take her to dinner," he continues. "Dress nice, though. You look like a bum."

I look down at the sweatpants and t-shirt I changed into when we finally got home with the rat. *Oh, I mean guinea pig.* Across the table, my son is dressed like a tiny 18th century gentleman. He certainly doesn't get his sense of style from me. God knows I hate the days I have to dress up and play boss.

"Toby, I think that's enough advice for your dad for one evening." My mom finally intervenes, leaning over to pat the top of his hand in warning.

She used to do the same thing to me growing up when I'd babble on about something.

Tobias shrugs, poking at his food with his fork in his opposite hand. "All I'm saying is, if he's nervous that's okay. Maybe I can ask her to go bowling with you?" he suggests, looking at me with wide innocent hazel eyes. "That way you don't have to do it, or go by yourself."

I scrub my hands down my face, my mom laughing once more.

My son trying to wingman me is hilarious, sure, but also mortifying. He's *seven*. What does he know about any of this? Maybe I should have a talk with this Tommy kid in his class and tell him to shut up about all talk of storks.

Yeah, I might've always thought I'd have more kids than one, but since I don't plan to ever go down the path of marriage again it's not in the cards for me. Tobias will have to learn to be okay being an only child. I was. It's not the worst thing ever.

"Do you have her number?" he continues, oblivious to my distress. "I can call her for you."

If ever in my life I wanted to be struck by lightning, now is the moment.

"You could send her flowers." He's on a full on rant now, and my mother is laughing so hard tears stream down her face. I want to fucking disappear. "You've never had a girlfriend, and I really think you should get one. I'm not going to be around forever, Dad, and I don't want you to get lonely."

My mom covers her face with a linen napkin, her whole body shaking. Tobias picks at his food like there is nothing wrong with what he's saying. And me? I've never felt so attacked in my entire life.

Clearing my throat, I look my son clear in the eyes. "I'm not lonely Tobias. I have you and Grandma Jo."

He rolls his eyes. "Did you not hear anything I said, Dad?" He lets go of his fork where it clatters against the plate. "I'm not going to live here forever. Grandma Jo is old, so she's going to die. Then it'll just be you."

My mom's mouth pops open and she swats him lightly on his arm with her napkin. "I'm not old!"

He tilts his head, looking up at her. "You have wrinkles on your neck, that means you're old."

She looks across the table at me and I shrug. She was fine when he was ragging on me, so she can deal with it now that the tables are turned.

"Just do me a favor, Dad, and *try*."

"I've suddenly lost my appetite," I grumble, though I'm mildly amused.

"Finish your vegetables, Jamie," my mother chides, a twinkle in her eyes.

With dinner finished, dishes clean, and Tobias fresh out of the shower I tuck him into bed, grabbing the book off his end table we're reading together.

"Are you cozy enough?" I eye his pile of blankets and stuffed animals. There's barely any room on his bed for me, but I always make it work.

Selfishly, I love this time with my son. I know one day, probably sooner than I'd like, he won't think it's awesome to lie in his bed every night and read a book together. It's the moments like this I know I'll cherish forever.

He nods, burrowing under his blankets. I move some things out of the way so I can lie down. Crossing my feet at the ankles I crack open the book to where we left off and begin reading. Tobias scoots closer to me, laying his head on my shoulder so he can read as I go.

The thought of Shannon dragging me to court again terrifies me.

I've fought so hard for my son from the moment I

knew he existed, but I'm scared in the eye of the law that won't be seen because I'm a man. That's un-fucking-fair.

Spending time with Tobias isn't a chore, it's a joy, and I know she really doesn't want to be involved in his life. I wish for his sake she was genuine. He deserves to have a mom in his life.

Maybe that's why he's so determined to make something happen with Miranda for me. My mom might be around, but I know it's not the same for him. The only blessing is, he doesn't know any other way. Shannon was never around so it's not like he lost something. However, he could *gain* something.

But I never planned to add to our world.

My feelings for Miranda are growing, but are they headed down the path to something like marriage?

I hadn't planned on it, but who fucking knows. My thoughts are a mess.

"Dad?" Tobias interrupts me, lifting his head.

"Yeah?" I lay the open book on my chest.

"I just want you to be happy."

"I am happy," I protest.

He shakes his head. "You could be happier."

I frown. I'm not lying when I say I'm happy, but kids ... they're pretty perceptive, and even though I don't want to, maybe I should listen to him.

CHAPTER TWENTY-ONE

Miranda

Swinging my door open, my backpack threatening to fall off one shoulder, I come face to face with a surprised Jamie, hand poised ready to knock.

"Hi!" I cry, breathless, since I'm running late and in a mad dash to leave. I certainly wasn't expecting to open my door and find Jamie waiting. "What are you doing here?"

"Can I come in?" He points inside at my messy apartment. I'm swamped with schoolwork, which means no time to clean. Besides, cleaning sucks.

"Nope. I'm in a hurry. I'm going to be late for class."

Thank God, I shut Fettuccine in my bedroom.

I close the door behind me and lock it.

"I'll follow you to your car, is that okay?"

"Mhmm." I power walk down the hall and he follows.

He's able to keep up all too easily with his long legs. "I ... uh ... wanted to ask you something."

"Um, okay?" I start down the stairs. "Why'd you have to come all the way here to ask me something? You have a phone. Text me like a normal human being."

He chuckles, but it sounds strained. When I glance behind at him I find his hands stuffed in the pockets of his jeans, his shoulders tense.

We reach the bottom floor and head for the parking lot.

"I wanted to ask you on a date. A real date. Dinner. Maybe a movie. Or dancing. Or ... um ... whatever you want."

I freeze and he bumps into the back of me.

I whip around and he backs up a few steps. "Did I seriously hear you right? I thought we went on a date? You showed me your plane and how you work your landing gear." I eye his crotch.

He wets his lips with his tongue. "It's as close to a

date as I've had in over a decade, but it's not the correct way to do things. I'm still holding myself back from you ... from myself ... God, from everything." He runs his fingers through his wavy reddish-brown hair, letting his arm fall to his side. "I don't know how to do this. To be a good guy who takes girls on proper dates, who isn't fearful of rejection, and the pain of losing someone they love."

I really have to go, but I can't help but linger in the parking lot with him.

"My son made a good point," he continues, taking a step closer to me. "I could be happier, and I realized, when I spend time with you I am. You make me smile and laugh. I don't feel so jaded. I think it's time I stop being so scared and take a leap of faith. So, yeah, here I am." He spreads his arms and releases a breath, his eyes wary. "Can you see now why I didn't text this?"

"So, we go on a real date and what then?"

He shrugs. "We go on another and maybe another until you decide I'm too much of a pain in the ass to continue to see, and then we break things off for good."

Despair fills me at the idea of never spending time with Jamie again.

"And what if we decide not to break things off? What if we decide it feels right?"

He takes another step closer to me. "Then I guess this little leap of faith of mine might pay off in a big way."

Another step. His shoes press to the edge of my combat boots. "I'd like to think I'm the kind of guy who can get the girl." He cups my cheek and I melt into his touch like a puddle of goo. Then he presses his forehead to mine, looking down at me reverently. "My son thinks he's the one holding me back from having someone to care about, but it's me. It's always been about me. Fuck, Miranda, I'm absolutely terrified of you and what this could mean, but I have to ask you on a date before Tobias does it for me."

He laughs and I laugh too.

"You are the most confusing man, ever."

It's been a week since I saw him at Petco. We texted some, but he seemed distant. I think I understand why now. He's had a lot on his mind.

"I confuse myself."

"So, I say yes—then what?"

He cracks a tiny grin. It's small, barley noticeable with our foreheads still bent together. I'd like to think it's a fissure in his rock hard exterior.

"Then I woo you."

CHAPTER TWENTY-TWO

Miranda

"Wait, you're going on a date—a real date, with Jamie?"

Lou shoves clothes on the rack aside, staring through the now empty slot at me on the opposite side.

I pull out a dress, holding it to my frame.

"Yes, who'd you think I was going with when I said I needed a dress for a date?"

She frowns, stepping around the rack to join me. "I don't know, I just didn't think it'd be him."

I'm not mad at Lou for her lack of support. I know she's only coming from a protective place, not a vindictive one.

I return the dress to the rack and turn to her. I know I owe her a real, honest explanation.

"I like Jamie." I hold up a hand when she opens her mouth to speak. "I don't know what exactly that entails, or where it'll go, but I have to give it a try. It's hard for you to believe, but he does make me happy."

"But a couple of months ago you hated his guts more than me. What changed?"

I move to another aisle, looking at a full skirt in a cobalt blue color.

"I can't explain it." She looks less than pleased by my response, but it's the truth. "I was mad at him for feeling used, for not giving us a proper ending even though it was only sex before, but he explained some things and it put a lot of my insecurities to rest."

"I don't want all the details, but I need more than that."

With a clatter the skirt goes back on the rack. "He said he rubbed the other woman in my face because he was scared of the feelings he was developing for me."

Lou snorts, crossing her arms over her chest. "Likely story."

I pause, considering my words. I don't want to get in a fight with her over a guy. Hoes before bros, always.

"I'm not asking you to be Team Jamie. I want you on Team Miranda and right now I'm taking a leap of faith." I smile to myself, realizing I used the same words Jamie did with me.

Lou shakes her head and pulls me into a hug. "Team Miranda, always."

I hug her back, relieved to have my best friend on my side. "I need to see where this goes," I murmur into her shoulder, holding on tight.

She pulls back, holding onto my arms. "Okay, then let's find you one bomb ass dress, get your nails done, make sure everything is waxed and shiny, so when he picks you up he loses his mind."

I snort. "I can make him lose his mind without all that."

She laughs, shaking her head. She drapes an arm over my shoulders, leading me further into the store. "Oh, I'm sure you can."

The white dress I bought looks fucking amazing on me. It hugs every curve and shows enough cleavage to be tantalizing, but not too much to be risqué. The thin spaghetti straps rest against my shoulders. They don't do much to hold up the dress, or my girls, but they add a small bit of *something* that helps make the dress.

I once read that big girls shouldn't wear white, but dare I say they're liars?

I can pull off whatever I want and I look sexy tonight. I figured since this is supposed to be an actual date, I should go all out.

Beyond the dress, I'm wearing a strappy pair of heals, a gold necklace at my throat, and some small hoop earrings. I curled my hair, but pulled the top half back with a silver butterfly clip, letting a few pieces fall out to frame my face. I spent way more time on my makeup than normal and I look like a dewy bronze goddess if I do say so myself.

I know I didn't have to go through all this trouble. Jamie's seen me lounging around in pajamas with no bra. But I did this for *me*, because *I* wanted to feel hot as fuck.

It's taken me a long time to feel confident in my skin.

I don't know when the change first happened, but I think it was subtle in the beginning.

Now, I don't give a damn what anyone thinks of me.

I feel good about myself. I know I'm beautiful, smart, and a boss ass bitch. It's like one day I finally woke up and the stress and worry of how my pants fit and if I'd ever be as thin as the women magazines claim are desirable just melted away.

It's been freeing.

I'm a butterfly finally spreading her wings, and it didn't take a man for me to do it.

I found it within myself, because everything we ever need to succeed in life exists insides us.

Smiling at my reflection I swipe some gloss over my lipstick and grab a coat and my purse. It's not technically fall yet, but the weather doesn't know that. The nights have been unseasonably cool and I don't want to freeze to death.

I hear a knock on my apartment door and I take a deep breath.

"I'll see you later, Fettuccine." I scratch the purring kitten behind his ears, closing my bedroom door behind me so there's no chance of Jamie spotting him. I purposely hid all the cat stuff littering my apartment.

I thought it'd be awkward if he showed up, saw the cat stuff, and we ended up in an argument before our official first date.

I swing the door open in a rather dramatic fashion, a breathless, "Hi," leaving my lips.

I look Jamie up and down while he does the same to me.

If Fettuccine wasn't currently occupying my bedroom —I'm too scared to put him in the spare where all my art supplies is—I would pull him inside and ask him to do wicked things to my body with his devilish mouth.

He's dressed in a pair of nice jeans—probably

designer, because I've never seen jeans look like these—a white button down shirt tucked into them, topped off with a gray jacket, and shiny chestnut colored leather shoes.

Finally making my way up the column of his neck, to his lightly stubbled cheeks and jaw, his lips quirk into a half smile as I study him. His reddish-brown hair tumbles over his forehead in that annoying way that you know is effortless—whereas my effortless hair look is called rolling out of bed looking like Medusa.

"You are beautiful."

"Thank you."

Stupid cheeks stop blushing!

"Tobias said that in order for this to be a real date, I had to bring you flowers, but flowers die, so I got you this succulent instead."

I laugh as he pulls out a beautiful succulent with a purple hue in a tiny white pot.

"Succulents can die too," I remark playfully, taking it from him.

The silly plant makes me ridiculously giddy. It feels like proof that something real is building between us and this living plant is like the budding of our new relationship.

Oh my God my mom has quoted way too many self-help books to me.

"Let me set this somewhere." I hold up a finger for

him to wait, but of course he comes in, closing the door behind him.

I look around for a place to put the little plant, preferably where Fettuccine won't get it.

My heels clack on the kitchen floor tiles and I feel the wall of heat that is Jamie follow me closely.

I rise on my tiptoes to set it on one of the open shelves in the kitchen.

"Let me get it." Jamie's large palm settles on the curve of my ass, his front plastered to my back. With his other hand he easily plucks the succulent out of my hand and places it on the shelf.

His now succulent-free hand skims over my shoulder and down my arm, eliciting a shiver from my body.

"If I wasn't trying to be a proper gentleman I'd tell you to forget the date, because *fuck*, Miranda, you're sexy as hell and I want to peel this dress off you."

I turn around in his arms, placing my hands on his chest. My butt bumps into the corner of the counter.

"I feel like we're doing this whole thing backwards."

He tilts his head. "How so?"

"Well, you said you were going to make love to me on your plane, which you did."

"And?" His eyes narrow speculatively.

"You weren't scared to make love to me, but you were to ask me on a date? Doesn't that seem backwards to you?"

He sighs, looking away. I know I've caught him off guard, but at least I know he's not entirely offended or he would've let me go.

Returning his gaze back to me, he says, "You're right. I think the physical stuff is easier for me when it comes to you, because that's what we started as. It seems easier to share myself sexually than personally. With sex, it's a feeling, a sensation. But something like this, a date, it's face to face. It's words. It's getting to know each other on a deeper level. There is no hiding with dating. Eventually you'll see every flaw of mine, every fear I hide."

I release a small laugh, softly stroking his stubbled cheek gently. "I hate to inform you, but I'm pretty sure I've seen all your flaws long before I ever had sex with you. You're kind of an asshole."

He chuckles, placing his hand on top of mine. "That's not me. It's a front, a fraud, to keep people away. So I don't have to get to know them, or talk about my life. The things that mean something to me, I like to keep them close and not share them with others. After my ex showed her true colors, I guess it made me jaded." He pulls my hand from his face, curling our fingers together. "The real flaws I'm afraid of are the stupid things. Like always leaving the toilet seat up, or how I *can't* make a cup of decent fucking coffee to save myself. Things that, over time, might become irritating."

I take his other hand, so now we're holding both

hands. "Don't overthink things. This is new for both of us. Neither of us are dating pros. I think it's better to take things one day, or maybe *date* is more apt, at a time."

"You're right." He kisses the tip of my nose not to mess up my blood red lipstick.

"Are you gonna take me on this date now, lover boy, or not?"

He shakes his head and gives a small snort of laughter. "Let's get you out of here, before I decide to get you out of your dress instead."

Jamie and I stroll the streets of downtown hand in hand. Lights are strung around the trees and the restaurants lining the walking area are all packed. We already ate at some fancy Inn I'd never heard of, and I was thankful I did decide to dress up. After the delicious meal, Jamie told me he had something else planned.

Color me intrigued.

"Where are we going?" My whole body vibrates with energy. I don't think I've ever felt so alive. It's a silly thing, to have someone make you so giddy, but with Jamie I feel this excitement I don't think I've ever had. I see everything in a new and different light.

"It's this way." He tugs me down a street, walking on the sidewalk passed parked cars and traffic. Ahead of us is the library, the tall looming dome above it haloed by a full moon.

"Come on, tell me," I plead, tugging on his hand as we walk.

He tilts his head down, giving me a crooked smile. "Such a nosy thing you are. We're almost there."

We turn left, walk a little farther, and cross the street.

"Here we are," he declares, stopping outside a small art studio.

There are already people inside and I realize it's one of those paint and sip parties.

I look from the lit up storefront to Jamie. "We're going to paint?" I can't stop smiling.

He shrugs. "I showed you what I love, my planes. Now I want you to show me what you love. You taught Tobias, but not me. I'm feeling a bit left out."

"Aww." I pat his cheek mockingly. "Jealous of a seven-year-old? Why am I not surprised?"

He laughs, shaking his head. "Get in there." He smacks my ass and opens the door so I can go in first.

The smell of paint hits me first, a mix of car exhaust fumes and a meadow. A lot of people hate the smell of paint, but I love it. It's my home.

"Oh, our last two." The woman whom I assume is the teacher claps her hands together and ushers Jamie and me to the final easels in the back row, passing us large aprons to put on. Hopefully it'll be enough to protect my new white dress. "Cecilia will be handing out the wine and hors d'oeuvres after instructions."

She flits back to the front of the room and with her small posture and pale pink hair I'm reminded of a pixie.

She motions with her hands for everyone to quiet down so she can be heard.

"I'm so happy to be spending the evening with all of you tonight." She bounces on her feet, a complete ball of energy. "It's going to be so much fun and at the end you're going to leave sated with wine and a new piece of art to hang in your house later on." She crosses over to the easel in front of the room with a completed painting. "This is what you'll be recreating tonight. Feel free to follow it exactly or take your own artistic abilities. I'll also be working up front, speaking about techniques, so you can watch it take form if you're a newbie and need more guidance. Feel free to ask any questions you might have. This is a safe space for all of us be a little weird and a whole lot creative."

Jamie clears his throat, tipping his stool slightly in my direction so he can whisper under his breath, "She's a bit ... uh ... eccentric."

I bump his shoulder, sending him back to his original position with all the legs of the stool solidly on the ground.

"You didn't tell us your name," someone from the front speaks, raising a hand.

"Oh, right." The instructor claps again, her cheeks tinged pink. "I'm Cynthia, and that's my sister Cecilia." She points to the blue haired woman in the corner of the room. "So ... um ... yeah, let's get to it then."

"Is she new at this?" I ask Jamie since she seems a little nervous.

He clears his throat, picking up a paintbrush and running the pad of his thumb over the bristles. "It's only been open a week."

"Oh." It suddenly makes sense, her chaotic nervousness and the fact that I haven't heard of this place before now. As an artist I usually hear about this kind of stuff from either online searching or my classmates.

I lean around my easel, peering at the finished canvas in front of the room. It's a simple painting of a starry night with black silhouettes for people. For me, this is an easy painting to do, but I look forward to putting my own spin on things. Plus, it'll be more than a little fun to watch Jamie try his hand at things. God, I love to watch that man squirm. I don't know what that says about me.

As promised Cecilia passes around glasses of wine and plates of fancy cheeses and crackers. I'm full, so I don't really want any but Jamie insists we take the snacks just in case.

He pays close attention to Cynthia's instructions while I paint my heart away.

Joy fills me, watching the colors bleed and blend

together, the spark of life I can create with color on a blank white surface. Art has always brought me a high that nothing else can.

Though, that may be in part to the fumes.

"Mine looks nothing like that," Jamie exclaims, causing a few heads to turn our way.

"It's not supposed to." I don't bother taking my eyes off my canvas. "It's your *interpretation*."

"Yeah, well, fuck my interpretation. Cecilia! I need more wine!" He holds his glass up, swinging around as he tries to spot the blue haired woman. Cecilia comes running over and tops his glass off. "You don't have anything stronger, do you? Some whiskey? A shot of tequila, perhaps?" She shakes her head and runs away. I guess Cynthia talks so much that she feels no need to utter a single word. Turning to me, Jamie brushes a lock of hair from his eyes with the back of his arm. "I'm going to need to be drunk to make this anywhere near decent."

I roll my eyes, returning to my painting. I brush the side of my pinky against the wet, midnight blue paint to swirl it. "Yeah, that's not how it works. But tequila, really? That shit makes me want to take my clothes off and wear a sombrero." My eyes shift to him. "Not that that's ever happened to me before."

His lips turn up on the left corner. "Interesting. When did that happen?"

"Spring break my freshman year of college. Went to

Cancun and that's pretty much the only memory I have —though it's not really a memory since Lou recounted the story to me." I ponder for a second. "Huh, maybe that means it didn't actually happen. Since I can't remember anything, she could've made up some bull shit."

"Would she do that?"

I sigh dejectedly. "No, Lou's not that type of person. Unfortunately."

"You guys are really close."

I know it's a statement not a question. "Yeah. She's like a sister to me."

He chuckles, but there's no humor in the tone. "I don't even know if you have any siblings or not."

"I don't. What else do you want to know?" My eyes slide to him. He's not looking at me, instead he's working intently on his painting. I wonder if he knows his tongue sticks out the tiniest bit between his lips when he's concentrating on something. "You can ask."

He doesn't respond for a minute. "Where did you grow up?"

"Delaware. That's where my parents still live. I miss them. A lot." I can feel my throat closing up. I don't talk often about how hard it is being away from my parents. We were the three musketeers, still are, I'm just hours away now. I needed to leave and spread my wings, and I'm thankful they understood that.

"Oh." I see his shoulders tense from the corner of my eye. "Will you go back there after you graduate?"

"I used to think I might, but this is where I belong. Something about this place..." I pause, looking out the large glass window to my right at the small town twinkling with lights and laughter. "It feels like home in a way Delaware can't. I'm hoping my parents will move here eventually, or at least closer."

He dips his brush into black, his eyes darting to me almost shyly. "Do you want to ask me something?"

"What exactly is it you do? I know you say you work for your family's company, but you've never stated what all that means."

He takes a sip—no, a gulp—of wine before answering. "Miller Enterprises dabbles in a bit of everything. Real estate, aviation, oil, the list goes on. My great-great grandpa built it from nothing into what it is today. As tradition goes, it gets passed down. You wouldn't believe some of the companies who have tried to buy us over the years for more money than you can dream, but my grandpa wouldn't sell and I won't either. Plus, I like working too much. I prefer handling what the bigwigs call the simple man stuff. Sometimes it's easy to forget I'm the CEO of a major corporation."

"Whoa." I wasn't expecting all that. "So, like ... you have to have other locations, right?"

He nods, picking up a cracker with cheese. He chews and swallows before finally answering me.

"There's one here in Tysons, that's our D.C. location, Manhattan, L.A., even London and Tokyo."

"How rich are you?" I find myself blurting out, probably a little too loud.

I knew Jamie had money, that much was obvious, especially when he showed me the planes, but I didn't realize he was *this* wealthy.

"Oh my God," I slap a hand over my mouth before he can reply, "you really are Christian Grey."

He looks sheepish and mumbles under his breath, "Yeah, pretty much."

My jaw drops.

My kinda-sorta-not-really boyfriend is a billionaire. Maybe even a multi-billionaire.

Billionaire.

Like a millionaire, but with a B for billion—as in more money than I can ever comprehend. So. Many. Zeros.

"But you ... you're ... *normal*." Okay, Jamie isn't exactly normal, but he's definitely closer to what I'd label normal than a billionaire.

"Is that a problem?" He raises one brow, his tone a little snappy.

I rear back. "No, it's a good thing," I assure him. "I *like* that fact about you. You're just *you*."

He drops his eyes, letting out a breath. "I'm sorry for snapping." He shocks me with his apology. "I ... I know now Shannon, my ex, only wanted to be involved with me for my money. It's a sore subject."

I let out a snort. "I'm only with you for your magic tea cup ride." He throws his head back and laughs. When he looks at me I can tell his shoulders are lighter. "Just remember, we started this thing *long* before we ever knew anything about each other. Chemistry is chemistry. That shit can't be denied."

His eyes spark with lust. "Believe me, I know."

We grow quiet for a little bit, focusing on our painting, before he speaks again.

"Anything else you want to ask me?"

I lower my paintbrush, hesitantly biting my lip. "You haven't dated anyone since your ex-wife, right?" I hedge and he nods in affirmation. "Why me? Why after all this time would you choose me?"

"Honestly?" He dips his brush in water and wipes it off. "I don't know. At first, it was easy, it was just sex. But then I kept coming back to you again and again. I hooked up with women after Shannon left, but not all that often. I have a son to take care of, a business to run, and a mom who watches me like a hawk." He laughs, shaking his head. "But I couldn't stay away from you, so I forced myself to." By using the woman I saw him with at the bar. "I wanted to hurt you, because I already knew how stubborn you are, and if you hated me then I knew that would be it for us." Something flashes on his face that I can't decipher, but disappears quickly. "Suffice to say, I couldn't stay away."

"Come on, Jamie, I need more of an explanation than that." I'm begging him, I know, but I don't care.

I need to understand what he truly thinks of me, of *us*.

Things have been headed in a new, blindly scary territory for us, and I just want to be sure before I end up with a broken heart.

I might have faith, but that doesn't mean I don't have the same doubts Lou has voiced to me.

"What Shannon did to me … it took me by surprise. She took some naivety away from me, and with you, I feel a little more like that old version of myself. Someone not so burdened with the hardships of a difficult past. Tobias had to have heart surgery after he was born." His voice grows incredibly soft, his hazel eyes filling with an old sadness. I reach over, placing my hand on his arm. It's strange to be having a heart to heart like this with Jamie in the midst of all these people, but I'm thankful he's opening up. "Having my infant son have open heart surgery was the scariest thing I've ever been through. Was Shannon there? No, she'd taken off to the Maldives thanks to one of my credit cards. She didn't even care that he was a *baby* having a major surgery." He looks like he wants to say more, but shakes his head. "Please, tell me something else about you. Something random and not nearly as sad and pathetic as all that shit I just unburdened onto you."

"Um." I scramble through my brain, looking for any minute detail about myself I can scrounge up. "I hate sweet tea. It tastes like piss. Clowns freak me out, they're weird as hell. Scary movies are not my jam. I still listen to Hannah Montana—Life's What You Make It is a *bop* and I will fight anyone on this fact. I love yoga, it relaxes me. Should I keep going?"

He shakes his head, a tiny grin tugging at his full lips. "What your favorite position?"

"Sex position?"

"No, yoga."

I snort, waving a dismissive hand. I sling a little paint on the woman's canvas a few feet away from me by mistake. Thankfully, she doesn't notice. "Corpse pose, of course."

"Ah," he breathes with a soft laugh. "It's not like Squiggly Snake or some shit like that?"

"That's not even a yoga pose. Don't be offensive," I mock playfully.

God, this is nice hanging out with him, being myself and seeing his walls come down more and more. I have to admit, this is the best date I've ever been on. Who'd have thought?

An hour later we've finished our paintings, leaving them to dry, as we head onto the street. I pull my coat tighter around me, thankful I had the forethought to bring it.

Jamie wraps an arm around my shoulders, pulling me against his solid side.

"I still say yours was the best of the whole class."

"You're biased." I bump my hip against his.

"I'm serious. You're an incredible artist, Miranda."

I glance up at him and I'm struck by how handsome he is. Jamie is my favorite type of art, one molded and crafted by time, circumstances, and sheer determination. His soul is the heartbeat of my existence. That might sound crazy, but it's true. If I never hear from him again after tonight it won't change that fact. Some people we are destined to meet and they become a tether, to a time, a place, to a feeling and I know he's that for me.

"Thank you."

He smiles at me and I say a prayer for us—a prayer for a tomorrow, a prayer for a future I suddenly, so desperately, want more than anything else.

CHAPTER TWENTY-THREE

Jamie

"So..." Miranda leans against her apartment's open door, holding onto my jacket with one hand. "I guess this is goodnight, then."

Tonight was more than I could've ever expected. Spending time with her is easy and it doesn't feel like hours have passed since I picked her up. It's after ten and I find myself sad at the prospect of having to say goodnight to her and walk away.

"Or you could always invite me in," I suggest, tilting my head to the side.

As much as I want to peel her dress from her body, I'm not having sex with her tonight even if she does say I can come in. I want this to be a *real* date, the beginning of something new, and I want to show her I do want more than sex with her.

Though, the sex is pretty fucking fantastic.

She twists her lips, looking over her shoulder and down the hall.

Fucking hell, I'd bet anything that stupid kitten is somewhere in this apartment.

I'm not a cat person, it's true, but I'd let her keep it if pets weren't extensively against the rules of the whole complex. I bought a few apartments here from her original landlord, but there's still a committee in charge of things like allowing pets and rules of the pool—shit like that.

"Not tonight," she finally says, placing her palm on my chest. Her fingernails are painted a silvery color. It's the first time I've seen them neat and manicured. Normally they're bare with scraps of dried paint from her projects caked under them. "My mom always told me a real lady never gives it up on the first date."

In a blink, she kisses my cheek and the door closes in my face.

I bust out laughing at the closed door.

"Always keeping me on my toes. Goodnight, Miranda," I say through the door.

"Night! Masturbate to only thoughts of me!"

I shake my head at her antics.

I head down and narrow my eyes when I see her neighbor Stan poke his head out of his apartment.

"Can I help you?" I glare at him when he stares at me.

"You got a smoke?"

"No." I shove my hands in my pockets, narrowing my eyes.

Am I going to have to punch this fucker?

He looks up the stairs behind me and licks his lips. "Miranda, she's pretty sexy, huh? I like 'em thick. We have that in common."

Anger boils in my bloodstream. I've never wanted to hit someone so much.

"I don't think we have anything in common," I come back with, sounding much calmer than I actually am.

He smiles and his nasty stained yellow teeth look ready to rot out of his mouth. How is it possible with dental care readily available people like this still manage to exist?

"Well, we'll see about that."

He laughs, the sound echoing off the concrete floor, and closes his door.

I stand there for a minute, giving my blood pressure a chance to go down. I'm going to have to do something about that guy, because my gut tells me Miranda isn't safe with him around.

Perhaps I'm being overprotective but I doubt it.

He's got to go.

My drive home is all too quiet without Miranda in the car. Normally I like the silence. It gives me time to think. But I miss the sound of her chatting passionately and her laughter that always seems to explode out of her suddenly.

I pull into my garage, heading into the darkened house and up to my master bedroom. Setting my wallet on my dresser I nearly shit myself when I hear Tobias.

"How'd it go, Dad? Did you give her flowers? I told you girls like flowers."

I shake my head at him. Tobias is far too young to be concerned with what girls do and don't like. If he's like this now God help me.

"What are you doing up?" I narrow my eyes on him, giving him my best *stern father* look.

He shrugs his small shoulders. Tonight he wears a pair of striped pajamas with insects. "Don't be mad at Grandma Jo, she thought I was asleep. I'm good at pretending."

I pinch the bridge of my nose between my thumb and forefinger.

"You should be sleeping, Tobias, not asking me about my date."

He frowns slightly, his shoulders drawing inward, and I instantly feel bad for what I said. "I just wanted to know. I'm sorry."

He turns to go back across to his room.

I let out a breath and follow him. The last thing I want is for my son to think he can't talk to me or ask questions. I don't want to be the kind of parent who holds my kid at arm's length, scared to have a real world conversation.

Tobias climbs into his bed and grumbles, "Go away, Dad."

I sit on the edge of his bed and he looks anywhere but at me. It's okay. I deserve that.

"I'm sorry, Tobias. This is just ... weird. I haven't dated in a very long time."

"Since my mom," he states, finally looking at me.

"Yeah, since your mom." My shoulders sag.

"But she doesn't love us."

This has always been the tricky part, trying to explain things to a young child so he understands while not bad mouthing Shannon. "I'm sure she loves you in the only way she knows how, but it's not the way I love you, if that makes sense."

"But she doesn't love you?"

"Not anymore."

"Does that make you sad?"

"Not anymore," I answer truthfully, picking up his

most-loved teddy bear. It's worn, missing an eye, and has more patches than I can count. I got it at the hospital the day he was born and it's been a permanent fixture ever since.

"But Miranda ... you like her?"

"I do," I admit with a soft laugh. It's crazy, but I do.

"Does she like you?"

I shrug, setting his bear up beside him. He immediately grabs it, curling one arm around it and tugging it against his body.

"I hope so."

"I think she does."

I chuckle, tickling his toes beneath the blanket. "Thanks, son."

"But ... did you remember the flowers?"

This kid and his damn flowers.

"I got her a flower."

"*A* flower? That's singular, Dad. One flower is not good enough."

"It was a succulent."

"A succulent? What's that?" His nose crinkles. I pull out my phone and show him a picture of one. He promptly rolls his eyes at me. "That is *not* a flower, Dad. Do better next time."

Schooled by a seven-year-old.

"Can you go to sleep now?" I ask him, raising a brow.

He looks around and I know he's probably trying to think of even more questions. "I guess so."

I lean over and ruffle his hair before kissing him on top of his head. "Night."

"Goodnight, Dad."

I cross his room and look back at him one more time before I close his door.

If there's anything I've done right in this world, it's that kid.

CHAPTER TWENTY-FOUR

Jamie

"Considering this is our third official date, and you still won't have sex with me for chivalrous reasons I have yet to understand, I think it's important for you to know my date of birth is in two weeks—October twenty-sixth—and if you're not putting out by then that might be the end of this relationship." She twists her lips back and forth contemplatively. "Because I think I deserve some birthday sex."

I chuckle, setting down my drink.

"That so?"

"Yep." She leans forward, elbows on the table, fingers clasped, and rests her chin on them. My eyes drop to her ample cleavage now on full display. When she took off her coat I nearly choked on my tongue at the sight of her in the dark blue dress. It's curve hugging with a plunging neckline that my dick likes very much. "You should totally get me an epic birthday present too. Like a star with my name, or sponsor some kind of animal."

I snort, turning it into a cough because I *do not* snort. "Pretty sure I'm already sponsoring the cat you're hiding in your apartment." Her jaw drops. "Did you seriously think I didn't know? You're not a very good secret keeper. Besides, when I picked you up the other night there was a cat food bag on the counter."

Her mouth flaps like a fish.

I take another drink and clear my throat. "If anyone asks, I know nothing. I'll deny everything. This is on you."

Her cheeks color and her hands drop to the napkin folded in her lap. I swear I hear a mumbled thank you but can't be sure.

If she wants the damn cat so bad, who am I to say no?

Well, *again*, since I already said no five-hundred other times and it always fell on deaf ears.

"Your birthday, huh?" I hum, wiping condensation

from my glass. "Do I get to spend the day with you for your birthday?"

She fiddles with her napkin more. "I was ... um ... actually wondering if maybe we could do something with Tobias for the day? If it's okay with you?"

She's been over once more to paint with him and I swear if my son was of legal age he'd try to steal her from me. He's in love with her.

I always thought if the time came where I did date I wouldn't bring a woman around my son, but I don't want to keep Miranda away. She makes him happy and I like seeing my son light up like that. He deserves to have another womanly touch in his life other than my mom.

"What do you have in mind?"

She smiles, sitting up straighter. "I was thinking we could do something in D.C.—maybe go to a museum, see the White House and monuments, have you guys ever done that before?"

I shake my head. "No, but he's been asking. I think he'd love it." I pull out my phone, looking at the calendar. "Would you want to make a weekend out of it? Spend Saturday night there?"

"That sounds amazing." She beams and looks ready to launch across the table to tackle me into a hug. "I won't even beg you for birthday sex."

"Yeah, that'd be a little complicated with my son around."

"I'm excited about this," she admits in a whisper, almost like she's scared to say it out loud.

Surprisingly, I am too. "You should be the one to tell Tobias. I swear he likes you more than me."

She sets her water glass down and swallows. A small droplet of water clings to her bottom lip and *fuck* what I wouldn't give to lick it away.

"Maybe that's because I call him Toby, you know, what *he* prefers to be called, and you insist on Tobias."

"Because, it's his name."

She sighs, shaking her head. Her dark hair is curled and lays long down her back. I itch to wrap my fingers in it and tug her mouth to mine, but I'm trying to behave myself and take things slow. It's possible I'm killing us both in the process.

"You're so stubborn."

"It's part of my charm." I wink, taking the check from the waiter when he arrives. I add the tip and sign my name to the slip of paper, tucking my credit card back into my wallet.

We stand, both of us shrugging into our coats.

Hand in hand we walk next door to the movie theater and since it's reserved seating and I already bought the tickets we don't even have to wait in line.

We walk up to our seats in the back row, Miranda's heels clacking, and sit down.

She picks up the menu and I chuckle. "We just ate."

She rolls her eyes at me and goddam *why* is that such a turn on?

"Yeah, and I'm getting popcorn anyway. You can't come to a movie theater and *not* get popcorn. That's sacrilegious."

"Whatever you say." I rub my fingers over my lips to keep from laughing.

She orders the popcorn and drinks, sticking the piece of paper in the air for one of the runners to grab.

She sits back in her seat, finally shrugging out of her coat.

"You know," she muses, turning around so she can drape the garment behind her seat, "the last time I was here was with Lou and Abel. I felt like such a third wheel. Now, I'm here with you."

"I'm way better company." I grab her hand, kissing her knuckles.

I'm so fucked when it comes to her. If I'm not touching her or kissing her I feel lost. She grounds me. It's like all this time I've barely been tethered to the earth. I had Tobias and my mom, but I was missing that one last, final piece, and it's her.

The lights begin to darken and she squeezes my hand.

I'm suddenly regretting my choice of dinner and a movie. I'd much rather have this time to talk to her, which is ironic since I normally hate talking. Miranda brings out a side of me I didn't know I had.

But watching her eyes light up at the previews, and later her excitement as the movie plays, popcorn pressed to her lips as she watches the climax with anticipation, makes it all worth it.

A few days after my movie date with Miranda, it's time for my second meeting with Shannon. She's already pushed it back twice, and if I arrive at the office and find that she's a no-show I'm going to lose my shit.

She's playing games with me and it's not okay, not when *my* son is involved.

Stepping into the building I adjust my tie. It's a stupid habit I can't seem to quit.

Heading down the hall I find Don waiting for me.

"She here?" Short, clipped, to the point. I have no time for pleasantries.

He shakes his head. "Not yet."

He ushers me into a similar conference room to the one we were in last time.

He passes me a small bottle of water. Unscrewing the cap I gulp down practically the entire thing.

I'm not nervous, I'm pissed, because this entire thing is a waste of my time and energy. I could be doing something productive instead of arguing with her greedy ass.

Don sits down beside me, laying his hands on the table.

He looks cool as a cucumber while I'm ready to bolt out of my skin. I'm particularly antsy after all the reschedules. Call it paranoia, but I'm pretty sure she's up to something.

The ticking of the clock grates on my nerves. I'm in hell.

"Calm down," Don chides me under his breath.

"I am calm," I growl.

Ten minutes pass.

Another five.

Even more until it's thirty minutes past our scheduled meeting time and Don sends me on my way.

I get in my car for the drive back home and anger boils my blood, because she's stringing me along on purpose.

Shannon officially has me right where she wants me.

Angry and desperate for her to be gone.

This has been her goal.

To drive me insane until she can get whatever she wants and go on her merry way.

But fuck it, I'm older now, sort of wiser, and I won't give into her demands so easily. I meant it when I said she wouldn't get another penny from me.

I pull out my phone, making a call I should've made a long time.

"Hey, Chase? Yeah, it's Jamie. I need your help with something."

CHAPTER TWENTY-FIVE

Miranda

Lou's name flashes on my phone screen, vibrating against my bed. I zip up my overnight bag, ready for Jamie and Tobias to pick me up any minute.

I can't believe I'm going to D.C. tomorrow with my *boyfriend*, I mean, I guess that's what he is. We haven't said anything official on the matter, but it feels like he's my boyfriend.

"Hello?" I pick up and immediately hold the phone at arm's length when Lou screams right in my ear.

"OHMYGODYOU'RENEVERGOINGTOBELIEVETHIS!" She slurs the words together at a volume only dogs could possibly hear.

"Uh ... what was that?"

"You're never going to believe this," she rushes the words. "Abel got us tickets to see the Jonas Brothers! Happy birthday, Bitch!"

"Uh..." I have no words and that's rare. I'm literally speechless.

"We see them next month at the Verizon Center! We can stay the night in the city and everything. We'll make a whole day of it."

I think Lou is more excited over my birthday present than I am. We both share a love of the Jonas Brothers, but where I love them, Lou is plain out stalker obsessed.

"That sounds like so much fun. Tell Abel thank you for me."

"He's right here, you're on speaker."

"Thank you, Abel. I guess I'll let Lou keep you."

He chuckles. "I'm glad I'm allowed in the pack."

"Are we going to do our traditional brunch? You haven't said anything about it," she rambles. "I didn't make reservations, but surely we can get in tomorrow if today is booked."

For the last few years on each of our birthdays we've

driven to Leesburg to have brunch at one of the fancy-schmancy restaurants there.

"Uh ... about that."

It probably makes me a horrible friend that I haven't said anything to her about my weekend with Jamie and Tobias. I *know* she's trying to be more open and understanding about my romance with Jamie, but she's still not one-hundred percent backing it either.

"What?" she sobers. "Is something wrong? You're not sick are you?"

I flop onto my bed, bouncing up and down slightly. My bag rolls off the side and splats on the floor. Thank God I zipped it because I would not be repacking all that shit.

"No, I'm spending the weekend with Jamie and Tobias."

"Oh."

I flinch at the hurt I hear in her voice.

"Yeah," I continue, covering my face with my free hand. "We're spending the weekend seeing the monuments. We'll probably go to a museum or two as well." It's quiet on the other end and I prompt, "Lou?"

"Things are changing, aren't they?" She sounds ... not sad, but a bit nostalgic.

"Yeah, I guess they are. We're growing up."

"I thought we swore we weren't going to do that?"

"Unfortunately I don't think we have much choice."

Her sigh echoes through the phone. "Okay, no brunch, but is there *something* we can do?"

I bite my lip. "We should have a girls date next weekend."

"Ooh, yes—that sounds fun. Sleepover at your apartment?"

"That'll be perfect. We can stay in our pajamas and watch movies all day."

"I knew there was a reason we're friends."

I hear a knock on my door and my heart starts beating faster. "Jamie's here. I have to go."

"All right, well I love you, beautiful, and happy birthday. Have fun with Jamie and Tobias, but if Jamie acts up kick him in the balls for me."

I laugh, covering my face with my hands. "Deal."

We hang up and the impatient dick face I like for some reason knocks again. I grab up my duffel bag and hurry to the door, kissing Fettuccine who lies sleeping on the corner of the couch. My elderly neighbor next door, a sweet lady named Fran, agreed to come over and feed him while I'm gone. Thankfully, she's so old she doesn't even know we're not supposed to have pets.

I swing open the door and can't stop the ridiculous smile that splits my face.

Big Jamie and Little Jamie stand in front of me looking like the most adorable father and son duo.

Big Jamie is dressed casually in distressed jeans and a

gray sweater. Little Jamie is all decked out in dark jeans, a white shirt, suspenders and a red bow tie.

"Hi, boys."

"Miranda!" Little Jamie crashes into my legs, giving me a giant hug.

I laugh and bend down, wrapping my arms around him. "It's nice to see you too, Toby."

He releases me and steps back beside his dad. He looks up at Jamie and then me as I stand up. "Dad says we're going to the museum. Which one? Is it the one with the dinosaurs?"

"Tobias," Jamie says in what I like to think of as his *dad* tone.

"Oh, and happy birthday."

"Thank you, Toby." Jamie rolls his eyes, but he's going to have to get used to it. If his son wants to go by a nickname, let him. "And yeah, we can do the dinosaur museum."

"It's your birthday," Jamie interjects, reaching for my bag. I let him take it and lock up my apartment. "Wouldn't you rather go to an art museum?"

"Dinosaurs sound more fun. I'm surrounded by art all the time."

"Yay!" Toby cries, shoving a fist in the air before the three of us start down the stairs.

I actually would like to go to the art museums, but I wanted to spend more time with Toby. If Jamie and I are going to do this thing, then Toby is going to be in my life and I want to get to know him better and vice versa.

At Jamie's car he adds my bag beside theirs in the trunk.

"Ladies first." Jamie swings the front passenger door open for me while Tobias scurries into his booster seat. When I look back to smile at him I swear his cheeks get pink and he looks down embarrassed, picking at the arms of his seat.

"My dad makes me use it even though I'm a big boy."

"Safety first."

He gives me a tiny smile. "Can we go to the museum first?"

"Tobias," Jamie warns, sliding behind the driver's seat. "It's Miranda's birthday, it's her choice. Remember your manners."

"Oh, right." Toby nods before I turn around to face the front. Behind me he says, "Miranda, do *you* want to go to the museum first."

"You know, I think I do."

Jamie chuckles. "I'm so screwed when it comes to you two. You gang up on me. Well, since the birthday girl says we do that first, then we will."

Exhausted from the museum, but in high spirits, we enter the Cheesecake Factory—aka heaven on Earth.

Jamie made reservations so we're led to a booth right away. He said since it was my birthday I could go wherever I wanted, so this is what I chose.

I slide into the booth and Tobias scoots in next to me, sitting up on his knees. Jamie sits down opposite us.

"Here are your menus," the hostess passes them out to us. "You're server will be by shortly."

"Can I get dessert, Dad? Since it's Miranda's birthday we're allowed to have dessert, right?"

Jamie shakes his head. "You make me sound so horrible, like I never allow you to do anything."

"You're a good dad, just overprotective," Toby says with a small shrug of his shoulder.

Jamie's eyes slide to me and he releases a breath. "I only let him have dessert once a week and on special occasions."

"Hey," I raise my hands, "you don't need to defend yourself to me. Like Toby said, you're a good dad. That's your *job* as a parent. To instill good habits and teach him things."

Jamie's lips quirk into a small smile and he mouths, "Thank you."

I think it's had to be hard on him being the sole disciplinary and rule maker. That gives him fewer chances to be the fun parent when he's trying to teach his son things. Like I knew back at my apartment he wanted Toby to understand it was my birthday and he should let me say what I want to do instead of him suggesting what he'd enjoy.

I peruse the menu, marveling at all the choices. Even though I've been to a Cheesecake Factory numerous times, I'm always in awe of the pages of dishes. Frankly, there are too many choices and I'm indecisive.

Jamie slides his menu aside and my jaw drops. "You know what you want?"

His brows furrow as he contemplates how to answer my accusing tone. "Um ... yes."

"How? There are so many choices."

"Simple." He shrugs, crossing his arms over his chest and leaning back in the booth. "I always get the same thing."

"Always get the same thing," I repeat in shock. "That is blasphemous. There are too many good choices to get the same thing every time. You must try all the things."

"I know I like it, why bother risking my dinner on something I might not like?"

I gape at him. "For the experience!"

"I'm with my dad," Toby pipes in. "I always get the chicken tenders."

I look between the two Millers. "This is ... unacceptable."

"Predictability is nice." A little smirk lifts the corners

of Jamie's lips, cocking his head to the side to appraise me.

"Predictability is the death of creativity," I scoff, cradling the menu to my chest.

"There is nothing wrong with being safe," he counters, leaning forward to rest his elbows on the table.

"Yeah and there's nothing wrong with being bold and taking chances either," I argue back playfully.

Jamie gets a wistful smile and nods in approval. "You have a point."

"Oh my God." I clap my hands, causing the older couple at the table beside us to look over. "Did I just win an argument with you?"

Jamie's tongue slides out, wetting his lips. "That wasn't an argument, sweetheart. It's called a disagreement, a spat if you will."

The waitress's arrival for our drink order breaks our eye contact.

Since the boys already know what they want that means I have to decide, and quickly since I'm starving. I'm pretty sure I burned an entire day's worth of calories walking through the museum it's so large. Besides, it's my birthday and everyone knows calories don't count on birthdays so I'm free to stuff my face.

By the time the waitress returns we place our order and dig into the bread basket she brought. It's safe to say I'm not the only hungry one at the table.

"This is fun." Toby grabs a pat of butter and opens it meticulously. Across the table Jamie does the same and I find it adorable how many traits Toby has picked up unconsciously from his father. "We should do this more often."

"It's such a shame Miranda only has one birthday," Jamie quips at his son, before taking a bite of bread.

Toby rolls his eyes at his dad and starts spreading his butter on the bread. He struggles and I take the knife from him, finishing it for him. He takes the buttered bread gratefully. "But *Dad* you have a birthday and *I* have a birthday. With Miranda that gives us three whole birthdays in a year."

"And," I point out, Jamie's amused gaze sliding my way, "you can go out without a birthday to celebrate. This information is life-changing, I know."

Jamie chuckles, shaking his head. His hair is a bet messier than normal from our chaotic day, but there's a happiness in him I never used to see. "Attacked, I am *attacked* by you two."

I look at Toby, then across the table. "You're definitely outnumbered now."

Toby giggles and blurts, "Did my dad ask you if you make cookies?"

I arch a brow, looking between both of them. "What is this about cookies?"

Jamie sighs and Tobias grins. "I like cookies and I told

my dad to ask if you make them. If you're going to be his girlfriend that means you should make cookies."

I bust out laughing and ruffle his hair. "You're a cool kid, Toby."

"So, do you make cookies?"

"No, but I can learn. I do eat cheesecake." I wink at him and his returning smile makes my heart soar.

I look across the table at Jamie and he's watching the two of us fondly.

It's scary how much I love this time with him, both of them, it's starting to scare me the idea of not having this.

Jamie walked away from me before, what's to say he won't again?

CHAPTER TWENTY-SIX

Jamie

"Whoa, this place is sweet!" Tobias rushes past us and into the suite. There's a living area, small kitchenette, and a door to the right that leads to two double beds.

Tobias runs from the couch, to the kitchen, bathroom, and finally bedroom like an out of control pinball.

The door shuts behind us and Miranda steps around me, inhaling a breath.

"This view," she croons, walking to the window that overlooks a lit up Washington monument. She wraps her arms around her body, drawing up her cropped sweater to expose a bit of skin. "Jamie ... I ... this is incredible." She spins around facing me. "This whole day. Dinner. This," she sweeps her arms to encompass the suite, "you, all of it. It's more than I could've asked for."

"It's your birthday."

I set down our bags and from the bedroom Tobias exclaims, "This is *awesome!*"

Miranda shakes her head, wrapping her arms around herself. "Nobody has ever done anything like this for me before."

I step forward, skimming the backs of my fingers down her cheeks. "I wanted to make it special for you."

I haven't gone out of my way like this in a long time, but for her I will. I want to see her smile, laugh, because selfishly that brings me joy.

"Miranda," Tobias bursts into the room, grabbing her arm until she gives him her hand, "come see this bathtub it's *so* big. Like a pool."

Miranda flashes me a small smile before letting my son tug her away.

I watch them head into the bathroom, shaking my head. I won't lie though, it makes me insanely pleased to see how much Tobias loves Miranda and that she cares for him too.

While the two of them are occupied I carry the bags into the bedroom area. Tobias drags Miranda through the suite like he's giving her a tour.

I set out a pair of his pajamas and his teddy bear. It's getting late and I need to coerce him to take a shower and go to bed. Easier said than done with Miranda around since he loves to talk her ear off.

"Can we watch a movie?" Tobias asks, popping back into the bedroom.

Miranda stands behind him looking amused, her head tilted to the side. "I told him he had to ask you."

"We can put one on," I agree and Tobias begins to bounce around, somehow still a ball of energy despite the late hour and walking most of the day. "But you have to shower first."

He frowns. "Fine. Now?"

"Now. March your butt." I point to the bathroom.

Once he's situated and thoroughly warned that he *must* wash his hair and body, not simply let the water run over him, I rejoin Miranda. She lies on the bed farthest from the window, looking at her phone.

I sit on the opposite bed and face her. She sets her phone aside and rolls over to face me, cradling her hands beneath her head.

"Thank you again for today, Jamie."

"That reminds me." I hop up and cross the room to my bag, bending down to dig out the small package.

"Happy birthday." I hold out the carefully wrapped package, feeling nervous. I'm not one for big gestures or to be overly cheesy, but I couldn't help myself when I saw it.

She sits up, her dark tresses cascading forward. She takes the box with an eager smile and rips the paper off.

"It's beautiful," she murmurs, pulling out the necklace.

I was able to pick charms for it and chose a paintbrush, airplane, and key.

She touches each individual charm reverently.

"I love it." Her smile eases my anxiety over the gift. "Put it on me."

She passes it over to me and stands up, turning her back to me and sweeping her hair to the side so I can drape the necklace around her collarbone. I struggle with the clasp, but manage to secure it. Before I step away I place a kiss to the back of her neck.

Turning, she wraps her arms around my shoulders, standing on her tiptoes.

"Thank you," she whispers, kissing the corner of my mouth. Inside the bathroom the shower cuts off. She takes a step back and grabs ahold of the necklace. "The paintbrush is me, the airplane you, but the key..." She quiets, musing on it. Her dark eyes meet mine quizzically. "I don't know what it means."

I kiss her again, just for a moment before Tobias invariably comes running out.

"You'll understand soon enough."

CHAPTER TWENTY-SEVEN

Miranda

Classes end for the day, exhaustion settling into my bones.

For some stupid, naïve reason, I thought senior year would be easy.

I think it's a lie I told myself in order to make it through last year.

I have to remind myself that soon enough school will be behind me, certainly not the loans, and I can embark on my journey in teaching. This is what I've wanted for years and it's finally in reach.

"Miranda! Wait up!" I whip around and find Lou running across campus toward me. She reaches me and bends over, clutching her knees as she gasps for breath. "We're supposed to have our sleepover."

I lower my head, groaning. "I completely forgot." Lou's face falls and I instantly feel like the worst friend ever. "It's been a rough week. I'm just exhausted from classes."

She pulls me into a hug. "All the more reason for a sleepover. How about you go home and nap, or whatever, I'll grab snacks and pizza, then hop over to your place."

"That actually sounds really good."

Frankly, I need to study, but if I don't rest I think I'll flunk everything anyway and it'll all have been a waste.

"I'll see you in a little bit." She starts to back away, pointing finger guns at me. "If there's a specific thing you want, just text me."

She heads to wherever she parked on campus and I hop in my car.

Thank God my apartment is only five minutes from campus. Parking, I grab up my bag and books.

I pause when I see a new couple moving into Stan's apartment. I didn't know he'd left, but I'm glad to know he's gone. His creeper vibes were intense.

I don't linger long, just give my new neighbors a wave, before climbing the stairs.

When I open the door Fettuccine immediately rubs himself against my legs, meowing loudly.

"You're gonna get me caught," I whisper at him, dropping my backpack on the floor and scooping him up. He nuzzles his head into my neck, purring.

I grab him a treat, sitting him on the couch to enjoy it.

I hop in the shower and change into some cute pjs for our sleepover.

Lying down on the couch with my books, I try to get a head start on my homework before Lou arrives. I know she told me to nap, but there's no way I can with so much homework waiting in the wings.

With one assignment done, I sit up and stretch my arms, grabbing my phone off the coffee table.

Me: Hey, hot stuff.

Jamie: What are you up to?

Me: Homework. Lou is coming over. We're having a sleepover.

Jamie: Sounds kinky. Can I watch?

Me: Don't be a dirty bastard.

Jamie: But you like it when I'm dirty.

Me: UGH EXCEPT YOU STILL WON'T HAVE SEX WITH ME.

Jamie: I'm taking things slow.

Me: It's not like we haven't had sex—you even

made love to me on your plane, remember? Just do me already, Miller.

Jamie: No. Not yet.

I collapse back onto my couch with a groan.

Me: Are you trying to give me a case of Blue Vagina. It's a thing. Google it.

Me: On second thought, don't Google it.

Jamie: I just laughed out loud and got some strange looks.

Me: Where are you?

Jamie: Griffin's. Grabbing a coffee before I pick up Tobias from school.

Me: Give Toby a hug for me.

Jamie: I'll give TOBIAS a hug from you.

Me: Toby.

Jamie: Tobias. Meaning God is good. A Greek name with Hebrew origins.

Me: Yawn. Thanks for the history lesson old man.

Jamie: Did you just call me an old man?

Me: You're twelve years older than me. Practically ancient.

Jamie: Hmm, well you seem to like this old man.

Me: Only a little.

Me: Is that why you named him Tobias? Because of the meaning?

He doesn't text back right away and I worry I've pried

too much. I nibble my bottom lip and finally the bubble pops up letting me know he's typing back.

Jamie: It's part of the reason. I just liked the name, and after I learned the meaning I knew there was no other name meant for my son. God was good to me when he gave me Tobias.

Fuck my feelings. I feel a tear slip down my cheek and brush it away.

Jamie: Hopping in my car. Have fun with Lou. You deserve it.

Me: Xoxo

I set my phone aside and clean up my books and trash scattered from last night's study sesh. I can't have my bestie showing up to a pigsty.

I've barely finished straightening everything when I hear a knock on my door followed by, "Bitch, open the door before I drop something."

I hurry over, swinging the door open. Laughter bubbles out of me. Lou holds a pizza box with a bag from Oh, Crepe balanced on top, a bag from Walgreens full of candy and chips, her overnight bag is draped over her shoulders, a pillow under her arms, and a backpack strapped to her.

"Wow," I mouth, taking the pizza box and stuff on top from her. "You went overboard."

"I can't help it." She pouts, following me inside and closing the door. "My *too much* gene took over and I went a little crazy. We have pizza, macarons," she points to the Oh, Crepe bag, "Starbursts, gummy bears, salt n' vinegar chips, and I even got cupcakes since this is your birthday and all." She slips her backpack off and digs inside. "I also picked these up." She pulls out a brand new blanket, twinkle lights, and a board game. "Target has everything, man. Oh, and drinks are in this bag." She hands me a plastic grocery bag I missed in the midst of everything else.

I open it and pull the box of White Claw out. "Oh, you're the real MVP." I set the box on the counter and open it up. She got a variety pack so I line up the flavors.

She swipes a grapefruit one and pops the tab open with a hiss. Tipping it to her lips she hums, "Ooh, that's good. It's like an adult Capri-Sun."

I snort, un-bagging the rest of the items. Lou has always amused me with her love of Capri-Sun, it used to be practically all she stocked in her fridge but now that Abel lives with her blue Gatorade and Smart Water have joined the pack.

"When you met Abel did you think you'd met the love of your life?" I blurt out, swiping one of the plastic bags away from Fettuccine before he can suffocate himself.

Lou pauses, tilting her head to the side. "No."

"Even you, the big believer in fate?" I gesture wildly with my hands.

"I believe in fate, so I knew we were meant to meet, to be roommates, but at the time I didn't know that we'd become more." She shrugs, reaching up to grab a plate and adds two slices of pizza.

I bite my lip, throwing away all the trash and lining up the snacks. Stalling for time I grab pizza too, a lime White Claw, and we move to the couch. I curl my legs under me and wiggle around until I'm comfortable. Lou waits patiently, knowing there's more I want to say.

"How'd you know?" I take a too-large bite of pizza, stuffing my mouth full so I can't say any more.

"Know what?"

Silence.

"That I love him?"

Ding, ding, ding we have a winner.

I nod and swallow grabbing my drink.

She bites her lip, thinking about how she wants to respond. "It's one of those things that for me, started slowly. It was this trickle of awareness that I was happiest around him, how I watched the time when I knew he should be arriving at the apartment. I want to be around him all the time, even when he makes me mad I don't want to be without him. I've never felt like I have to impress him, because he's always made me feel special for who I am." She nibbles on the end of her pizza, waiting a moment. Then she asks, "Are you thinking about Jamie?"

I duck my head. "I'm trying to understand my feelings for him. I ... I've never been in love before. Infatuation, sure. Lust, all the time. But not love and I'm scared to put a label on my feelings because then it makes it real."

She snorts in amusement. "It's already real, even if you don't put a label on it. It's a mistake to think something doesn't exist if you don't give it a name. If you feel it, it's already true."

I set my pizza on the coffee table, suddenly not hungry. "But I don't know if what I feel is love." I sound defensive and instantly want to punch myself. Fettuccine must sense my distress because he jumps into my lap and starts kneading my bare legs, which hurts like a bitch. I pick him up, cuddling him to my chest before I end up looking like I trekked through a jungle. "It's not like I've known him that long."

She rolls her eyes and finishes her bite before she speaks. "You've known him since sophomore year, that's over two years."

"Not *know him, know him*."

"He's not a stranger, though, Miranda. Besides, Khloe and Lamar met and married after nine days. Love is love and you can't put a timeline on that."

"But they're divorced," I point out.

She waves a dismissive hand, swatting away my thoughts like a pesky nuisance. "But they still *loved* each other. Probably still do. Circumstances got in their way. Besides, I'm pretty sure at some point all divorced people love one another." Her face drops into a frown. "Well, unless you're held at gunpoint down the aisle, then you probably never loved your spouse, but like that's rare I'm sure."

"Do you think that's happened?" My jaw drops at the prospect of being forced to marry someone with a gun at my back.

"Probably. Anyway, my point is, sometimes love goes away, or it changes, love can dissolve like any other feeling, but when you feel it you should embrace it, because it's worth it."

"I don't want him to break my heart," I admit softly.

She picks up her White Claw. "We all get our hearts broken at some point by something. Heartbreak isn't synonymous with a partner. You can be heartbroken by the loss of a pet, or even a failed grade, or not getting a job you really wanted. Shit happens, you might as well enjoy the good things while you can. It's a mistake to think things are always rainbows and sunshine. Life's not like that. Sometimes we have to bleed, figuratively and perhaps literally, to have the willpower and drive to fight for what we want."

I blink at her.

Once.

Twice.

Three times.

"Who the fuck are you?"

"No idea." She looks at the can of her drink. "This stuff isn't that strong." She clears her throat and reaches over to rub Fettuccine behind his ears. "So, Miranda, do you love my evil landlord?"

"He's my landlord now too," I defend, which is absolutely ridiculous. Ducking my head into Fettuccine's soft fur I mumble, "I think I do." She squeals and starts clapping. I reach over and grab her hands so she'll stop. Fettuccine hisses at me in the process when he drops to my lap. "Stop that. I'm not telling him."

"My little Miranda, all grown up and in love." She looks wistfully at my ceiling, probably mentally planning my wedding. "Wait, what do you mean you're not telling him?"

"Not yet," I emphasize, picking up my plate of pizza once more. "I ... I need to be sure of how he feels first. We haven't been *together-together* for long. I don't want to send him running."

She huffs a breath, clearly disgruntled with me. "You're such a party pooper. You should totally drive over to his house with a boom box and declare your love like some cheesy 80s movie."

"I'm not doing that." The words rush out of me vehemently with a massive shake of my head. The idea of doing something so dramatic and public makes me want to throw up. I can't imagine actually doing it like Lou did once for Abel.

"Well," she tucks her legs under her, "I hope Jamie knows how lucky he is to have someone as beautiful, smart, kind, and amazing as you, love him. If he ruins this I'll gut him like a fish."

I have no doubt she would.

CHAPTER TWENTY-EIGHT

Miranda

"Seriously, Miranda, you have got to start ordering your groceries online."

"Excuse me?"

I look across the produce selection at an elderly woman. "Sorry, I was talking to myself."

She gives me a disgusted look and leaves the apple selection behind.

Apparently it's totally unacceptable to talk to yourself at the grocery store. Who knew?

I grab three apples, dropping them in a plastic bag and into my cart.

It's not that I mind grocery shopping all that much...

Lies. I hate it. Totally hate it.

Why can't food just appear in my fridge like some sort of magic trick?

You say alakazam and *bam* open it up and there's your food for the week.

Instead, I have to adult, put on real pants, a bra, and go to the store. Not to mention, with the start of November the snow has started to come, which means extra layers of a sweatshirt, coat, and furry boots. It makes me look like a well-fed grizzly bear.

Looking down at my clothes hastily thrown on I realize the woman probably thought I'm on drugs or something, because I look like a vagrant.

A week straight barely showering, holed up in your apartment studying, will do that to a person. Finals are only a few weeks away before our extended holiday break, which means I'm determined to get in as much study time as I can.

Moving down the aisles I toss in things I need to stock up on.

Which basically equals everything.

It's a miracle I've survived.

Raising up on my toes I grab a box of cereal.

"Excuse me?"

"Whoa." I nearly get whacked in the face with the box, but after flailing my arms I manage to catch it. I whip around, my eyes meeting those of a blonde haired woman. She's dressed in a sleek looking pantsuit, an expensive purse hangs off one shoulder. Her makeup is flawless, her red lips pulled into a smile. It's not a kind smile. Sort of condescending, and I feel my hackles rise since I don't even know this woman. She looks me up and down, her lips pursing. Her cheekbones are sharp like a Disney villain. "Can I help you with something?"

If anyone looks down this aisle I'm sure the two of us will be quite the sight. Her all dressed up and shiny looking while I appear to be fresh out of hibernation.

"I just wanted to see you."

"See me?" I blurt, pointing at my chest. I don't even know this woman. Maybe she's on drugs? High off some fancy perfume?

She ignores me, continuing to size me up. "I don't know what he sees in you."

"Who?" My brows furrow and my heart sinks.

Who is a silly question, who else could she be referring to but Jamie.

Sure enough, her lips curl into a coy smile. "Jamie," she says in a sickly sweet voice. "We're quite opposite don't you think? He married me, after all, so I'm much more his type."

She's a prissy white Barbie, all straight lines and plastic smile. Meanwhile, I'm a mixed darker skinned, curvy, Bratz doll compared to her.

This time I size her up. "You're right, we are. I'm much better looking."

She scoffs and jabs a finger at me. "Jamie will never stay with someone like you."

I bristle at her tone, wondering how she even found me, and why she thinks she can intimidate me.

"Why? Because I'm funny, smart, artistic, and a pretty amazing catch, if I do say so myself?"

She looks flabbergasted. She truly thought she could corner me and I would cower from her hurtful words.

She gets right up in my face, trying to appear as menacing as possible. "Stay away from him."

"No, can do. I really quite like Jamie, Tobias too. You walked away from Jamie, your son, everything. I won't do the same because I know a good thing when I have it."

Her jaw tightens. She looks tempted to pull off one of her pointed heels and beat me with it.

"You can't scare me," I tell her.

I'm only beginning to understand the depths of my feelings for Jamie. I'm not some scared little girl she can chase off. She has no claim on Jamie anymore. I don't know a whole lot about her, but I do know she's been absent for the last seven years. There's no way Jamie would let her come waltzing back into his life as if nothing had happened.

She twists her lips back and forth, eyes icy with murderous rage.

"I don't have to frighten you," she warns, looking all too conniving. I cannot believe Jamie was ever with her, that she's Tobias's mother. "All I have to do is scare *him*."

She flounces off and I sit there with a leaden feeling in my gut.

Somehow I manage to finish my shopping, go home, and unpack my groceries.

After that, I can't take it anymore.

I get in my car and drive.

Showing up at Jamie's house in a near flat out panic seems silly, but I have to see him.

The conversation with his ex has shaken me.

When it comes to us, my foundation is solid, but what about his?

I park on the street out front and practically sprint up the walkway.

I didn't change. Or do anything with my hair.

I look like I escaped a mental institution.

Do I care? No. But that's probably what someone mentally insane would answer with.

I push the doorbell repeatedly like a kid who enjoys pushing buttons.

His grumbling can be heard from the other side and then the door opens.

"Jamie," I breathe with so much relief it kind of frightens me. I dive into his arms, wrapping mine tightly around his middle and resting the side of my face against his solid chest.

"Whoa, what's going on?" He hugs me back but he sounds worried.

I allow him to tug me into the warm confines of his home. Once he's shut and locked the door he grabs my hand and pulls me to his office. He closes that door behind us, giving us privacy if his mother appears. Not that I'm worried about her overhearing the conversation but Jamie doesn't know that.

"What's going on?" He basically pushes me into a chair and then leans his ass against the desk, crossing his arms over his chest. Normally I would be turned on by how in charge and sexy he looks, but now isn't the time for my libido to surge.

I blurt out the incident at the grocery store. When I'm finished he curses quite creatively and begins to pace his office.

"I was afraid of this."

"Of what?" I stand and follow, placing my hand against his back when he stops. He braces his hands against one of his bookshelves.

He turns around, cupping my cheeks in his large hands. "Using you against me, to get what she wants."

"Which is what?"

He releases a humorless laugh. "What she always wants. Money. She's not getting a penny from me this time," he says vehemently.

He lets me go, stepping back to pull out his desk chair. He sinks down into it, resting his elbows on his knees and head in his hands.

I open my mouth to speak, but pause when I notice a small canvas on his bookshelf.

"That's mine." I point unnecessarily.

He looks where I'm pointing. "Yeah," he admits rather sheepishly.

"It's the one you said got damaged." It's in perfect shape, not a smear or scratch. When I picked up my paintings it was the one missing. Toby had told me Jamie said one was ruined and I didn't think of it again.

But here it is.

On his shelf.

"I lied." His voice is soft, but with a husky edge and he stands up, towering above me.

"Why? Why would you lie?"

It's a simple black line painting of the side of a

woman's face, nothing fancy at all, so I don't understand why it would've caught his eyes. I'm not mad at him for keeping it, just confused.

He shrugs, his eyes soft. "It reminded me of you, and you painted it which makes it special, I guess. So, I took it."

"You could've asked. I would've given it to you."

His lips crook. "Sweetheart, since when do I ask for anything." He lowers his head, skimming his lips over my right cheek. "I take."

My heart stutters, my eyelids fluttering closed.

I can't control the small moan that passes through my lips when he kisses me, angling my head back. I twine my arms around his neck, our bodies plastered together. He quiets my soft sounds with his mouth.

A small gasp leaves me when he grabs the back of my legs and picks me up, turning me around to set me on his desk. He spreads my legs, stepping between them.

"Jamie," I breathe as he continues his onslaught of delectable kisses, "your mom."

"Left hours ago to visit friends out of state and Tobias is staying the night at a friends."

"You're home alone," I accuse as he peppers small kisses down my neck. "Were you going to tell me?"

"You're supposed to be studying, but I thought I might surprise you later."

"Hmm," I hum as he unzips my coat, pushing it off

me. I forgot I was wearing it, but it could be the reason I'm unreasonably hot. Or that could just be Jamie and his devilish mouth. "You've been withholding sex from me for weeks. Changing your mind now?" I lift my arms above my head when he starts tugging impatiently at my sweatshirt.

He lifts it off and tosses it into the corner of his office.

I'm far from being naked, still completely fully-clothed, but he looks at me like I'm a work of art he can't help but admire. I feel sexy, worshipped.

"It's been too long since I've touched you like this," he murmurs, diving in for another kiss.

I get lost in the feel of him. I've been craving his touch more than anything. Not that he hasn't been touching me, but he's been holding back, not wanting to cross this line.

"Are you going to fuck me on your desk?" I croon.

He bites my bottom lip, fingers wandering under my shirt. "You have no idea how many times I've visualized you spreading those pretty legs right here, then kneeling to eat you out."

"Mmm," I purr, my body vibrating with pleasure at the visual, "then do it."

He flashes me a dangerous grin before tangling our tongues together in a long, not safe for the public, kiss. He pulls slightly away until his hazel eyes meet mine, darker than normal and filled with desire. "I will, but I fully intend on savoring this."

"Don't tease me," I pout.

"It's not a tease," his smile is wicked, "it's a fucking promise."

He undresses me slowly, kissing each piece of skin that's exposed with such reverence it makes me ache and fill with that emotion I'm so afraid of voicing.

Love.

He deserves to know, but I don't know how to tell him, and now doesn't seem like the best idea. I want him to know I mean it, that it's not some lust-filled confession, but the truth that beats inside my heart.

Goddammit, the man has turned me into a sap.

"Fuck, you're so beautiful," he whispers in admiration, stepping back to take in my naked body splayed on his desk. My fingers drift down, stroking my clit. He has me so turned on I'm already wet and can easily slip two fingers down and into me. I pump them in and out, his eyes zero in, watching every movement. He swallows, his Adam's apple bobbing.

He drops to his knees in front of me, placing his hands on my thighs to open me more to him.

I slip my fingers out, sliding them into my mouth and licking them clean for the sole purpose of seeing what it does to him.

His eyes flash, deepening in color, a shudder racking his body.

"God, Miranda," he murmurs, "do you have any idea how sexy you are?"

I do—and I feel it even more when he looks at me like this.

He lowers his head, the strands of his reddish-brown hair tickling my thighs as he does. My hips buck a moment later when he circles his tongue around my clit. He licks down the seam of me and back up, swirling his tongue again around the bud.

"Jamie, right there," I plead, sliding my fingers into his hair, tightening them around the strands. If it hurts he makes no protest. When his fingers slide into me pleasure zips through my entire body. "Jamie, Jamie, Jamie," I chant his name like a prayer.

He takes his time, bringing me close to the edge and then pulling away. Tempting me. Teasing me. Torturing me.

I tug his hair harder, forcing him to look at me. "If you don't let me come, I might kill you."

His chuckle vibrates against my pussy and I bite my lip to stifle a moan.

"Good things come to those who wait," he taunts with a wicked groan.

My planned retort vanishes when his tongue swipes my pussy and a low moan leaves me instead.

This time when he brings me to the edge he lets me fall over, my back arching and legs shaking with the force of the orgasm. He holds me steady against the desk. Perspiration clings to my skin and he backs a step away, taking off the last of his clothes.

I watch hungrily as each piece of tanned skin is exposed.

He watches me like I'm his prey and when all his clothes are in a pile on the floor he grabs my legs, stepping between them.

"God, I've missed this," he murmurs, a moment before sinking inside me.

I bite down on my lip, my eyes rolling back from the pleasure.

Goddamn Jamie and his magic cock. Forget the Genie's lamp in Aladdin, all you need is to rub Jamie's cock and all your sexual fantasies will come true.

I lift my arms above my head and a stack of papers falls. I hope they're not important but neither one of us seems to care.

His fingers press into my hips as he fucks me. It feels ridiculously good to have sex with him again, but I understand what he meant about waiting. This is infinitely better, and despite the time on the plane this truly feels different. Our masks have fallen, the bars around our hearts loosening.

All that's left now is what's real.

He starts pumping faster and I cry out as my second orgasm rushes unexpectedly through me. His orgasm follows, and he collapses nearly on top of me, only his hands flat on the desk keep him above me. His cock twitches inside me and he makes no move to pull out.

"I want to keep you forever," he admits in a quiet confession. His eyes widen and he looks surprised, like he didn't mean to say it out loud.

I take his face between my hands, his stubble rasping my palms. I pull him closer, meeting him halfway until our foreheads are nearly touching.

"I love you."

It's the first time I've ever told a man I love him. I didn't realize how powerful three words can be. If you separate them they're pretty innocuous, but when you put them together it's packed with meaning.

"Fuck," he rubs his nose against mine, "I didn't know it would feel this damn good to hear you say that. I love you, too."

I close that tiny bit of distance between us and kiss him.

This is a new kind of kiss.

One filled with understanding and a newfound, pretty powerful, love.

CHAPTER TWENTY-NINE

Jamie

After we're dressed and I clean my office up, I make us each a cup of coffee before we settle in the family room.

Miranda curls into the sectional, grabbing a blanket and getting cozy.

I love that she feels comfortable here.

"So, about your ex," she cringes, blowing lightly on the steaming liquid.

I stretch my legs out on the leather ottoman, exhaling a weighted sigh. "Don't worry about her." I rub the back of her neck, trying to ease her uncertainties.

"I don't trust her." She seems hesitant to admit this to me.

I don't know why. It isn't like I've given her any glowing endorsements. Shannon isn't an evil person, but she is misguided and way too focused on material things. But that's her life to live, not mine.

"I'm taking care of it." My voice rings true with the promise. I'm having her looked into carefully, the whole last seven years of her life torn apart for any crumb I can use to get her to walk away peacefully. I won't have her dragging me to court to fight over Tobias when it's not him she wants. My son won't be taken from me and forced to live with a stranger, because that's what she is.

Miranda shakes her head at me.

"What?" My lips quirk, waiting for her response.

"You're just so ... capable. Guys my age aren't like this."

I huff a laugh. "I'm thirty-four, sweetheart. I'm definitely not like guys your age."

She sets her coffee mug on the table behind the couch and lays down with her head on my leg, looking up at me.

"Do you think we were meant to find each other?" Her gaze is speculative, her lips rubbing together nervously. "That's what Lou would say, you know—that fate brings people together. We make the choices and decisions, but fate guides you to where you belong."

I stroke her dark hair, nearly black. The silky softness of it sifts through my fingers.

"What do *you* think?"

She ponders the question. "I think you're undoubtedly perfect for me. Not that you're perfect, don't go getting an even bigger ego on me now. But I can't imagine being here with anyone else."

I don't tell her this, but it's crazy how I wasn't looking for anyone, never planned to fall in love again. But she just happened. There's no controlling how I feel for her. I was so scared of my growing feelings for her that I ended things in a jerk move and I'm lucky as hell that things worked out like they did.

Maybe it is fate.

CHAPTER THIRTY

Jamie

"Dad, you have to smile," Tobias groans, "you're scaring all the old ladies away and everyone knows they love this shit."

My eyes narrow dangerously on my son, the chaos of the bake sale held inside his school's gymnasium is giving me a migraine. "Where did you hear that word?"

His eyes slide to Miranda who is counting change to hand back to a man who just bought a whole basket of baked goods my mom and Miranda whipped up yesterday. I'm pretty sure the man is interested in more than the baked goods the way he's staring at Miranda's rack.

Leave it to my son, though, to announce the day before yesterday that his school is having a bake sale and he signed up.

Two weeks ago.

My child had two weeks to inform us we needed to make a minimum of five-hundred items. Did he? No. It'll be funny later, to look back on this day, but for now I'm still irritated and it doesn't help that apparently my seven-year-old has developed a potty mouth thanks to my girlfriend.

"What?" Miranda blinks over innocently when she notices the silence. "I didn't do anything."

She doesn't even know what we're talking about.

"Have you said shit in front of Tobias?"

"Of course not." She looks mildly offended I would suggest such a thing, but then her face drops into horror. "Maybe," she admits softly.

To Tobias I say, "Don't use that word. Adults can use it, kids can't."

"Will I go to jail?" He looks terrified at the idea, his eyes drifting to the police officer manning the door.

"No, but you will be grounded. Consider this your warning. Next time, I'll take away ... I don't know what

I'm going to take away, but rest assured you don't want to find out."

My mom returns to the table, having left to go chat with one of her friends here with her granddaughter.

"I'm not in trouble am I?" She raises a brow, sliding into the seat on the other side of Miranda.

Miranda snorts. "Don't worry, it's just Jamie being his usual grumpy self."

My mom laughs and whispers something to Miranda.

I might be irritated if I wasn't so fucking happy that they like each other. My mom looks at Miranda like she's some long-lost daughter. She never liked Shannon all that much, and even though I know she'd never say anything to me, I know she's glad things didn't work out with us.

"How much longer do we have to be here?"

I can handle most school events. I don't mind being a hands-on parent and actually enjoy most of it, after all it's memories with my son. Call me a sap, I don't care, but he won't be this age forever. But the bake sale is a snore fest. It's mostly elderly people and other parents in attendance, slowly milling around the echoing gym like they have all day.

Which, I guess they do.

Miranda knocks her hand against my knee, silently scolding me.

"Dad," Tobias drones, rolling his eyes, "we've only

been here..." He squints at the clock above the set of doors leading into the school. "Twenty-seven minutes. We have a lot more to sell." He waves dramatically at the table full of desserts.

I exhale a weighty sigh and pick up a saran-wrapped brownie, opening it up.

Tobias looks horrified, but I quickly drop a five-dollar bill—over-priced if you ask me—into the jar and he's satisfied once more.

If I'm going to sit here I might as well get to enjoy something sweet.

My girlfriend has officially lost it.

She dances in front of the table to MC Hammer's *U Can't Touch This*.

It's gathering a crowd, which I guess is what she intended, because people are drawn from other tables to ours.

"Come on, Dad." Tobias tugs on my shirtsleeve. "Dance with her."

"I don't dance."

"Fine. I'll dance with her. One of us has to."

I feel like I just got owned by my kid.

Tobias hops up from his chair and joins her in front of the table. He doesn't know the actual dance so he improvises some sort of chicken looking dance, arm flapping included.

My mom scoots over until she's beside me. "You're missing out."

I watch as Miranda laughs, taking Tobias's hands. The two of them spin in a circle before she draws him to her in a hug. Letting him go she joins him in freestyle dancing.

"I'm fine here," I tell my mother.

I'm not trying to be stubborn, but that's not me. I'm not as free as Miranda is. She looks beautiful, confident, *alive*, but I would look like I was lost if I got up there. I don't like attention, it gives me indigestion. Okay, maybe that's a tad bit dramatic of me, but point is I'm just fine right where I am.

"Fine," my mother says in a tone that says she thinks she knows better, "suit yourself."

Before I can retort she's standing, rounding the table to join them.

Her and Miranda bump hips, the crowd clapping along to the new song playing. Tobias looks like he's having the time of his life.

I loose a breath, pinching the bridge of my nose.

Am I really going to do this?

With a groan, I stand up. My legs are stiff from sitting so long—that's what happens when you're old—and stretch them inconspicuously.

I join the three crazies. I feel like a fool, but as I take Miranda's hand, spinning her into my arms, Tobias dancing around us and my mother smiling at us, I know my mom was right. I was missing out. I need to remember to get up and *live* these moments, not let them pass me by.

Miranda giggles, placing her hands on my mom's shoulders. "Conga line!" She chants. Within moments one starts forming. My hands rest on Miranda's shoulders while behind me Tobias holds onto my belt loop.

I can't stop smiling. It feels a bit weird, after all this time, to smile so easily.

She's thawed my icy heart like it was nothing.

Across the room the doors leading in from the parking lot open. I notice the blonde hair first and it causes me to pause. A quick inspection of the expensive dress and heels tells me it's Shannon.

I slip out of the line, feeling Miranda's eyes on me.

I know she's worried about Shannon, but I'm not.

I'm a planner and I don't go down without a fight.

Shannon doesn't make any move to meet me halfway. She just stands there, arms crossed over her slender chest, giving me the stink eye.

I reach her, giving a stiff nod to the door. "Outside."

She follows easily enough, she always does.

"Jamie, you're being unreasonable," she spats vehemently.

My brows rise, a humorless laugh pushing unbidden past my lips. "I'm the unreasonable one?"

"Yes." Anger vibrates from her, pulsating around us. She's jittery, unable to look me in the eyes. "I never wanted to have that baby. You *owe* me. Give me the money dammit, or I *will* take you to court, so help me God."

"How much do you want?"

She freezes, lips parted with surprise. She's desperate enough to think I'm agreeing, not playing her.

She squares her shoulders, lifting her chin haughtily into the air. "One million. That's chump change to you."

I stifle a snort. "We'll set a meeting."

Her lips twist as she fights a pleased grin. "My lawyer will contact yours."

"Sure thing." I shove my hands in my pockets, amused that *now* she has a lawyer.

She nods, not seeming to know what to do since I've done the complete opposite of what she expects. If she only knew. "Well, I'll see you soon then."

She turns, heading to wherever she's parked. She looks back at me over her shoulder.

I wave mockingly.

Shannon thinks she can pull one over on me because of how much I love Tobias, but she's playing the wrong game.

CHAPTER THIRTY-ONE

Miranda

"I can't die like this," I whine into the phone, curled on my side beneath the covers. Fettuccine meows from nearby.

"You're not going to die," Lou's voice echoes across the line.

"If I pass away Fettuccine is going to eat my corpse."

A hefty sigh from her. "I take it you can't go to the concert tonight?"

"I am dying, Louise! Forget about the concert. Ugh," I groan at the end, because raising my voice made my head throb from the pulsating headache that won't go away.

I had fun the other day participating in Toby's bake sale, but I must've caught the flu or some other vicious virus, perhaps even the bubonic plague, and now I'm on my deathbed.

"It's the Jonas Brothers," she gasps, scandalized. "I can't just forget about them!"

"You mean you're not going to come over and help your ailing friend?"

"Is that a trick question? No, I'm hanging up with you and texting Abel to see if he can get off early and go with me."

"And what about me?" I whine. "I need medicine. Perhaps a casket."

"Yeah, I think Walgreens is fresh out of caskets. Call your boyfriend though, maybe he can help."

"I need a new best friend." I roll onto my back, crooking my arm over my eyes.

"Hey, it's not my fault you got sick on what is to be the best night of my life."

"Excuse me, missy, those tickets were for *my* birthday."

"Um ... yeah ... sorry, it's the Jonas Brothers, I'm going."

I laugh and it turns into a cough. I could be burning

alive and Lou would still choose them over me. For her, the Jo Bros are life.

"I see how it is."

"Seriously, though, text me a list of things you need and I'll bring it by. I might show up wearing gloves and a mask because I don't want whatever it is you have, so don't judge me."

"Nah, it's okay." I stifle another cough. "I'll bug Jamie later."

She laughs. "Send me a pic of Jamie playing doctor."

"That's kinky, Lou."

Her gasp echoes through the phone. "That's not what I meant, you psycho."

I cackle, which yet again leaves me hacking up a lung.

"Seriously, though, let me know if you need anything."

"Thanks, have fun at the concert. Send me pictures."

"I will."

"Love you, loser."

"Love you, sicko."

I hang up, tossing my phone onto the opposite side of the bed.

My body is exhausted from all the coughing and puking I've been doing. I need to sleep, but it seems like every time I doze off I end up rolling out of bed and running for the bathroom.

I stifle a yawn and Fettuccine pads across the bed, curling against my side.

"Mama's sick." I pet his head and he begins to purr. "Go fetch me a Sprite."

He tilts his head back and gives me what I swear is a disgruntled expression. I think he's telling me he's not a Golden retriever.

My stomach rolls and I push him out of my way as I surge out of bed, running for the bathroom.

I drop to the floor, throwing up.

I haven't been able to keep anything down since yesterday. My stomach and sides are sore from the incessant coughing and puking. On shaky legs I stand up, gripping the sink so I can brush my teeth and rinse with mouthwash.

"Ugh." I rub the back of my hand over my mouth.

Then I look in the mirror.

It looks like at least ten birds have built a nest in my hair, twigs and leaves included, my eyes are bruised looking and sunken in, even my skin is several shades lighter than normal with a grayish twinge.

"Fuck." I rub my face.

I waddle my tired self into my room, digging around in the mountain of blankets for my phone.

Me: I think I need to go to the doctor.

I hate the doctor with a fiery passion, but there's no way I can survive another day or longer of this.

Jamie: I thought you said it was a bug?

Me: I feel like death, don't argue with me.

Jamie: I can take you. I can be there in thirty minutes. Do you feel up to packing a bag?

Me: Why would I need a bag? I'm not going to be admitted to a hospital.

Jamie: You're sick. You don't need to be on your own. You'll stay with us.

Me: I'm not going to be able to go to the concert.

I tried to brush it off to Lou, but I am bummed. I've been looking forward to going and now I'm dying instead.

Jamie: I'm sorry, sweetheart.

Jamie: If you can't pack a bag I'll do it for you.

Me: You just want to play with my panties.

Jamie: ;)

I sigh, sitting on the bed as another round of coughing assaults me. I whimper from the pain in my ribs.

Jamie: Be there in 20.

Me: Fettuccine is coming.

Jamie: He'll be fine for a night.

Me: He. Is. Coming.

Jamie: Why are you so stubborn?

Me: Why are you?

He's not here but I swear I can hear him groan.

Jamie: Fine, point made. Bring the gremlin.
Me: Thank you.
Jamie: I'm a sucker.
Me: But you're my sucker.

My stomach rolls and I set the phone aside, closing my eyes. That's another thing, bright lights are killing me.

Somehow, I muster the energy to get up and pack my bag. I know if I don't Jamie will make good on his promise and I don't feel well enough to make sure he doesn't forget something important. I even pack a little overnight bag for Fettuccine.

Right on time I hear a knock on the door. Before I can get off the couch the door opens. It's the first time Jamie's ever made use of his landlord key.

"Fuck, you do look awful."

"Well, gee, thanks," I snap.

Having my boyfriend tell me in so many words I look like shit isn't going a long way to helping me feel better.

"I didn't mean it like that." He bends, picking up my bag and swinging it over his shoulder, then grabs Fettuccine's. I scoop up the wiggling kitty into my arms and grab my blanket from the couch. When I'm ill I resort to a childlike state where all I want is my blanky and a milkshake. Not ashamed of it either.

I follow him out the door, locking up.

On the bottom floor I blurt, "Oh, did you know Stan moved? Good fucking riddance." I cover my mouth with my left elbow as a cough wracks my body. From my other arm Fettuccine looks at me with disgust.

Come on, cat, give me a break. I'm trying to cover my mouth here to not spread germs. I can't help it I'm sick.

When I look over at Jamie he wears a sheepish expression.

"What?" I ask, the sunlight nearly crippling me as we step onto the parking lot.

"Nothing."

"Oh my God." Cough. "You totally..." Cough. "Got..." Cough. "Stan kicked..." Cough. "Out."

It's official, I definitely have a bruised rib with all this coughing. Whatever devil illness this is can take a hike.

"Maybe."

"Jamie!" I would swat at him if I wasn't afraid of losing my balance and toppling over. It'd be a crime to squish Fettuccine. I'm not sure he'd survive the weight of my boobs if I landed on him.

"He was a creep, rude, and I didn't like the way he looked at you. So, yeah, I may have influenced things to speed up his departure."

"You didn't kill him did you?"

We reach his car and he unlocks it, letting the back lift-gate up. He puts the bags inside and closes it, proceeding to open the passenger door and help me inside with the cat. He braces his hands on top of the car and lowers his body to peer in at me.

"No, I didn't kill him. Besides, I could pay someone to do it for me."

He laughs wickedly and shoots me a wink before closing the door in my awestruck face.

It might seem dumb, or silly perhaps, that I forget so easily about Jamie's money. But to me, he's just Jamie, a normal, sometimes grumpy, guy.

He slides behind the driver's seat and I look at him, ready to ask a question until another coughing fit hits me. My stomach rolls and I pray to the feline Gods above that I don't throw up on Fettuccine or Jamie's car.

When I'm recovered I ask, "How does that work? You being a billionaire? Like do you have a billion dollars just sitting in the bank?"

He snorts, "A lot of it is in stocks or tied into the company, so no, I don't have a billion dollars just sitting in the bank. You ready to go to the doctor?"

I pout. "Can't you be my doctor?"

He frowns, eyes narrowing as he shifts the car into reverse. "You're the one who texted me saying you needed to see a doctor."

"That was just a ploy to get you to pick me up and take me to your house so you can take care of me."

Why the hell did I have to ask him to take me to the doctor? I don't want to be poked and prodded.

"Nuh-uh." He pulls out of the apartment complex. "You're not getting out of this one."

I gulp.

Fuck.

CHAPTER THIRTY-TWO

Jamie

Miranda is terrified of the doctor.

Not only is she scared to death of every person in the Urgent Care, but she made me smuggle the stupid fucking cat in here in her purse which I have to carry on my shoulder. Something tells me if she wasn't so worried she'd be making fun of me right now, but this is her fault and I'm doing the best I can to make the whole cat purse thing look sexy.

Miranda swings her legs back and forth, the paper beneath her crinkling with each movement.

"Do you think they're going to give me a shot? I don't like needles. Like I would rather face a swarm of talking angry spiders Chamber of Secrets style than get poked with a needle."

"I don't think shots are typically given in the case of a virus."

"Well, at least that's good news." A sigh whizzes out of her.

I probably shouldn't be nearly as amused by all of this as I am. But considering I'm the man hiding a cat in a bag I don't have much room to judge.

There's a knock on the door and it opens a moment later. Miranda visibly recoils as the nurse enters the room.

"I'm going to get your blood pressure and temperature. It'll just be a second," the nurse tells her.

Miranda looks a bit green and I'm not sure if it's from the nurse being in the room or if she has to throw up.

"Do you need a trashcan?" I ask just in case.

She shakes her head, holding out her arm to the woman.

Inside the bag Fettuccine meows. The nurse's eyes shoot to me.

"He has really bad gas," Miranda blurts. The nurse's gaze slides to her, narrowing with suspicion. "Oh, yeah."

She tosses her thumb at me and I try not to cover my face. "He had Taco Bell. It gives him the toots and something else if you know what I mean." Miranda whispers the last part behind her hand as if I'm not right there to hear it.

I stare up at the ceiling, saying a silent prayer even though I'm not one for praying.

Dear God, give me the strength to survive this woman.

"Blood pressure is good," the nurse says, wrapping her stethoscope around her neck, "heart rate is a tad high, but not bad." She types something into the computer. "Tell me about your symptoms."

"Coughing, throwing up, achy," Miranda rattles off, ticking each thing off on her fingers. "I'm miserable."

"When did this start?"

"Yesterday."

She adds something else into the computer.

"Date of your last period?"

"Uh ... it was last week. I think. I don't remember, but I had it."

The nurse looks at her doubtfully.

Miranda rolls her eyes and pulls out her phone, opening an app. "Yep, last week for sure."

"Sore throat?"

"No."

"The doctor will probably want to test for Strep anyway. It's going around right now."

Miranda's eyes widen in horror. "You are not shoving a Q-Tip down my throat."

My head jerks back with amusement.

The nurse sighs. "Any other symptoms I should know about?"

Miranda wrinkles her nose in thought. "No, I don't think so."

"I'm going to give this information to the doctor."

She walks out with the laptop in hand and I turn to Miranda. "You're terrified of having a Q-Tip swab your throat, but you'll deep-throat my cock?"

Her cheeks flush. "Well, when you put it like that I feel dumb."

She does end up needing the throat swab, even though it comes back negative. It's an hour before she gets a non-diagnosis and is released with an antibiotic. She falls asleep in the car, not waking until I pull into my garage.

"Where am I?" She looks round blearily.

"Home."

A wistful smile graces her lips. "If I wasn't sick, I would kiss you."

I chuckle and get out of the car, unloading her bags. Fettuccine snoozes in her lap and only cracks one eye open when I go to help Miranda out.

She swats my hand away, giving me the cat instead.

"I'm sick, but I can still walk." She groans as she gets out, wobbling a bit.

Always so fucking stubborn, but I don't argue.

Inside, she looks around like she's seeing it for the first time, or perhaps with new eyes.

"Come on," I nod at the stairs, setting Fettuccine down, "you're staying in my room."

The cat runs away like the idea of Miranda in my room terrifies him.

You and me both, buddy. I might never let her leave.

"Your room?" I swear her voice shakes. "I've never seen your room."

"Well, now you are. Try not to throw up on the sheets. They cost me a grand." Her jaw drops and I laugh. "Kidding, I got them from Target."

"A frugal billionaire. I dig it." She stifles a yawn.

"You're exhausted," I accuse. It's pretty obvious, but I hate knowing she's tired.

She brushes her unruly hair behind her ears. "Sleep has been evasive. That tends to happen when you cough every thirty seconds and throw up every hour."

"Well, the doctor said to get rest and drink lots of fluids. Let's get started on the rest part."

She pouts but follows me upstairs, her eyes widening as she sees my master bedroom for the first time. I wonder what the dark gray, nearly black walls, mahogany furniture and other accents look like to her. Is it what she expects? Does it tell her more about me?

She doesn't say anything, just reaches for her bag and changes into pajamas, quickly climbing beneath the thick covers.

She sighs dreamily, sinking into the bed. "It's official, Jamie Miller, you have the most comfortable bed on the planet. You could rent this bed for a fee."

"That so?" I raise a brow.

"Mhmm," she hums, closing her eyes. Her body then shakes with yet another coughing fit and I frown.

"I have to pick up Tobias from school. Are you going to be okay?"

She nods, not opening her eyes. I hope she can get some sleep because she seems to need it.

"My mom is around here somewhere so if you need something while I'm gone just holler for her or text me."

"Just go, I'm going to try to sleep." She curls her arms under her head.

Fettuccine scares the shit out of me as he appears out of nowhere, plowing through my legs. He tries to jump onto the massive bed, but he's still too small. I lift him up and runs up to Miranda, curling his body beside her. She absentmindedly strokes the top of his head.

It's ridiculous how fucking happy it makes me to see her lying in my bed, making herself comfortable. If only she wasn't sick.

I can't linger for long, so I head downstairs. I find my mom in the family room, curled up reading a book.

"Miranda is upstairs in my bed, she's really sick and shouldn't be alone."

"Oh." She closes her book, removing her bright orange reading glasses. "Is she okay?"

"The doctor couldn't be certain what it is since she only got sick yesterday, but she has some antibiotics. She's feeling pretty rough."

She frowns and hops up. "I'll make some homemade vegetable soup for her."

"You don't have to do that, Ma."

"Nonsense." She brushes past me, already on a mission to get to the kitchen. "I'm making the girl soup, and that's final."

I shake my head, following her. "I have to go get Tobias from school. I'll be back. I told Miranda to get you if she needs anything."

"I've dealt with sick people before. I can handle this." Her eyes twinkle with assurance. Raising to her tiptoes, she grabs my chin and kisses my cheek. Stepping back, I see tears in her eyes. "I raised you good, Jamie."

"Don't get sappy on me now, Mama," I joke, pulling her into a hug.

"I like seeing you happy."

She smiles up at me and I know she means it. She's thrilled that I've found someone I love.

"I like feeling happy."

It's not that I haven't been happy, per se, but there's been something missing.

Someone.

Her.

Miranda.

"I gotta go." I dig my keys out of my pocket. "Have fun with your soup."

She laughs at me as I stroll from the room to the garage.

Tobias's school isn't far, but already the pick up line extends into the road.

I pinch the bridge of my nose in impatience. I hate waiting in the pick up line, it's the bane of my existence. It's also the place where on far too many occasions one of the single moms has tried to ask me out. Not interested in your PTO approved vegan, gluten free, nut free, and fun free cookies, Karen.

The line moves forward slowly.

Oh-so-fucking-slowly.

Eventually Tobias spots the car and climbs in the back, buckling into his booster. I'm able to pull out and around, passing all the other suckers who still have to wait.

"How was school?"

"Fun."

"What did you learn?"

"Stuff."

I sigh heavily. The one word answers have already begun.

"Miranda's at the house."

"She is?"

I look in the rearview at his glowing expression.

"Yeah, but she's sick. So don't expect her to play board games or paint with you."

"She was going to play Just Dance with me the next time she was over." I hear the sadness in his voice as I turn onto the main road. "If she's sick we should bring her something to cheer up. Like chocolate or a teddy bear."

"You want to pick something out for her?" I look back at him briefly.

"Yeah!"

"I'll stop at Walgreens."

Fifteen minutes later I'm buying a bag of Reese's cups, a small bouquet of sunflowers, and a squishy cat stuffed animal. All for my son to give my girlfriend.

He grabs the items after I've paid, saying, "Thank you very much," to the cashier before heading for the automatic doors.

I have a total ladies man on my hands.

The drive home is only a few minutes and the smell of the simmering soup permeates the air as soon as I open the door.

"Smells delicious, Ma!" I call out, closing the garage the door. Tobias's feet already pound up the stairs. "No running in the house!" I yell after him. "And don't wake up Miranda if she's sleeping!"

The master bedroom is all the way on the opposite end of the upstairs so I don't have to worry about waking her up yelling.

I poke my head in the kitchen, finding my mom occupied with cooking and singing along to the radio.

Deciding I better go upstairs before Tobias steals my girlfriend, I pause when I reach the landing and hear them laughing all the way down the hall. Miranda's laugh turns to a cough. I can't help smiling. I've fallen for a woman who loves my son and who my son loves. It couldn't be more perfect than that.

I walk down the hall and into the open room. Tobias is sitting on the end of the bed and the goodies are piled around Miranda. Fettuccine rubs against Tobias and he giggles.

"Dad, we should've gotten a cat. Do you think Fettuccine will like Oreo?"

"He might think he's a snack."

"Jamie," Miranda scolds, fighting a smile. "Don't

worry, Toby, I have a feeling they're going to be best friends."

Tobias grins at her and looks back at me. "Dad, can Miranda live with us? If you don't want her to live in your room she can live in mine."

Miranda presses her lips together, stifling laughter as her eyes connect with mine.

"And where, precisely, will you live then?"

"I guess you'll have to build me that tree house I keep asking for." He shrugs his small shoulders.

"Ah," I breathe. "I see."

"You should live with us." He turns to Miranda once more, pleading. Fettuccine climbs up and curls into his lap. "We're a lot of fun."

"I know you are." She starts coughing. "I think you better go, Toby. I don't want you to get what I have in case it's contagious."

"Fine." He looks down dejectedly. "I hope you like the stuff."

"I *love* it." She cuddles the stuffed cat. "Thank you for thinking of me. You're so thoughtful."

He beams and hops off the bed, running out of my room.

"I love him," she tells me, and the confession rings with truth.

I step closer, bracing my hands on the bottom of the

bed, feet of space still separating us. "But you love me more, right?"

She holds up her thumb and forefinger a tiny bit apart. "Only a little bit."

I throw my head back and laugh. "I see how it is."

"Dad!" Tobias calls from down the hall. "You better hurry, you don't want to get sick."

I shake my head at Miranda's grin. "He doesn't want me alone with you."

She laughs, her smile fading when she starts to cough again. "Oh, shit." She hurtles her body out of the bed and across the room to the master bath. A moment later I hear her throw up and my chest aches that she's so sick. I carefully make my way into the bathroom, dampening a cloth and bending down to press it to the back of her neck. Her eyes flick to me. "Jamie, go downstairs. You really don't want this flu or whatever it is. At least I'm not pregnant," she jokes, then groans as she throws up again.

After she's recovered I brush her hair back from her face. "Is that something you want some day?"

"Yeah, I do. I've always wanted to be a mom."

I realize then how important it is to me to be a father again. If I never had another child I would be fine, but I love being Tobias's father and feel it in my heart that I have more room to love others just as much.

I don't reply, just help her clean up and stay as she

brushes her teeth. Once she's back in bed I finally leave and find Tobias downstairs sitting at the table with a massive glare and arms crossed over his chest. "It's about time, Dad."

It's official. My son is going to end up being the biggest cock block ever.

CHAPTER THIRTY-THREE

Miranda

"I feel loads better already." Stretching my arms above my head I smile. "A lot of the achiness is gone and I haven't thrown up in hours."

Coughing, on the other hand, hasn't gotten much better.

Jamie lies in bed beside me, long legs stretched out. His pajama bottoms sit dangerously low on his hips and he doesn't have a shirt on. He's reading something on his iPad, completely engrossed in it. His hair is still damp from a shower, curling around his ears.

I might be sick, but I can still appreciate a sexy man. Sue me.

His eyes flick over to me. "I'm glad you're better."

"Can you hand me my phone?" I point to it at the end of the bed beside Fettuccine.

Jamie said the cat couldn't sleep on the bed tonight.

I said he was going to.

I won.

He leans over, picking up my phone. He passes it to me and I frown at all the texts from Lou. Photos from the concert that's just begun.

"I can't believe I'm not there," I whine.

Only his eyes move in my direction—he's good at that, must be a dad thing. "You do realize I could get you tickets to any concert and fly you there."

My jaw drops. "I legitimately hadn't given it any thought."

He chuckles. "I love that about you."

"What?" I sound slightly defensive as I type a text back to Lou, telling her I'm happy she's having fun. Poor Abel looks really unsure in a selfie she sends right after. The poor guy is surrounded by thousands of screaming women.

"That the fact I'm wealthy is the last thing you think of if you even think of it at all."

"Your money isn't why I like you." I bring up a browser, getting onto Buzzfeed to spend some mindless time scrolling articles and taking quizzes. "I like you for you, even when you're an asshole."

He chuckles, the sound vibrating the bed.

"Thanks, I guess."

"It's a compliment."

I click on a quiz that says it'll tell me what Disney princess I am.

I already know, though, I'm Jasmine. She's always been my favorite princess.

When the results pop up I let out a disgruntled breath. "Merida? Freaking, Merida? She got her mom and brothers turned into bears. Yeah, she's a bad ass with a bow and arrow, but I am *not* Merida."

Jamie sets his iPad down, looking at me in surprise. "Um ... what was that nonsense? I didn't understand any of it."

"Ugh, it's this quiz," I wave my phone wildly, "that tells you what Disney princess you are and it says I'm Merida. I call bullshit. Here, you take it." I text him the link and it pops up on his iPad. He gives me a look that says, *really?* "Humor me."

He sighs and clicks on the link. It only takes him two minutes to take the quiz and he flips his iPad to show me the results. "I got Merida too."

I flop back onto the fluffy pillows. "Do you know

what this means?" I cry before falling into a coughing fit.

When I'm recovered he says, "We're soul mates?" He winces, seeming to know that's not the right answer.

"It means we're both annoying as fuck and missing a very vital piece of being Merida."

"Which is?" He arches a brow, clearly indulging me at this point.

"Neither one of us has a fire crotch," I whisper conspiratorially.

He busts out laughing. "Only you, Miranda."

"What? It's a valid point." I click onto another quiz that's supposed to tell me how many kids I'll have.

He leans over, seeing what I'm up to. "This ought to be interesting."

I finish the quiz and get my results, jaw dropping. "Five? Five, kids? No way in hell is my vagina pushing out five kids. I can't do it. That's just ... too much." I'm horrified at the very idea. I want kids, but not that many. Five is an entire sports team, practically an army.

"How many do you want?"

"I don't know. Two? Three? I know I want kids, but I haven't given much thought to how many. Five seems like a lot, though."

"Send it to me."

I do and roll onto my side, watching his iPad screen for his results to roll in once he's done.

"Six?" I scoff. "This thing is insane. Can anyone even

afford six kids these days?" He gives me a look and I release a breath. "Right, *you* could afford six kids."

He chuckles, wetting his bottom lip with his tongue. "Got any more quizzes we should take?"

And that's how we spend our night, taking Buzzfeed quizzes and arguing over the results.

It's stupid, silly, probably a bit weird, but it's perfect and it's us.

I think it might be one of my favorite nights ever, despite being sick.

CHAPTER THIRTY-FOUR

Miranda

"The concert was amazing," Lou gushes, wrapping her fingers around her Starbucks pink drink.

"Rub. It. In." Tanner stirs sugar into his black coffee, giving her a pinched look. "I could've gone with you."

Lou smiles sheepishly. "It was so last minute, Miranda not being able to go. I honestly didn't think of you."

Tanner lets out a dramatic sigh and turns to me. "What am I? Last year's Gucci? I think not. I am brand new, unreleased Gucci."

"Of course you are." I pat his shoulder.

"At least we're on break." Lou sips her drink and it doesn't go unnoticed by me that she's trying to change the subject. "Any Christmas plans?"

"I'll be with Jamie."

"You guys are really serious," she remarks. "I honestly didn't think it would last this long, but ... I am happy for you. You're glowing."

"Seriously, you look amazing." Tanner looks me over. "Love is the skin's natural glow." I blink at him. "What? I totally read that in a Cosmo magazine." Propping his elbow on the table and head in his hand, he pouts. "When am I going to find love?"

"When it's ready for you."

Lou, always dropping her wisdom.

"Don't think I've forgotten the concert snub, missy."

She sinks down into her chair looking sheepish. *"I'm sorry."*

"Don't worry," I pat Tanner's hand, "Jamie can get us tickets to anything we want to see *and* a private plane. We won't invite Lou."

"Hey!" She pouts, setting her cup down on the table. "Not fair."

Tanner ignores her—I know he's not actually mad at

her, but this is what friends do, or at least the three of us, we mess with each other. If you can't make fun of each other and laugh together how can the friendship possibly last the test of time?

"Jamie coming in clutch with the big dick and big jet. We love a true Daddy."

I snort and Lou spews her drink across the table.

Tanner grins widely, faking a hair flip.

"Serious topic," I try to get the conversation back on track, "what are you and Abel doing for Christmas?"

"My mom's planning to come visit, and we'll spend the day with his sister's family."

"Wait," I pause, fighting a laugh, "is your mom going to stay with you guys?"

She drops her head onto the table. "Yes." Her voice is muffled by the wood.

Tanner sips his coffee, eyes wide. "That's going to be fun for you guys ... or you know, not fun."

"Yeah, no fun-stick time for you, girl."

"I'm not even worried about that." She runs her fingers roughly through her hair, mussing the blonde strands. "It's such a small space, and you know how close I am with her, so I have a feeling boundaries will mean nothing so all sexy times are off the table until after she leaves."

"What about when you guys went to visit her over the summer?"

She winces. "We stayed in a hotel."

"What?" I blurt in surprise, leaning on the table like I'm trying to get close enough to shake the information out of her. "I thought you stayed with her."

She shakes her head. "We planned to, but at the last minute I panicked and we got a hotel instead."

I lean back in my seat, letting out a low whistle. "Damn."

"Yeah." She drops her head in her hands. "It's going to be so awkward."

"Well, I mean, you're adults. Your mom knows you bang."

Lou gags. "Oh my God, do not mention my mother and *banging* in the same sentence ever again."

Tanner's eyes dart from side to side and he leans in, lowering his voice like he's spilling a secret. "What if the bathroom door doesn't lock properly and your mom walks in on Abel naked?"

Lou squeals, covering her eyes again. "I can't do this! My mother and boyfriend in one tiny ass apartment is too much for me to handle." She starts breathing heavily.

"Before you have an anxiety attack, remember how much you love your mother. You guys are close. It'll be fine."

She lowers her hands. "I know it'll probably all work out in the end, but the idea of it still freaks me out. She's my mom, I want her to—"

"What? Think you're a virgin forever? Please." I wave a dismissive hand. "You tell your mom everything, so I know she already is aware of that sordid tale. Your mom is awesome and loves you, stop freaking out."

Lou exhales a breath. "You're right. I'm being dumb. I guess since this is the first time she's driving up here to see me I want it to be perfect."

"What about you, Tanner? Any plans?"

Tanner sighs heavily and frowns. "Not really."

Sadness clings to him and I can't help but reach out and wrap my arms around him. "Aw, Tanner."

"It's okay, don't feel bad. I'm used to being on my own. I haven't found love yet, not like you guys."

His eyes slide away and I follow his gaze to where his eyes linger on one of the baristas.

"Maybe one day," he adds softly.

"No maybe about it. It's going to happen." Lou reaches over and takes his hand. I still haven't let him go.

"You should totally come over and celebrate with Jamie and me. His mom will no doubt make enough food to feed the entire neighborhood."

"I couldn't. I don't want to be a burden."

Lou makes a squeak of protest while I shake my head. "We're friends, friends are never a burden. Friends are family."

"But never food," Lou interjects with a soft laugh.

I roll my eyes at her piss poor Finding Nemo joke.

"Maybe I will."

"And who knows," I add, nodding in the direction of the barista he was checking out—a tall guy with shoulder length blond hair tied back, full lips, and straight nose, "maybe if you wish hard enough Santa will bring you a boyfriend for Christmas. You've been nice this year, right?"

Tanner busts out laughing and I sit back, picking up my coffee to finally take a sip.

He looks between us and cracks a crooked smile. "Oh, ladies, I am *always* naughty, there's no other way to be."

"Amen to that."

We clink our cups together, laughter filling the air.

No matter what, I'm forever thankful I've found these two incredible people.

Friends like these are worth more than anything and it's all too easy in today's chaotic world to forget the power of friendship—the power in the people we *choose* to be our family.

CHAPTER THIRTY-FIVE

Jamie

It's time for this to end once and for all.

I have to drive to Sterling for another meeting with Shannon.

She doesn't know it, but it's going to be the last. I won't play her stupid games anymore. I won't allow her to use *my* son as a way to scare me into giving her money. I won't cower to her threats.

But I want Miranda with me. I want to stand as a

united front and let her be a part of this. If she's a part of my life that means she's a part of Tobias's. I want her to see that I'm not afraid of Shannon and any lies she might hurl against me, or any tactics she might use to persuade me to stay away from her. Shannon might not want me anymore but she's the type to not want anyone else to have me either.

Picking up my phone, I ring Miranda.

"Hello oh Masterful one, what can I do for you today? No really, can I do you?"

I shake my head, trying not to laugh. I need to be serious. "What are you doing?"

"Not you."

"Miranda," I chide.

"Sorry," she whines slightly. "I'm leaving Target. I came to get some cat food and now I'm the proud owner of not only cat food but three new shirts, a pair of jeans, a purse, two pairs of shoes, and a blanket. I can't resist a good blanket. It's purple, my favorite color, and I'm a sucker."

"Do you think you could come to my house and ride with me to Sterling?"

"Sterling? Why?" I hear her open her car door in the background.

"I need to see my lawyer."

"Jamie, we can't get divorced, we're not even married yet."

I laugh at her deadpan attitude. "It's about custody. I have to meet with Shannon again."

Miranda grows silent on the line.

"She's not going to keep me from loving you, sweetheart."

"But what if she threatens you—I won't be the reason she tries to take Toby from you."

"Miranda," I say softly, trying to calm her. "I have a plan. I won't let her threaten us."

"Us?"

"That's right, baby, you're stuck with me now."

"What are you up to?" She sounds suspicious. I suppose she has a right to be. I've been working on this for a while now. I knew it would be the only way to get rid of Shannon for good. It's a shame she doesn't want to be there for Tobias for the right reasons, but since she doesn't want to be she needs to know she can't use my love for him against me.

"You'll know soon enough."

"You're being so cryptic. You really aren't going to tell me anything? Just let me walk in here blind?" Miranda clutches the edges of the passenger seat in her hands.

I put the car in park, taking my seatbelt off. Twisting my body toward her I take her hands in mine.

"I hired a private investigator buddy of mine. We use him sometimes for the company when certain situations arise and I had him look into Shannon." I rub the back of her neck, trying to soothe her. "He found enough that there's no chance of her ever sniffing around again for money. She doesn't know that, though, and since she basically threatened you I want you to be here. We're in this together." Her eyes soften as I speak. "I don't want you kept in the dark, not anymore. You're a part of my life, one of the biggest parts, and you deserve to be a involved in things. You love Tobias too, and that's more than I can say for Shannon." Ducking my head, I admit softly, "It breaks my heart for my son that his mother isn't capable of loving him the way he deserves."

She gently extracts one of her hands from mine, cupping my cheek. She forces me to look at her and God, when I do, I see how much she truly loves me. I see everything I've denied myself, thinking I didn't deserve it, but I guess that's the thing, I didn't deserve this until her. She's the one I was waiting for all along to pull me out of the dark.

"You love him so much that it doesn't even matter. He has your mom. He has me. He has more than a lot of kids do. Give yourself credit, Jamie. You've shown your son what it truly means to feel loved."

"You always know what to say." Pulling her hand away from my face I kiss her palm. "We better head in."

Inside, Don is already waiting for us. His face is steely, like he's preparing to go into battle.

"Don, this is my girlfriend Miranda. Miranda, this is Don, my lawyer."

"Nice to meet you." He shakes her hand. "Let's head on back."

He takes us to the dreaded room I've come to hate so much over the last few months.

"Chase should be arriving any minute," I inform him, pulling out one of the chairs for Miranda before I sit down myself.

Don passes us bottles of water. "I'll go wait for him."

"Thanks."

I might pay the man, but he truly goes above and beyond.

Miranda props her head in her hand. "Shannon is going to lose her mind."

I chuckle but there's not one bit of humor in the sound. I don't relish in having to do this, but if she wants to threaten me she won't like what's coming for her.

I cross my arms over my chest, ready to get this over with. I feel like I'm preparing for the fight of my life. It's a good thing I've come prepared.

"Yeah, she is," I finally say. "But it's what has to be done."

Her hand wraps around my bicep. "The way you fight for Toby makes me love you even more."

"He's my son." I gaze down into her warm brown eyes. "I'll always fight for him. Until my last breath and maybe even after that." She smiles at my vow, kissing my cheek. "I would do it for you too. For anyone I love. I love wholly, with no ounce of doubt, and when your love is true you'll fight through hell and back to protect them."

"Jamie, Jamie, Jamie," she murmurs softly, rubbing her plump pink lips together. "You're the man who wears a mask, who tries to hide your true self from the world, all because your heart is purer than we deserve."

I snort in amusement. "I wouldn't go that far."

Her lips twitch in amusement.

Don enters the room again, Chase behind him.

"Thanks for coming, man." I stand, shaking Chase's hand.

"It's not a problem," he assures me.

I introduce him to Miranda and then all of us sit to wait for Shannon to arrive with her lawyer.

Minutes tick by, and I'm not surprised when she's over thirty minutes late. I swear she gets enjoyment out of knowing she's made people wait for her.

She breezes in with a toxic cloud of perfume. Her lawyer closes the door behind them, and they sit down.

"Who are these people?" Her lawyer asks, smoothing a hand over his tie. He then waves a hand to Miranda and Chase indicating they're who he's asking about.

"This is Miranda, my girlfriend, and Chase is my private investigator."

Shannon's lips pinch, eyes narrowing at this news.

That's right. I've got you now.

I'm truly not a vindictive person, but I'm thoroughly going to enjoy scaring the shit out of her.

"Let's get down to business then." Her lawyer shuffles some papers, banging them on the table to straighten them. "My client is asking for one million dollars or she'll pursue custody of one Tobias Ezekiel Miller."

Miranda gives me a what-the-fuck look at the reveal of Tobias's middle name.

"Considering your net worth," her lawyer continues in a monotone, "one million dollars is a very generous request. I informed my client she shouldn't ask for any less than ten million." He smacks the papers on the table again before laying them flat. "This back and forth has been going on for months. If we walk out today with no agreement our next step will be to bring this to family court."

Shannon clears her throat, wiggling her shoulders as she does. It's a clear sign she's asking for the floor.

"It would be a shame," her voice is sickly sweet like a sticky syrup, "for a court to learn how much time you're spending with your *girlfriend*," she spits the word venomously like it's sour and rotten on her tongue, "and not with your son."

Your son.

Not hers.

Or ours.

But only mine. At least she got one thing right out of that whole pointless spiel of hers.

"I spend just as much time with Tobias now as I always have. Your threats are pointless."

"I have photos!" She bangs a fist against the table.

She's fucking unhinged.

"Really?" I sit back, lacing my fingers together. Miranda watches me curiously. "So do I." I wave my hand at Chase at the end of the table. "Photos, bank statements, credit card statements, email chains. I have everything Shannon. Are you sure you want to take me to court and have to discuss why you're in debt?"

Her lips thin.

"Oh, come on, Shannon. Plenty of people have a drug problem."

She swallows, eyes darting from side to side as if seeking escape.

"Although, I'm sure most don't exploit they're child in order to get money from their ex-husband to fuel said drug problem. Chase, if you'd please."

The burly mountain looking man gets up and strides to the end of the table, handing Shannon and her lawyer each a folder with all the evidence I need. No judge would ever grant Shannon custody rights with all the proof we have on her now.

I knew something had to be up with her. She's been too desperate to get money from me, almost rabid. So, I had Chase start digging and he didn't have to dig far before the image became clear.

"You're never getting custody of Tobias. It's a real shame, Shannon, that you're willing to use your son this way. He's a brilliant, funny, amazing kid."

"I ... I..." She stutters, no words forming. I'm sure her brain has shut down at the sight of the photos and evidence in front of her.

Shannon might not be the typical picture of a drug addict, but that's the thing, it's not one size fits all. Anyone can be an addict.

Laying my hands flat on the table, I propose my offer. "I'm willing to offer to pay for a five star rehab center if you'll agree to stay there for a full year. If, at the end of the year, you're clean and a therapist thinks you're on the right path I'll pay off your debt and give you one-hundred thousand dollars to start over. That's it. No more. You'll have to sign an agreement to never contact me again for money. But if you leave this room without agreeing or signing the paperwork, this proposal is null and void." Clearing my throat, I lower my voice. "I don't like who and what you've become. But I loved you once and you're the mother of my son. I don't want to see you fail, or God forbid hear you've overdosed. Because I loved you I'm giving you this chance to make something better of yourself."

Beneath the table Miranda squeezes my knee.

Perhaps it's crazy of me to give her this chance when I've been adamant on not giving her a penny more, but I hate seeing her life spiral down this deep dark hole.

"You have a moment to think this over." I wave my hands and sit back.

Miranda looks at me with tears shimmering in her brown orbs. I take her hand, entwining our fingers together beneath the table.

Exhaling a breath, I add to a stunned Shannon, "Everyone deserves a second chance. Even villains."

Miranda and I make eye contact. Her lips tip into a small smile.

Once upon a time she saw me as nothing but a villain. Now I'm the hero of our story.

Shannon whispers something to her lawyer and he clears his throat.

"My client would like to know where she needs to sign?"

CHAPTER THIRTY-SIX

Miranda

Jamie's house is the perfect idyllic Christmas scene. Greenery and twinkle lights twine around the banisters. Stockings hang from the fireplace hearth—one for Jamie, Toby, Mama Jo, and even one for Fettuccine and me.

The tree is the tallest I've ever seen, decked with homemade ornaments that the three of them have made over the years, including ones from Jamie's childhood.

Some new ones have been added this year that I made and even a mold of Fettuccine's paw.

The whole house smells of pine and cinnamon. I've decided it's my favorite scent in the entire world. Mama Jo is constantly baking some sort of pie or other holiday treat.

I spend more time here than I do at my apartment anymore. This is where I'm happiest.

Curled up on the couch, tucked against Jamie, I can't stop smiling as I watch Toby tear through his presents with that contagious joy only children seem to possess. The magic of the holiday spirit fills the air.

Tanner came over and I think Mama Jo wants to adopt him. The two of them have snuck off to the kitchen to bake more things, as if the kitchen isn't already fully stocked with every holiday treat imaginable.

"Ah, yes! I wanted these so bad, Dad!" Toby holds up a set of dinosaur toys.

Despite his excitement he tosses the box to the side, tearing into another one.

Jamie brushes his fingers delicately over my bare shoulder where my loose sweatshirt has dipped, exposing the skin there. "What do you want for Christmas?"

I turn to him, my hands wrapped around a mug of peppermint hot chocolate. "Not a thing. I have everything I've ever dreamed of right here."

"Not a thing? Not one?" His smile is playful and I feel like he's messing with me.

"I mean, if you're hiding a cat somewhere to feed my new-found cat lady life, that'd be great." His lips twitch. "Jamie?"

He holds up a finger and gets off the couch, heading out of the family room.

Toby is oblivious to his departure, now looking intently at the art kit I got him.

"This is amazing. Thank you, Miranda!"

"You're welcome."

Fettuccine snoozes on my lap and I scratch him behind his ears.

A moment later Jamie returns with a box and holds it out to me with a smile he can barely contain.

I trade him my mug of hot chocolate for the box.

It moves.

Like something literally wiggles inside of it.

"You didn't?"

He just smiles, nodding for me to open the box.

I do. A squeal erupts out of me, scaring Fettuccine who runs off my lap to hide under the chair in the corner.

"Jamie," I shriek, "you got me a kitten!" I pull out the fluffy white kitten wearing a green collar with milkshakes on it.

"Yeah, well, I'm learning I'm quite the sucker. Every

time I asked you what you wanted most you always said a cat. I thought about being a smart ass and giving you a stuffed animal, but that was too mean."

I kiss the kitten on top of the head. "Boy or girl?"

"Boy. The last thing I need is *more* animals around this place. I couldn't have them procreating."

"Don't worry, you'll always be the head alpha in charge." I wink at him.

"Is that a cat?" Toby exclaims, finally noticing the fluff ball in my arms.

"It is." I hold the kitten out for him to take.

He cuddles up to it. "What are you going to name it?"

"Yeah, what can possibly top Fettuccine?" Jamie scoffs playfully.

"Alfredo, duh."

"You're naming the cat Alfredo?" Jamie raises a brow. "Fettuccine and..." He lowers his head. "Alfredo. I got it."

"I'm brilliant, I know." I shrug.

"You're something, that's for sure." He pulls me in for a kiss.

"Thank you for the kitten. He's going to be spoiled silly."

"Mhmm," he hums, kissing me again.

"And thank you for something else."

He tugs away a bit. "What?"

"Giving me the key to your heart." I grab the necklace

he gave me for my birthday, letting the charms dangle where the light reflects off of them.

He chuckles. "Yeah, well you kind of forced your way in there. You're impossible not to love."

Dropping the necklace, I grab the collar of his shirt and pull him into a deep kiss.

This is only the beginning for us. I know it.

CHAPTER THIRTY-SEVEN

Five Months Later
Jamie

Miranda and Lou pose in front of a backdrop that says: The One Where They Graduate. Miranda explained to me about their love for the show *FRIENDS* and they based their entire graduation party around that shared bond. Watching her smile and laugh with her friend, excited by this next step in her life, makes me happy.

They pose for another photo, holding their decorated caps in front of them.

Miranda, ever a smart ass, wrote JUST GOT HOTTER BY ONE DEGREE on hers then surrounded it with flames made of tissue paper.

She might be crazy, but she's mine.

"Dad, that man has a *monkey*. Can I have a pet monkey?"

"No, Toby, I draw the line at two cats, a guinea pig, and a Miranda."

He looks at me in surprise. "Uh ... Dad, you called me Toby." He says it as if I've made some grievous mistake, his hazel eyes speculative.

"Well, you're eight now. I figure if you want to be called Toby I should respect your wishes."

He wrinkles his nose. "I think you should call me Tobias. It's weird when you say Toby."

I choke on a laugh. "Okay, son."

"I'm going to see if I can pet the monkey."

He runs off and Miranda stalks toward me. She twirls her arm in the air and pretends to lasso me. Off to the side Lou hugs Abel, resting her chin on his chest as she looks up at him. Her eyes meet mine briefly and I feel her approval for what's about to come. We had a heart to heart a couple of months ago and smoothed things out. Abel still hates my guts, but that's fine.

I meet Miranda halfway, taking her face in my hands. "Look at you college graduate."

"I can't believe I did it."

"I can." I rub my thumb over her bottom lip. "You can do anything."

She laughs. "Yeah, I am pretty brilliant."

I kiss her and she smiles against my lips.

"Having fun?" I nod to indicate the entire party.

"It's perfect. You didn't have to do all of this for us."

"I wanted to. When it comes to you there are lots of things I want to do."

"Naughty things?" Her eyes sparkle.

"Yeah, those too, but there's something else I really want."

"And what's that?"

I drop to one knee and her mouth drops.

Pulling the small black box from my pocket, I open it to show her the purple sapphire ring. "I really want to call you my wife. So, Miranda, will you marry me?"

She presses her hands to her face, tears streaming. Behind me I hear my mom and her parents all crying.

"Yes! Oh my God! A thousand times, yes!" She dives for me and I nearly lose the ring.

I hug her back, kissing her deeply.

Still crying, she finally allows me to slide the ring on her finger.

"It's beautiful, Jamie. I love you."

"I love you," I murmur, kissing her again. We're both still kneeling on the ground and seem to have no plans to move.

"I get to call you my husband."

I groan. "God, that sounds fucking amazing when you say it."

She grins mischievously. "You know what sounds even better?"

"What?" Curiosity fills me.

She leans in and I hold my breath as her lips press to my ear.

"Baby Daddy."

EPILOGUE

#1
Eight Months Later
Jamie

"I hate you! You are never ever coming near me with your Devil dick ever again!" Miranda screams at me, squeezing all feeling from my hand.

She can do whatever she wants to me. I don't care. She's bringing our son into the world and I'm happy to be her verbal and physical punching bag.

"It hurts," she begins to cry, and I wipe away her tears with a damp cloth.

"You're doing amazing. You're so strong, sweetheart."

Miranda wanted to do a home water birth, with absolutely no drugs. I was adamantly against it, but she's the one who has to go through this part, so at the end of the day I wanted her to do what's best for her.

"I want him out," she whimpers.

"You're almost there," the midwife tells her. "A couple more pushes."

"Lies," Miranda shrieks at her. "You said that twelve pushes ago."

"Hey," I gently take her face in my hands, "you can do this. You're so fucking strong and powerful. You're so close to bringing our son into the world. You can do this. Don't underestimate yourself."

She begins to cry, wrapping her damp arms around my shoulders. "I l-l-love you."

Before I can respond she cries out with another contraction.

"Push, baby, push."

She squeezes my hand again, her screams filling the room.

"Almost there, come on," her midwife encourages.

And then, in a single moment, our baby enters the world with a cry.

He's placed on Miranda's chest and her cries turn into sobs as she cradles him, his hair as dark as hers.

Shock and awe fills me just like when I watched Tobias be born.

Tears warm my cheeks and Miranda turns her body into mine where I lean over the birthing tub.

"You did it, sweetheart," I murmur, kissing her. She kisses me back, face wet with tears. "He's beautiful."

My hand swallows his tiny head whole. His cries quiet but his full lower lip trembles.

"Hi, Caleb," I whisper to him, "I'm your daddy."

Miranda touches the back of her finger to his cheek. "And I'm your mommy."

I kiss the side of her forehead, gazing down at our tiny and perfect baby boy.

"Thank you," I murmur against her ear.

"For what?" She glances at me with surprised eyes before she can't help but look at our newborn again.

"For giving me a chance I probably didn't deserve. For showing me I can love again. For becoming my wife. For loving Tobias. For giving me another child. For everything."

"Don't worry," she laughs, tracing her finger around Caleb's tiny ear, "I'm charging you interest."

I laugh too, kissing her again because I just can't seem to stop.

Miranda took my black and white life, splattering it

with all of her colors. There's no erasing the mark she's left on me and I would never want to. She's everything I never knew I wanted, needed, or deserved.

Hours later, once everything is cleaned up, a tired Miranda lays in bed holding the baby and Tobias finally arrives home since we had him go to a friend's house during the birth.

"Where's my brother?" he exclaims, bursting into the room.

Ever since we told him we were having a baby he's been ecstatic to be a big brother. I never thought I'd give him a sibling, so I'm thrilled he's getting this opportunity.

Miranda holds out one arm to him and he runs to hug her, completely passing by me at the door.

"What am I? Chopped liver?" I grumble, walking over to join them.

My breath catches looking at my wife and two boys.

This is the life I always pictured for myself but thought I wouldn't have.

The world works in mysterious ways, I guess.

"I missed you." Miranda hugs Tobias.

"Missed you, too. Can I hold him?" Tobias points at the baby who yawns. "Aw, look, he's sleepy."

"Sure, go sit in the chair." She points to the chair in the corner of the room. "Dad will give him to you." She extends the baby to me and he gives a little squawk, not pleased at being disturbed. I mean, if I was cuddled up next to Miranda's boobs I wouldn't want to move either.

I carry Caleb over to Tobias. "Curl your arms like this." I show him how I'm holding the baby. "And you have to be careful to support his head."

"Okay, Dad, I've got this."

I chuckle. I'm sure he does. He's wanted to be involved and learn things about taking care of a baby. It's been a pleasure to watch him be excited about the whole process. I don't have to worry about any resentment from him—after all, he's the one who asked about a sibling this time last year.

"Hi, little baby, I'm your brother."

Caleb wiggles his tiny body, but Tobias doesn't freak out and worry about dropping him. Besides, I'm right there.

Miranda watches us from the bed, looking at me with tears in her eyes. "My three boys," she mouths.

I smile back at her.

"He's very cute." Tobias rubs his hand over Caleb's downy soft hair. "We have the same nose, but he has Miranda's lips." He looks at me and then over at her in the bed. "Miranda?"

"Yeah?" She wiggles, wincing a bit from the pain.

"I've been thinking..." he hesitates, looking down at his brother. "Can I call you, Mom?" My breath whooshes from me in surprise. Miranda starts to cry and wipes her tears away hastily. Still looking at Caleb, he adds, "It's just ... he's going to call you Mom, so I think I should too. I ... so ... um ... is that okay?" He bites his lip and finally looks at both of us.

Miranda sniffles. "Toby, that's more than okay. Can I have a hug?"

"Um ... sure but I'm not done holding my brother."

She laughs around her tears. "That's okay. You can give me a hug when you're done."

"How about this, let me take the baby, and you hop in the bed beside Miranda then you can hold him up there. Sound good?"

"Okay."

I take Caleb and Tobias runs over to the bed, jumping up and next to Miranda. He gives her a hug and she helps him pile up the pillows so he'll be sitting up straight.

I hand him back the baby once he's situated and lay down beside him.

Stretching out my arm, I grab Miranda's hand twining our fingers together.

My wife. My boys.

It doesn't get more perfect than this.

EPILOGUE

#2
Approximately Five Years After That
Miranda

Who decided it would be a *smashing* good idea to ask me to be Maid of Honor at eight and a half months pregnant?

Lou. My so-called best friend. That's who.

"I'm dying." I fan myself with a magazine.

Lou gasps as her mom tightens the corset on her

wedding gown—because of course Lou would decide to get married in an explosion of princess ball gown tulle in a pale pink color.

"Please, just make it through the ceremony," she begs, holding her hands beneath her chin. "That's all I ask."

"God, it's hot as Satan's balls sack today. Did you have to get married today of all days?"

"We're in air conditioning right now, Miranda. You can't possibly be that hot."

"Until you're practically nine months pregnant at the end of July I don't want to hear a word out of your mouth."

"I can't believe you're having your third and fourth kid."

Twins. That's right.

Jamie Fucking Miller impregnated me with twins.

Actually, they're identical twin girls so technically my own eggs revolted against me and brought this upon me. Traitors.

I continue to fan myself and once Lou is strapped into her dress it's minutes away from show time.

I hug her as tight as I can which is tough with my pregnant belly in the way.

"I'm so happy for you. You're marrying your soul mate."

"Thank you. I can't wait."

She's absolutely giddy.

"I'm still mad I'm not the Man of Honor. I'm way cooler than Miranda. Just sayin'," Tanner says from the corner of the room, feet propped on an ottoman. He's already drinking what looks like a gin and tonic. Only Tanner.

The wedding planner appears out of nowhere, fussing over us, and then guides us to get lined up to head outside where everyone waits.

I'm worried I look like a sweaty cow but everyone assures me I look great.

That's good news I suppose considering I'm miserable. The heat is killing me, and I haven't told anyone but I'm pretty sure I started having contractions this morning.

Yeah, I'm crazy, what's new?

I loop my arm through Abel's brother-in-law's arm, plastering a smile on my face as we head out and then down the aisle.

We're halfway there when I feel it.

The telltale wet trickle and then the feeling of a balloon popping.

Oh. Shit.

Lou is going to murder me.

Abel's brother-in-law pauses, looking down. "Did your—"

"Yeah, yeah it did."

People are beginning to look and Jamie, bless him,

stands up. He immediately spots the problem and with Toby's help wrangles Caleb and Logan.

Every single eye is on us and I hear whispers spreading.

Yep, that's right. Best friend and Maid of Honor extraordinaire, stealing the spotlight by going into labor at the wedding. I'm available for other events for a hefty fee.

Jamie helps me out, while a teenage Toby holds onto Caleb and Logan.

Passing by a stunned Lou on our way out, I mouth, "Sorry."

She shakes her head, stifling laughter, calling out, "Good luck!"

Jamie drives me straight to the hospital, the boys in the backseat. As soon as we were in the car he called his mom to meet us at the hospital.

I had a home birth with my first two but I knew I couldn't risk it with twins, much to Jamie's relief.

Chaos ensues and six hours later, two tiny, perfect, identical human beings enter the world.

Our two boys look more like me, but the girls are *all* Jamie.

They have the same reddish brown hair, nose, eye shape, mouth, and even his long fingers.

Sophia Grace and Abigail Madison might already have their daddy wrapped around their fingers even more than their brothers do. Watching my husband hold them both, rocking them in his arms as he looks back and forth between them, chokes me up.

When I first met Jamie, never in a million years would I have believed I'd marry the guy, let alone have *four* kids with him.

It was a gigantic lesson for me—don't judge a book by its cover.

Jamie smiles at me, eyes crinkling at the corners.

I know whatever decisions I made that led me to him, I'd gladly do it all over again.

EPILOGUE

#3

Another Four Years After That
Miranda

"Look at our little boy," I cry, wiping way tears as Tobias's name is called.

He strides across the platform, accepting his high school diploma. He ducks his head when Jamie and I cheer, along with his five siblings.

Toby's grown into a brilliant young man who's going to go far in the world.

It's going to kill me when he goes off to college in the fall. He wants to be a doctor and despite the years of studying ahead of him, I know he'll make for a compassionate and kind doctor when he does.

It takes a while to get through the rest of the names but when it ends, and the caps have been tossed into the air, we storm the field.

Jamie and I rush after the kids trying to keep up with them as they plow through the crowd for Toby.

Somehow, they find him easily, sniffing him out like some sort of little human bloodhounds.

They pile on Toby, tackling him to the ground. He laughs beneath their weight.

"I love you guys, too."

"Don't leave us, Toby!" Sophia pleads.

"Yeah, you have to stay," Logan chimes in, stealing his cap and sticking it on his own head.

"I'm not leaving until fall and I'll visit as much as I can."

His school is only two hours away, which I know isn't too far, but it feels like forever. The kids pull away, letting Toby up.

He hugs Jamie first, then me.

"I'm so proud of you. Watching you grow up has been

one of the greatest blessings I've ever been given. I love you."

"I love you too, Mom." He kisses my cheek.

His wavy hair, the same color as Jamie's—though Jamie is starting to sport some gray at his temples—tumbles over his forehead. He shoves it out of the way smiling. I can't believe this is the same boy I met eleven years ago. It's like I blinked and he became a man. He might not be of my blood, but he's my son nonetheless, and the fierce protectiveness I feel for him is all-consuming. He's the sweetest teenager, who loves his siblings, even the unexpected six-month-old, Jade, who cries all the time. Sometimes I fear he's too kind and precious for this cruel world, but I know he has to be allowed to go on his own and spread his wings.

At least I know without a doubt, he'll be successful at everything he does.

Except maybe when it comes to girls. The poor guy clams up and turns into a bumbling fool, but I know even with that he'll figure it out in time.

Toby picks up Abigail and she wraps her arms around his neck. "If you're not here who's going to protect me from Caleb. He's mean."

"Caleb, are you being mean to your sister?" Jamie scolds in his dad voice.

Caleb groans. "I told her she couldn't come in my room. Boys only. She's such a tattletale."

Jamie opens his mouth, but I shake my head and tell him, "Later."

Today is Toby's day.

We wrangle the five little ones—Goddamn that stupid Buzzfeed quiz for being right, I gave birth five kids and Jamie fertilized six eggs—and head off the football field.

"You know," I begin, looking up at Jamie, "our life might be the definition of crazy, but I wouldn't have it any other way."

He bends down, kissing me. "And I wouldn't want anyone else at my side to handle it with."

ACKNOWLEDGMENTS

I can't believe this is the end of yet another book. Every time I finish one there's this "whoa" moment where I can't believe I did it. So many people helped shape this book and I hope I don't forget anyone.

Kellen, you are such a combo of Thea/Miranda, and your comments on this book cracked me up. I love that when you beta for me you don't hold back and tell me where you think I can improve. You totally whipped this baby into shape. Now we both need to find our Jamie's.

Raquel and Stefanie, words cannot describe how

thankful I am to have you guys beta for me. I don't say it enough, but truly, thank you. You put so much work and love into my books and it never goes unappreciated.

Emily, Emmers, Wifey, hahaha, you've been here since practically the literal start of my career. You started as a reader, then became a friend, and now you're a sister. I seriously feel like we're a part of each other's families at this point. You're wonderful and I love and miss you so much. Oh, and we can't forget to add designer to that list! You knocked this cover out of the park. It's incredible and I'm obsessed.

Thank you to the early readers who take time out of your busy lives to read and review early copies of my books. It means so much. Thank you!

And to you, dear reader, whether you're reading me for the first time or the thirty-seventh, thank you. Thank you times a million. You're the reason I can do what I do. You're the real MVPs.

Haven't met Lou and Abel? That's okay! Start their story today. Here's a peek at chapter one!

WANTED: A ROOMMATE

Requirements

Don't be a smoker. That's gross.
Don't be a jerk. I have no time to deal with your mood swings.
Clean up after yourself. Is it really so hard to put dirty clothes where they belong?

If you meet these qualifications, call me.

Sincerely,
Desperately Seeking Roommate

When I put the ad in my university's newspaper, the last thing I ever expect is for the star football player to respond.

From what I know of him, Abel Russo is a womanizer and an absolute jerk.

Sadly, he's the only thing stopping me from being evicted by my annoyingly gleeful landlord.

It should be easy enough—there's no chance we'll fall for each other. But then he gives me lingering looks, and I might just be looking back.

All I wanted was a roommate, but I'm about to get so much more than I bargained for.

Desperately Seeking Roommate
Chapter One
Lou

"I can't believe I have to do this," I sigh, staring at the ad I've typed up.

"It's not like you asked your landlord to be King of the Douchebags and raise your rent," my best friend Miranda chimes. She's lying across my bed on her stomach, swiping madly on Tinder. I don't know why she likes the stupid app. I find it insulting more than anything. The *one* time I used it I got a message within five minutes of a dick with a bow wrapped around it. I immediately replied that that was not the gift I was asking for at the moment, thank you very much.

She turns her brown eyes to mine and heaves a dramatic breath. She reaches past me and pushes the pad on my laptop, sending the ad through to our university's newspaper.

I cry out, hands fumbling toward my laptop. "Miranda, I wasn't ready! I needed to proofread it again."

"You would've been here all day reading it and then talked yourself out of posting it. It needed to be done."

She rolls off my bed and strides over to my closet door, swiping through the clothes on the hangers.

Miranda is the first friend I've ever had who I could

share clothes with. I'm short and curvy—or what many would call plus size—and most of my friends growing up were either thin or average-sized. I always felt like the odd duck out, until Miranda and I met during English 101. Neither of us are from Winchester—I came from the southern part of Virginia to here in the north, and she ventured all the way from Delaware.

Somehow, we ended up sitting beside each other in our English class and the rest is history.

She holds up an oatmeal colored over-sized sweater. "Can I borrow this?"

"Sure," I reply with a shrug, shutting the lid on my computer. With a groan, I stand up, stretching my stiff muscles. I'm twenty-one going on eighty. If I'm sitting or in any position for too long my limbs lock up despite my nearly daily yoga routine. It's ridiculous.

"Thanks." She drapes the garment over her arm. Her dark brown curls swing around her shoulders. With her father being Hispanic and her mother Asian, the girl is the epitome of the word *unique*. She's stunning and I tell her all the time, but she never believes me because of her size.

I don't know why us bigger girls are shamed by society. We're *normal-sized*—I'm sorry your media standards are candy-cane stick thin. I'd rather *eat* them than look like one.

"I wish you could move in with me," I whine, as she

goes back to flipping through my closet. I've been pouting about this fact for a solid week—ever since I found out rent was going up and I was no longer going to be able to afford my two-bedroom apartment in the historic district. The idea of living with a stranger isn't appealing at all, and since I have no time to spare, I have to be open to a guy for a roommate too.

The prospect of going to pee and falling into the toilet doesn't sound like my idea of getting wet, but desperate times call for desperate measures, and I need a roomie *stat*.

She sighs, her lips twisting downward in genuine apology. "I know, babe, but I just re-signed the lease on my apartment. There's no way I can get out of it. Living here would be so much nicer. My place is a dump."

She lives in an older apartment beside the small airport of privately owned planes. I still don't know how I lucked out getting my cute place downtown—but right now I don't feel so lucky and want to punch my landlord in his smug face. He's young, probably late twenties or early thirties, and inherited this building over the summer when his grandpa passed away. Now, the greedy bastard wants to make more money off broke college students like me.

"Does this match?" she asks, pairing the sweater with a maroon skirt that ends above the knees with buttons down the front.

"Yeah, it'll be cute," I tell her honestly. "But ... what do you need it for?"

Color blossoms across her dark skin. "Charlie asked me out."

"*Charlie?*" I shriek. "Why am I just now hearing about this? I thought you hated him." I jolt upright from this news, in desperate need of hearing the tea on how this came about.

Charlie is in our history class—he's the type who answers every question correctly and then looks around smugly like we all care that he's so much smarter than us.

Newsflash, we don't.

She shrugs. "It happened yesterday. I bumped into him in the library and he asked. I don't really like him, but ... Lou, it's been *forever* since I got laid and I'm desperate. My kitty needs more than some sweet vibrations. I need a man. On top of me. Inside me. All around me."

"But *Charlie*?" I can't get over this. He's not hideous, but if looks were determined by personality he'd be one ugly guy—like Smeagol.

"He's not horrible looking," she reasons, her bottom lip jutting out in thought. "And you never know, he might be cool."

"Well, when he bores you with his vast knowledge of

the size of every shit a president took, don't come crying to me."

"I doubt he knows *that*." She spreads the clothes on top of my bed and stands back, assessing how they look together. Glancing at me she adds, "I'm giving him the benefit of the doubt, okay. Can you do that, too? For me?"

I hug my best friend. "I'd do anything for you."

"Thank you." She smiles, her dark slanted eyes looking relieved. Her relief transitions into worry and her lips flatten. "What are you going to do if no one responds to your ad?"

I sit down on my bed, looking out the old dirty window onto the street below.

"Live on the streets, I guess."

"You know I'd never let that happen," she vows. "My place might be small, but I can make room for you somewhere—maybe add a cat cushion in the bathroom."

I grab a pink pillow and toss it at her. "My ass wouldn't even fit on it."

"At least it's a nice ass." She gives it a tap. "Can we get something to eat now? I'm starving, and you bribed me with the promise of dinner only to spend two hours writing a measly four lines for your stupid ad."

It was more like seven, but even that *is* a pathetic amount of time to spend writing it.

"Fine," I grumble. "I do owe you food."

Her eyes roll as she sticks her tongue out at me. "At this point you owe me a whole fucking pizza."

Twenty minutes later we're seated in a booth inside the cozy wood-fired pizza place—aptly named *Woody's*.

The place has a warm and cozy vibe with browns and blacks used for much of the décor. Our booth is beside the bar, packed with people—mostly fellow college students and the random old guy interspersed. I watch one old man leer down the shirt of the woman beside him.

Nasty old bastards.

Picking up my beer glass, I let the warm liquid slide down my throat. Across from me, Miranda texts on her phone, and I don't dare ask to whom, because I don't want to hear the name *Charlie* leave her lips. The thought alone makes me want to gag.

Who knows, he could prove me wrong, but as her best friend it's my job to have reservations about any guy she dates. She's a queen and deserves to be treated as such. A guy will be lucky to get my stamp of approval, and chances are it won't be Charlie.

She sets her phone aside and stretches across the table toward me. "How much longer until the pizza is here? I'm withering away by the second."

"Considering we ordered five minutes ago, I'd say you'll be waiting a while."

"Dammit." She tosses her head back in aggravation. "Good thing I always have snacks in case of an emergency." She rifles through her purse and pulls out a small bag of popcorn. She proceeds to open it and starts shoving pieces into her mouth.

"If you had that why didn't you eat it earlier?" I remark.

She shrugs and answers around a mouthful. "Forgot I had it."

I shake my head amusedly. Miranda is one of a kind.

I wasn't hungry before, but now that we're here I'm positively *starving*. It feels like it's been a whole day since lunch, not hours. I was too busy agonizing over the stupid ad to think about my stomach.

"Give me some of that," I plead, holding my hand out for some popcorn.

She cradles it against her boobs. *"Mine."*

"Miranda," I gripe. "Please?"

"Fine." She drops a stingy three pieces in my hand.

"That's all you get." She grins and shoves more in her mouth.

I glare at her, but at least it's better than nothing. I eat the three pieces slowly, savoring them. The food is on its way, and once it's here all will be right in the world again. I'm pretty sure pizza can solve any problem. Honestly,

I'm not sure why the idiots in government haven't just ordered some damn pizzas already. Nobody can fight when ooey-gooey-cheesy goodness is in front of you. It's like, against the laws of nature or something. I'm sure of it.

She finishes her popcorn and stuffs the empty bag in her purse.

"I'm full, let's go."

I narrow my eyes.

"Kidding," she adds. "God knows it takes more than that to fill me up."

As much as I don't want to bring up Charlie again, I have to. "When is this date of yours?"

"Tomorrow." She bites her lip.

Studying her, I narrow my eyes into slits. "If you've never really liked him why are you acting nervous all of a sudden?"

She tucks an errant piece of dark hair behind her ear. "I honestly haven't liked him. He's arrogant, rude, condescending ... but also kind of hot in a dork-ish sort of way. The glasses, the floppy hair." She rests her chin on her hand and gives a dramatic dreamy sigh. I'm friends with a complete and utter nutcase.

"Don't go falling in love now," I joke. "I can't be left alone in my singledom."

She rolls her eyes and fans her hand through the air. "Not going to happen. I doubt Charlie can handle all of this." She wiggles her body. "I have needs that need to be met and I'm not certain he's the guy for the job. It's only a date though—free dinner and a movie? I'm not going to complain one bit about that shit."

"True." When you're a broke ass college student, getting to go out and have a free meal is the equivalent of the Holy Grail. Toss a movie into the mix and you've found Jesus himself.

It's been so long since I've dated I've become a Scrooge. Freshman year I went a bit crazy, going out all the time to parties and on dates with guys that usually only led to sex. Then last year I decided I wanted something more serious, but most guys still only wanted a one-and-done experience and the few looking for a relationship didn't want someone like ... well, *me*.

I never used to be insecure about my size. I don't think anyone at any size should ever be ashamed of their body. You never know someone's personal struggles, so who are you to judge? But suddenly, I *did* start to become insecure and wondered if men didn't see me as the type they wanted to have a future with—that I was only good for a quick lay.

After that, I swore off men, determined to build up my confidence again.

Junior year is supposed to be *my* year, and I won't let myself get dragged down by pining for some ideal that exists solely in my head.

Love will come along when it's meant to. Until then, I'll be living my best life, which includes pizza nights with Miranda, manicures and pedicures once a month, and whatever else I want to do—which let's be real, after I spend the money on the mani-pedis I'll be sitting in my apartment contemplating my life choices and if I *really* had to buy those Cheetos from the campus vending machine two years ago for three dollars and fifty cents, because surely if I had that money today I'd be better off. You might say I don't need the mani-pedis, which might be true in theory, but I don't need that kind of negativity from anyone in my life, so you can kindly fuck off.

"Here you ladies go," our usual waiter Joe says with a smile, setting down each of our pizzas—Miranda's meat lovers and my veggie. Joe is an older guy, probably in his fifties, bald, and has a black goatee. He's awesome and always makes us laugh. "Don't do anything I wouldn't do tonight."

Miranda snorts. "Like devour this pizza whole? You bet your ass that's happening."

He merely chuckles and walks away to tend to another table.

I cut two slices of pizza and set them on the plate Joe brought earlier to cool down.

Miranda stares longingly down at her plate. "I want to eat it now, but I know if I do I'll have severe regrets when my tongue is burnt for a week." She raises her eyes to mine and shrugs. "Eh, you only live once, right?"

Before I can stop her, she grabs a piece and takes a huge bite. *"Regret,"* she cries, pulling a stringy piece of cheese away from her mouth. "Instant. Regret." She pants, spitting out a blob of too hot pizza.

Stifling a giggle, I gesture toward the unfortunate mess of cheese and other toppings in front of her. "Now look what you've gone and done. You ruined a perfectly good piece of pizza."

She frowns. "Such a tragedy. Let's have a moment of silence in its honor for its service to my mouth." She claps her hands together and bows her head. Lifting it two seconds later she announces, "Enough of that."

She proceeds to pick up the rest of the piece she bit into and blows on it to cool it down.

Once a few more minutes pass and I feel sure my own pizza is green-lit to eat, I take a bite.

Nope! Abort mission!

"Ah!" I cry, as the hot cheese and sauce burns my tongue, bringing tears to my eyes. "Get it out," I plead stupidly, because it's not like a stranger is going to shove their hand in my mouth to yank out the scalding piece of pizza. I manage to spit it out and reach for my beer, but the starchy drink does little to soothe my tongue. I spot Joe walking by and wave madly, nearly falling out of the booth. "Water," I beg when he sees me. "Need. Water."

He chuckles. "Coming right up."

Looking across the table at Miranda, I sigh. "We shouldn't be allowed out in public. We're both walking disasters."

"I like to think my awkwardness brings joy to those around me."

"As opposed to what?" I inquire, thanking Joe with a nod as he sets down a glass of water for each of us. I gulp greedily at the cold liquid.

"Horror at the realization a walking wrecking ball exists, ready to take down anything and anyone around her. I can't help it that I'm clumsy and stupid things happen to me."

"Same, girl." I can relate to that on every level.

When I was six, I fell from the top of the playground slide onto the ground, banging my head into a piece of wood that was a part of the area separating the grass from the mulch. Suffice to say, there was a lot of blood, more than five stitches, and a scar on my forehead that I carry with me to this day.

"Let's try this again," she says, and takes a tentative bite. She gives me a thumbs up. "All clear."

I follow suit, thankfully, it's not scorching hot anymore, but my sore tongue makes it less enjoyable than it should be.

I eat a total of three pieces before asking for a box. After we've both finished our drinks we grab our things and head outside onto the cobblestone road in front of the restaurant.

The sun is only beginning to set, and it's a little before eight, but already starting to get dark earlier every night. I personally love the times when it's nine at night and still light out. Fall and winter are the bane of my existence. I thrive on the energy the sun brings me. If I could hibernate through the winter months I might like them more, but since I have to get out and brave the cold on the daily it's a hate-hate relationship.

We walk a couple of streets over, both of us much more subdued thanks to the pizza and drinks.

If you put food in me, suddenly I'm ready to sleep. It makes eating breakfast and lunch a game of Russian roulette of will I or won't I fall asleep in class.

Miranda and I say our goodbyes as she gets in her car, and then I enter my apartment building. It's a ground floor unit, which I hated at first because it didn't seem very safe to me, but I've come to love it—when I have groceries at least I don't have to walk up any stairs.

I close the door behind me and sweep my gaze around my place, my *home*. I've spent so much time buying things and making it mine. The white and gray décor with pops of pink in the main space brings me peace. The same theme carries into my bedroom. The spare room has been my office, housing a desk and two bookcases that didn't fit in the main room—though I do have bookcases lining the wall behind my couch.

Tomorrow, I'll have to clean out the office. I don't know where I'll put the things in there, but I'll figure it out. Anything I can't keep will have to be donated, or Miranda can have it if she wants.

I stand in the doorway of the room, wondering who on Earth my roommate will be. I hope we get along and that is doesn't end up being a complete and utter disaster.

Though, knowing my luck, a disaster is exactly what I'll get.

ALSO BY MICALEA SMELTZER

The Wildflower Duet

The Confidence of Wildflowers

The Resurrection of Wildflowers

The Boys Series

Bad Boys Break Hearts

Nice Guys Don't Win

Real Players Never Lose

Good Guys Don't Lie

Broken Boys Can't Love

Second Chances Standalone Series

Unraveling

Undeniable

Trace + Olivia Series

Finding Olivia

Chasing Olivia

Tempting Rowan

Saving Tatum

Trace + Olivia Box Set

Willow Creek Series

Last To Know

Never Too Late

In Your Heart

Take A Chance

Willow Creek Box Set

Always Too Late Short Story

Willow Creek Bonus Content

Home For Christmas

Light in the Dark Series

Rae of Sunshine

When Stars Collide

Dark Hearts

When Constellations Form

Broken Hearts

Stars & Constellations Bundle

Standalones

Beauty in the Ashes

Bring Me Back

The Other Side of Tomorrow

Desperately Seeking Roommate

Desperately Seeking Landlord

Whatever Happens

Sweet Dandelion

Say When

The Road That Leads To Us

The Game Plan

www.ingramcontent.com/pod-product-compliance
Lightning Source LLC
LaVergne TN
LVHW031609060526
838201LV00065B/4783